TEAROOM
mysteries

Dear Reader,

This series makes me homesick for Maine. Fort Knox in Prospect, Maine, was a favorite outing for our children. Whenever we had company from out of state, we liked to pack a picnic and flashlights for everyone and go over to the fort. When my editors and I began talking about the plot for this book, I decided to find out more about General Knox and make him a part of the story.

Writing another adventure for Elaine and Jan was pure joy. I hope you enjoy their story, as they try to figure out who stole a historic letter, penned by a famous Maine statesman, from the church.

As I think of Jan and Elaine sitting on their deck near the lake in the evening and looking out over the still water reflecting the moonlight, I can smell the pines and hear the loons calling.

Whatever your location and favorite destinations, I hope you have fun reading this book. Fix your favorite hot beverage and curl up for a visit with Elaine and Jan.

Blessings,
Susan Page Davis

## Tearoom Mysteries

TEAROOM
mysteries

# Trouble Brewing

## SUSAN PAGE DAVIS

**Guideposts**
New York

Published by Guideposts Books & Inspirational Media
110 William Street
New York, New York 10038
Guideposts.org

## Acknowledgments

Every attempt has been made to credit the sources of copyrighted material used in this book. If any such acknowledgment has been inadvertently omitted or miscredited, receipt of such information would be appreciated.

Scripture quotations are taken from *The Holy Bible, New International Version.* Copyright © 1973, 1978, 1984, 2011 by Biblica, Inc. Used by permission of Zondervan. All rights reserved worldwide. www.zondervan.com

Cover and interior design by Müllerhaus
Cover illustration by Ross Jones, represented by Deborah Wolfe, Ltd.
Typeset by Aptara, Inc.

Printed and bound in the United States of America
10 9 8 7 6 5 4 3 2 1

# Trouble Brewing

# CHAPTER ONE

J an Blake placed a yardstick and a notebook on the back-seat of her car. Her cousin, Elaine Cook, got in on the passenger side and set a bulging tote bag on the floor.

"Got everything?" Jan asked.

"I think so."

Jan backed out of the garage and headed for their little church. They had a lot of work to do to prepare for Lancaster Community Church's Mother-Daughter Tea the following week. Their tearoom on the lakeshore had been busy that morning, but Rose and Archie, their hired servers, had assured them that they would be fine for the next hour or two. Since they usually didn't serve full meals, fewer customers came into Tea for Two during the noon hour most days.

They would have gotten away a little earlier, but Elaine's twenty-six-year-old daughter had called minutes before they planned to walk out the door. Jan didn't mind. She and Elaine adapted to each other's schedules and whims. Jan, for instance, had gotten up at 5:30 a.m. to bake fresh scones and cream puffs for the day's customers. She liked to be up early and get her baking done well before opening. She usually had time for devotions on the screened-in back porch or, in nice weather, the deck down near the water. She loved that still time of day when the sun was rising and, if it wasn't windy, the water was absolutely flat. Elaine, on the other hand, preferred to sit up at night and read, then get up a little later than Jan in the morning.

"So what did Sasha have to say?" Jan asked in the car.

"She's flying up here Tuesday for a few days."

"Wonderful!" Jan said. "Will you have to drive to Portland to pick her up?"

"No," Elaine said. "She's renting a car."

"She could use one of ours." Jan was ever mindful of expenses.

"It's all right," Elaine said. "I think she'd rather do it this way. She's got to drive over to Sugarloaf Thursday. She's meeting with the management to set up a biathlon event there in the fall."

Jan nodded. Sasha was an Olympic-class biathlete. Elaine could hardly wait to see her compete, and Jan caught the excitement whenever she talked about it.

"Do you think we can get tickets to the event?"

Elaine smiled. "I sure hope so. It would be so much fun." The biggest ski area in Maine, Sugarloaf, hosted many winter sports events, and the prospect of seeing her daughter ski and shoot there made Elaine's eyes glow. She glanced at Jan. "So how was your date with Bob last night?"

Jan nodded, but didn't smile. "It was good." To tell the truth, she was a little worried. Her old school friend, Bob, who had over the last year become her romantic interest, had a job offer that would move him out of state.

"He hasn't made up his mind about the job yet?" Elaine asked.

"Not yet." Bob was an attorney with a practice in the nearby city of Waterville. He was usually decisive, and the fact that he had not yet made a firm decision about the job change was stressful for Jan.

"Here we are." The short drive was over, and Jan pulled into the church parking lot. "Just keep praying about it, okay?"

"I will."

They climbed out of the car, and Jan looked toward the church's side door, at the top of the handicapped ramp. "I wonder if Pastor Mike's in his study."

"I think we should go knock at the parsonage," Elaine said, reaching for her tote. "Besides, we brought them cookies." She led the way across the lot.

The maple trees on the edge of the yard were leafing out, and the sun shone on the tender spring grass. Jan pulled in a deep breath. "I love spring."

"Me too." Elaine stepped up to the front door of the pastor's house and pushed the doorbell. A few seconds later, Pastor Ryder's wife, Sarah, opened the door and surveyed them with pleasure.

"Hello, ladies! What can I do for you?"

"I hope we're not interrupting your lunch," Jan said. "We'd like to get into the fellowship hall so we can firm up our plans for the Mother-Daughter Tea."

Elaine held out a small cardboard box. "Some of yesterday's leftover cookies and a couple of fresh scones."

"Oh!" Sarah's whole face lit. "Yum! Thank you. I'll get the key for you."

From inside, they heard a chair scrape the floor, and Pastor Mike came to the doorway. "No need for that. I unlocked the side door this morning. The Murphy boys were cleaning up the lawn, and I opened it in case they needed to get trash bags or use the restroom."

"Oh, all right," Elaine said. "Thanks, and enjoy the cookies."

Pastor Mike grinned. "I'm sure we will."

They walked across to the parking lot again, and Jan looked toward the church's front lawn. "The boys must have finished and gone home. The yard looks nice though."

"Yes," Elaine said. "They've moved the branches that were on the lawn, and the gravel the snowplow shoved off into the grass too."

Jan smiled as they walked up the ramp. "Those twins are hard workers."

"And they weeded the flower beds," Elaine said, nodding toward the tulips that would soon be blooming in the bed below the ramp. She reached out for the knob on the side door and turned it.

They stepped into a dim entry and went down the back stairs to the cool basement fellowship hall. Inside it was dim, with light coming through a few small, high windows in the foundation. Jan flipped the light switch.

Elaine gasped.

They both stood staring at the mess in the fellowship hall. At first glance, Jan saw two tables overturned, and folding chairs removed from their racks and thrown around the room. Paper towels and tablecloths lay crumpled on the floor. A broom, dustpan, and other cleaning implements were strewn about. Worst of all, someone had spilled cleansing powder and dishwasher detergent all about, making it impossible to cross the room without stepping in it.

Jan looked at her cousin.

Elaine wore a shocked expression. "Someone's ransacked the church."

"WE'D BETTER GET Pastor Mike," Elaine said. Jan's cheeks were pale and her eyes wide as she surveyed the damage.

"Maybe I should run home and get our fingerprint kit," Jan said.

Elaine looked inspired for a moment, but then she frowned. "No, we should tell Pastor Mike first."

"You're right. Come on." Jan turned on her heel, and Elaine followed her.

They scurried up the stairs, out the door, and across the parking lot to the parsonage. This time the pastor answered their ringing of the bell. His gray eyes surveyed them in surprise, and his eyebrows arched.

"Hello again. What's up?"

Nine-year-old Caleb peeked out from under his tall father's elbow. He had one of Jan's cookies in his hand.

"We need you to come over to the church," Elaine said, not wanting to alarm the whole family.

"Oh?" Pastor Mike picked up on her concern immediately. He turned and called over his shoulder, "Sarah, I'm going over to the church for a minute."

"That's fine," Sarah replied from near the sink. "Caleb, sit down and finish your lunch."

"Sorry to take you away from your meal," Elaine said as the three of them hurried across to the church.

"Is something wrong?"

"I'm afraid so," Elaine said.

"Very wrong," Jan added. "In the big room downstairs."

The pastor's mouth set in a grim line as he flung the side door open and descended the steps. He walked into the large room and stopped, gazing about. Nothing had changed. Elaine watched his expression fade from mild concern to deep dismay.

"Well." He shook his head. "Who could have done this?" he asked.

"I have no idea," Elaine said.

"Me neither," Jan added. "You said Des and Jo Murphy's boys worked here this morning?"

He nodded. "Outside. I guess we'll have to ask them if they came in here."

"You don't think Nick and Chris would do this, do you?" Elaine frowned as she looked around again and noticed more items tossed from their usual places. A trash can lay on its side near the door to the kitchen, with wads of paper spilling out of it. A box of straws had been scattered, and a framed Bible verse lay on the floor, the glass cracked. The Murphy twins worked in their parents' store, and she found it hard to believe they

6

would make such a mess when they knew how hard it was to keep the general store shipshape.

"I wouldn't have thought so, but they may have seen something. I'd better call the store and talk to Des right away." Pastor Mike patted his pockets. "I left my cell at home. I'll call from the office." He headed up the stairs, toward where his office lay behind the auditorium.

Jan looked bleakly at Elaine. "Should we clean up?"

"I don't know. He might want someone else to see it first."

Jan walked cautiously closer to an area covered with greenish powdered cleanser. "Look. There are footprints right through it."

"You're right. Don't touch it."

"Don't worry about me." Jan had her cell phone out and raised it to eye level.

"Good idea," Elaine said as Jan popped off a photograph.

Elaine turned toward the stairway as Pastor Mike's "Oh no" reached them. She hurried up the stairs, calling, "What is it, Pastor?"

"They've been in here too."

# CHAPTER TWO

Elaine noticed powdery footprints on the stair treads. She turned and said over her shoulder, "Jan. Footprints."

"Got it." Her cousin walked cautiously toward the stairs, her cell phone at the ready.

Elaine stepped carefully close to the wall to avoid ruining any evidence. She gained the upper level and strode down the carpeted hallway to the pastor's office. No footprints here.

She paused at the office door, and a moment later Jan crowded in beside her to see. Two file drawers had been pulled out and dumped, the papers in disarray all over the floor. All of the drawers on the pastor's desk were open and the contents scattered. The desktop was littered with church bulletins, paper clips, pens, memo pads, markers, a ruler, other office supplies, and, incongruously, jelly beans every color of the rainbow—plus black.

Elaine's chest ached as she pulled in a deep breath. "What else?"

Pastor Mike turned toward them, his eyes troubled. "My thoughts exactly. You ladies check the classrooms and restrooms downstairs. I'll see if they touched the sanctuary or the other rooms up here."

Jan dashed downstairs and to the door of the ladies' room, and Elaine took the men's. Toilet paper, towels, and soap were the weapons of choice here. The liquid soap was smeared across the mirrors, and the paper goods thrown everywhere. A complete roll of toilet tissue was stuffed into the bowl of one toilet.

Elaine backed out of the men's room and met Jan in the hall. Her cousin's ashen face told her that the scene in the ladies' room was no better.

"At least they didn't break the mirrors," she said.

"Yeah." Jan's lips twitched. "That would have meant bad luck." Her face crumpled. "Sorry. I shouldn't have said that."

Elaine swooped her into a hug. "It's okay. I just hope it's not this bad upstairs."

They looked into the classrooms and the nursery. All were in disorder. They would need help if they wanted to put everything back in order before tomorrow's Sunday school hour.

Care lines creased the corners of Jan's mouth. "I was thinking I'd go get our fingerprint kit, but then I remembered. We used up all the powder, and I forgot to order more."

"So did I," Elaine said.

Pastor Mike's steps thumped down the carpeted front stairway. They moved toward him and met him near the glassed-in display case that held memorabilia from the church's history.

"They didn't touch this," Elaine noted with a nod toward the case.

"That's good," Pastor Mike said. "It looks like they didn't make it as far as the sanctuary. Everything's okay up there."

"The library?" Elaine asked.

"Not touched. Or the restrooms."

"Thank the Lord," Jan said. "It's bad down here."

Elaine nodded. "Yes. I'm sorry to report that this display case seems to be the only thing they didn't touch down here."

"The bathrooms are bad?" he asked.

"Real bad."

"Could be worse, actually," Jan said.

They both stared at her, and she shrugged. "I'm just sayin'."

"I suppose you're right." The pastor's shoulders sagged.

"It looks like they tossed things around in the classrooms," Elaine told him. "They tipped chairs over and dumped out the Sunday school material and supplies. But I don't think much is broken."

"Same in the nursery," Jan said. "Disposable diapers all over, and some powder was spilled, but it will vacuum up."

"Let's go back to my office." The pastor turned toward the stairs. "I think it's time to call the police. They can decide what to do next." They followed him to the office door, and he stood there, looking inside. "On the other hand, would you mind giving Dan Benson a ring?"

"Not at all." Elaine took out her phone and scrolled through her contacts for Dan Benson's number. The state trooper lived in town, just a couple of miles away, and he was a member of Lancaster Community Church. He had helped Elaine and Jan several times before. He answered the ring, and Elaine explained that there had been a break-in at the church.

"I can be there in ten minutes," he said. "Leave everything as is until I get there, okay?"

Elaine relayed the message. "Maybe we should wait outside."

Jan nodded. "What do you think, Pastor?"

"I suppose you're right. I want to just tear into it and get things back to rights."

They all went out into the parking lot and stood close together, waiting.

A breeze stirred the limbs on the maples, and Pastor Mike ran a hand through his light-brown hair. "I can't imagine who would do this. I was out visiting most of the morning. I'll have to ask Sarah if she saw anyone."

"Did you go into the church at all before you left?" Jan asked.

The pastor shook his head. "I was planning to spend the afternoon in my office, getting ready for tomorrow's services. This morning I just unlocked the door for the boys and left."

Sarah and Caleb came out of the house and strolled toward them. Sarah's dark-auburn hair was in a ponytail, and she wore jeans and a pink plaid flannel shirt, definitely "off duty" and out of her nurse's uniform. Caleb had his dad's light hair, and he wore sweat pants and a T-shirt, ready to play.

"Everything okay?" Sarah asked.

"No," Pastor Mike said. "We seem to have been visited by vandals."

Sarah's jaw dropped. "No!"

"What's vandals?" Caleb asked.

"People who break the law by making a mess of things," his mother said. "Can I help?"

"We've called Dan Benson," Pastor Mike told her. "Just keep the kids away until he's done looking things over. You all might be able to help clean up afterward though."

"All right. Is it bad?" Sarah glanced apologetically at Elaine and Jan.

"Bad enough," Pastor Mike replied.

"No paint or anything like that," Elaine told her. "I think we'll be able to clean up in a couple hours if we get a good crew to help."

"Maybe we can call a few women on the social committee," Jan suggested. "I'm sure some would be willing to come."

The pastor nodded. "Just wait until Dan gives us the go-ahead. I'll let you know when."

"Got it," Sarah said.

"You didn't see anyone go in this morning, did you?" her husband asked.

"No. I saw the Murphy boys working on the lawn." Sarah's eyes widened. "You don't think..."

"They're good boys. But maybe they saw someone hanging around," Pastor Mike said.

Elaine was glad he was already sticking up for the twins.

"I'll put on some coffee and mix some iced tea," Sarah said. "Tell me when you're ready for help. Come on, Caleb."

"I want to see," the nine-year-old boy protested.

"No, you come back to the house with me."

Caleb scowled but went with his mother. They had barely shut the house door when Dan rolled in, driving his state police SUV.

"Afternoon, folks." He got out of the car and walked over to them. "What have you got here? Someone broke in?"

"They may not have needed to break in," Pastor Mike said. "I unlocked the side door this morning. I don't know that it was done after that, but it's possible. I suppose it could have been any time since yesterday afternoon. That's the last time I was in the church."

"You unlocked it but didn't go in?"

"That's right," Pastor Mike said. "I just wanted to make sure the Murphy boys could get in if they needed to while they did some yard work."

"Let's have a look."

The pastor led Dan inside. Elaine and Jan crept in behind them and stayed near the door while Dan walked through the rooms taking in the damage and making notes in his pocket pad. After Dan had inspected and photographed the office and taken a quick look into the other upstairs rooms, the cousins followed the two men down the stairs.

"I'm surprised they didn't smash that glass case," Dan murmured when they paused by the memorabilia case at the bottom of the flight.

"We said the same thing," the pastor replied.

"Odd that they didn't do anything upstairs except trash your office, but they went wild down here."

Jan spoke up. "Maybe they came down here first."

"Maybe," Dan said, picking his way across the fellowship hall.

"Or maybe the office was their target, and they just wrecked things down here for fun afterward," Elaine mused.

"Well, I'm very thankful they didn't do anything in the sanctuary," the pastor said. "At least that room is ready for church tomorrow. But the Sunday school rooms..." He shook his head.

"Yes, and it's Mother's Day tomorrow," Elaine reminded him. "We'll have lots of visitors."

"We've got to make sure those restrooms are in good order," Jan said.

After Dan had completed his tour, he gathered the three of them upstairs in the hall outside the office. "Have any of you noticed that anything was missing?"

Elaine and Jan looked at each other and shook their heads.

Pastor Mike sighed. "I don't know. I don't think so. There was nothing of particular value in my office. My computer and printer are still there."

"You wouldn't keep offering money here, would you?"

"No, the treasurer takes everything right to the bank," Pastor Mike said.

"Well, keep your eyes open as you clean up," Dan said. "Sometimes a thief will mess things up to draw attention away from a theft. If anything turns up missing, I want to know about it."

They all nodded.

"All right. Now, somebody mentioned that the Murphy twins were here this morning."

"Right," Pastor said. "I had to make some visits this morning, and I didn't actually see the boys. My wife said she did though."

"They're not mowing the lawn already, are they?" Dan asked, frowning.

"Not yet. Maybe by next week. But there were limbs down and gravel in the grass. They were supposed to do some weeding. I think they did all of it, but I haven't looked closely."

"And you don't know if they came into the church?"

"No. Do you want me to ask them?" Pastor didn't look eager to do that.

"I'll go past their house and see if they're around," Dan said. "Did anyone else have access?"

Pastor Mike sighed. "Obviously, anyone could have come in this morning, but the Murphy kids are the only ones I know of for sure. They were probably around for at least an hour, maybe two. Sarah was home, but she'd have told me if she noticed anyone else going in. You can see most of the area where they were working from our kitchen and living room windows."

"What about last night?"

Pastor Mike shook his head. "We didn't see anyone or hear anything unusual."

"Who has keys?"

"Me, the deacons, and the head trustee."

"Cleaners?"

"The families take turns," Pastor Mike said. "They come to the house, and we either lend them the key or go over and open the door for them."

"Who cleaned this week?"

"Uh...the McInnises, I think. I can check the list to make sure."

Dan wrote it in his notebook. "So the damage is mostly nuisance stuff. Nothing stolen that you know of, and not much actually broken."

"I saw one picture downstairs with the glass cracked," Elaine said.

Jan raised her chin. "A lot of supplies were ruined."

Dan wrote it down. "Make a list of anything else that's damaged or will need to be replaced."

"Can we start the cleanup?" Jan asked.

"I guess so. I've got enough photographs. But do stop and call me if you find anything serious. I'll take a look around outside, and I'll check the front doors."

"They should still be locked," Pastor Mike said. He led them all into the front of the building. After checking the front doors in the foyer, which were indeed locked, Dan went around and checked all the windows throughout the church

"Nothing seems to have been tampered with," he said. "Go ahead with your cleaning. Pastor, I'll let you know if I learn anything about this."

"Thanks, Dan." The trooper left them, and Pastor Mike said, "I'll go tell Sarah she can make those calls and come over to help clean. I guess you ladies can start. Unless you need to get back to the tearoom."

"I'm sure Rose and Archie will be fine without us, but I'll give them a call," Elaine said.

Archie answered the phone cheerfully with "Tea for Two. May I help you?"

Elaine smiled at his lilting British accent. She quickly told him the situation.

"That's hard luck," Archie said softly. "We're fine here. Bristol Payson just popped over from the Bookworm to get a box of muffins. Seems her son is home from college and has a hankering for Jan's cranberry-orange."

"Oh, I'm sorry I missed her." Elaine looked over to where Jan was stooping for a close look at the footprints. "Is the tea-room busy right now?"

"Four tables occupied, and a party coming through the door," Archie replied.

"I'll let you go then," Elaine said. "Thanks!"

Sarah soon arrived at the church with her three children. Sarah carried a mop and a plastic bucket full of cleaning products and sponges. "Just in case we need extra," she said. She scrunched up her face as she surveyed the fellowship hall. "I called Annie Richardson, and she's coming over. I'm afraid the others I called were out or busy. Rue said she'd try to get over if she could."

While the pastor went to begin restoring his office to order, Sarah let the kids begin on their Sunday school classrooms. She went with Caleb, the youngest, and allowed twelve-year-old Leanne and fifteen-year-old Asher to work on their own, since there weren't any cleaning products spilled in the classrooms.

"I wonder if Chris and Nick saw anyone come in here this morning," Asher said as he and Leanne went down the hallway.

"Trooper Benson is going to ask them that," his mother said. "Just straighten up the chairs and supplies as best you can, and tell me when you're done. The cleaners vacuumed through yesterday, but we may need to do it again."

"I'd like to work in the kitchen," Jan said to Elaine. "Is that okay?"

"Sure," Elaine told her. "I'll start out here, because people might see this room when they come down for Sunday school tomorrow. When Annie gets here, maybe she can help you."

"What about the bathrooms?" Jan asked. "The upstairs ones weren't touched, but the two down here are pretty bad."

"Right," Elaine said. "I'll do those first. If anyone else shows up, put them to work in this room, okay?"

"I think there are some rubber gloves in the kitchen. At least there *were*." Jan hurried through the debris into the kitchen. She returned a moment later waving a pair of yellow latex gloves. "Here you go." She tossed them, and Elaine surprised herself by catching both.

"All right, into the breach," Jan said in stentorian tones and headed for the ladies' room.

The first order of business was to clear the floor. Elaine bent and picked up the items she could salvage first—a couple of rolls of toilet paper and a half-empty bottle of liquid soap. She rinsed the bottle at the sink and wiped it dry, then put it in place. A stack of paper towels had apparently been taken from the cupboard and flung about without purpose. Most of them had wet spots or had touched the pool of soap on the floor. She started gathering them into a trash bag.

Beneath one clump, she found a small object that made her catch her breath. She picked it up gingerly by one end.

A pocketknife. Not a thing one would normally find in the ladies' room. She carried it out to the kitchen.

"Jan? Have you got a zipper bag?"

# CHAPTER THREE

Two hours later, the women gathered in the now clean fellowship hall. Sarah had sent the children home after their classrooms were straightened. Rue Maxwell, who owned the Northwoods B and B with her husband Ned, had come to help them, and she had pitched in with inspiring energy.

"I'd say we did some good work," Jan proclaimed, looking over her shoulder into the kitchen, where the appliances gleamed and the cleared floor shone from a fresh scrubbing.

"Yes, we just need to get these bags of trash outside," Annie said, eyeing the four large bags they had filled.

"I'm so glad the toilets are functioning right," Rue said, pulling off the bandanna she had tied around her hair and giving it a shake.

Elaine smiled at them. "You ladies are troupers. Rose called me a few minutes ago and asked if she and Archie could serve complimentary tea and pastries to all the workers who want to stop by the tearoom. Of course, I said yes."

"How lovely," Rue said.

Sarah frowned. "I'd love to, but I'd better get home to the kids."

"Bring them," Jan said. "They helped."

"Do you think?" Sarah asked.

"Sure," Jan said. "They don't get in there often. I'll bet they'd like it—at least Leanne would."

"Okay, I'll ask them."

"I guess I could stop for a few minutes," Annie decided.

"Great," Elaine said. "We have to pop into Murphy's on the way home for some butter. Rose's request, but we'll be quick. We'll see you all there."

"Oh, make sure Pastor Mike knows," Jan added.

Sarah shook her head doubtfully. "I don't think we'll be able to pry him away from that office before suppertime. He was still working on his files when I peeked in last. He says no one else would understand his system, so he has to do it all himself."

"Too bad," Elaine said, but she sympathized with him. She would feel the same way if someone dumped out all her file drawers in the tearoom office.

"Oh, Jan!" Annie called as they headed for the door.

Jan turned back. "Yeah?"

"My daughter Ella is turning twelve next week, and I've invited all the girls in her class over after school on Wednesday. Ella wants cupcakes instead of a cake. Is there any chance you could do them for me? Gavin's getting ready to plant, and I've got a lot going on."

"Sure, I can do that," Jan said. "How many do you want, and do you have a theme?"

Annie's relief was written all over her face. "Thank you! That's one thing I can cross off. Four dozen, I think. Not that there will be that many girls, but I know my men. They'll want samples. If you can put lots of pink on them, it'll be great. Maybe pink and white?"

"You got it. You can pick them up that morning, or I can take them to your house if you want."

"Oh, that would help me a lot."

Jan winked at her. "Don't you worry about a thing."

In the car on the way to Murphy's store, Elaine asked Jan, "Are you sure Brian will remember to pick up my mom tomorrow and bring her to dinner?"

Jan smiled. "Paula knows, so yeah. You don't have to worry about it. Brian might forget, but not Paula." Since Brian's family and Elaine's mother both lived in Augusta, Jan's son had offered to bring Virginia with them so they could all celebrate Mother's Day together at the lakeside house.

"Good. I hope Tara and Amy can make it too," Elaine said, referring to Jan's two daughters.

"They all said they could. Amy and Van are going to visit Van's mother later and take her out to dinner tomorrow night." Jan pulled in at the general store. "I'll run in for the butter."

Before Elaine could answer, she was out of the car and dashing inside. She went straight to the dairy case, grabbed two pounds of butter, and hurried to the counter.

"Hi, Jo," she said to Mrs. Murphy, who was manning the cash register.

"Jan. Hi."

Jo seemed distracted as she rang up the butter. Jan hesitated to bring up the morning's events, but Jo had become a friend. When she handed back the wrong change, Jan decided she should say something.

"Oops, you gave me too much. Here you go."

"Oh, thanks." Jo stared blankly at the dollar Jan had placed in her hand.

"Are you okay?" Jan asked.

"Not really. My stomach's churning."

Jan looked around. No other customers were near. She said softly, "Elaine and I just came from the church."

Jo's eyes widened. "Oh, that's right. Dan Benson said you were the ones who discovered the vandalism."

Jan nodded. "It was quite a mess."

"You don't think my boys did it, do you?" Jo asked.

"No, we don't."

"Because Dan was here to see them. He talked to them for quite a while about what they did this morning at the church. They told him they didn't know about it, and they didn't even go inside this morning. They took all the tools they needed with them, and I even had them take along a box of trash bags for the sticks and things they gathered. They didn't know anything about the break-in. But I don't know if Dan believes them or not."

"He'll get to the bottom of it." Jan looked around the store. "Are the boys here now?"

"I sent them home."

Jan nodded, thinking of the footprints and pocketknife they had found. It would be nice if they could truly rule out the twins.

Jo sighed. "Was it really bad?"

"Bad enough," Jan said. "So far as we could tell, nothing was stolen. But it was a real mess. It will take the pastor a while to straighten out his files."

Jo shook her head. "That's so senseless. Listen, if the church needs to have anything replaced—lightbulbs, paper products, anything at all—please tell us. We'll happily donate whatever's needed. But Chris and Nick didn't do this."

ELAINE AND JAN spent a pleasant hour at the tearoom with Annie, Rue, Sarah, and the kids. Asher and Leanne Ryder had been especially eager to see inside the house, and Jan took them all down to the dock when they had finished their snacks.

"Do you swim here?" Asher asked.

"Yes, and if you'd like to this summer, you just call ahead."

"That's very generous of you," Sarah said. "We wouldn't want to intrude during your business hours."

"Well, it's possible to get out here without going through the tearoom," Jan pointed out. "We wouldn't mind."

She and Elaine saw their guests off and cleared away the dishes they had used.

"Shoo," Rose said, coming behind them with a damp cloth to wipe down the tables.

Jan looked at her watch. "I was thinking, maybe we should take a little walk over to the Murphys' house."

"What for?" Elaine asked.

"The boys."

"They said they didn't go in the church," Elaine said, frowning.

"I know, and we might be able to help them prove it. Whoever was in there might have evidence on their shoes. If we wait too long, it will wear off."

"You're thinking of the scouring powder?"

Jan nodded. "And we could ask about the pocketknife."

Elaine hesitated. "You said Jo was pretty upset already. I think we should ask her or Des before we talk to the boys."

"Okay."

Elaine took the bagged pocketknife from her purse, and they walked over to the general store.

"I suppose we should give this to Dan."

"Probably," Jan said. "After we talk to the Murphys." She looked ahead. To her surprise, one of the boys was outside, helping his father unload crates from the back of Des's pickup. "Hi, Des," she called.

He straightened and turned toward them. "Hello, gals." Des was only a few inches taller than Jan, with wavy brown hair. He pushed back a lock that had fallen over his forehead. "Can I help you?"

Jan and Elaine stepped closer.

"We wondered if you'd mind if we talked to the boys about the church incident," Elaine said.

Des frowned, looked at his son, and shrugged. "Guess not. What do you say, Chris?"

The fifteen-year-old ducked his chin. "We didn't go in. We already told Mr. Benson."

"We know," Jan said, smiling. "By the way, you and Nick did a terrific job on the church yard this morning."

24

"Thanks," Chris mumbled.

Jan looked down at his feet. He was wearing black high-top sneakers. The white rubber edge, where the top met the sole, was covered with grass stains and dirt.

"This may sound a little odd, but are those the shoes you wore over there?"

"Yeah." Chris frowned and shot a look at his dad.

"It may not be important," Elaine said quickly, "but we found some footprints in the mess in the fellowship hall and on the stairs."

Jan wished her cousin hadn't revealed so much, but she could roll with it. "We figured if your shoes didn't match them, everyone would know it wasn't you."

Des said slowly, "Sounds reasonable to me." He looked at Chris and arched his eyebrows. "What do you say?"

"We didn't go in there."

Des clapped him on the shoulder. "Then there's no problem, right?"

"I...I don't know."

"What do you want?" Des asked Jan. "Should he take off his shoe?"

Jan took out her phone and brought up the pictures she had taken of the shoe prints.

"Take a look, Des. This picture is the clearest, so far as the pattern goes. See it? I thought by looking at the bottom of the boys' sneakers, we could tell if the shoes were the same. I also measured the prints."

Des looked pointedly at Chris. The boy sighed and bent to untie one of his shoelaces.

"Oh, the right one, if you don't mind," Jan said quickly, since the clearest photo showed a right shoe print.

Chris complied, pulled the shoe off, and handed it to her. He stood awkwardly, holding his stocking foot up off the pavement of the parking lot.

Jan turned the shoe over, ignoring the slight odor that emanated from it. Des leaned in, holding her phone, so she held the shoe where he could easily make the comparison. The tread of Chris's sneaker had a markedly different pattern from the print in her photo.

"I guess that clinches it," Des said, turning to Chris. "It wasn't you."

"I told you it wasn't."

"I know," Des said evenly, "but now we have proof to show the world."

Jan held the shoe closer to her face, quickly looking for traces of the cleanser or other substances he might have picked up at the church. She didn't see anything suspicious. With a smile, she held it out to Chris.

"Here you go. Thanks very much."

"Yes, thank you, Chris," Elaine said.

He took the shoe without speaking and sat on the tailgate of Des's truck to put it on.

"Are Nick's shoes like yours?" Jan asked.

"No, they're different," Chris said.

"Did you want to see his too?" Des asked. "He's not here right now. I let him go over to a friend's house."

"*Hmm.* Are their shoes the same size?" Elaine asked.

Good point, Jan thought.

"Yeah, they're pretty much the same all over," Des said with a chuckle.

"Jan measured the shoe prints," Elaine said. "If we could measure Chris's shoe, and Nick's are the same size, maybe that's enough for now."

"I didn't bring a tape measure," Jan said.

"I've got one right here." Des went to truck bed and flipped open a metal toolbox. He took out a carpenter's tape measure and went to stand in front of Chris, who still sat on the tailgate, tying his shoe. "Stick your foot out, buddy."

Chris scowled but held his foot out straight before him. Des pulled out the tape and held it to the bottom of his shoe. He looked at Jan.

"About ten and a half inches, you think?"

"Almost eleven."

"They're size ten," Chris said.

Jan nodded. "Thanks."

Des let the tape snap back inside the case. "Anything else we can do for you?"

"Actually, yes," Elaine said, stepping forward. "Chris, do you or Nick carry a pocketknife?"

Chris shook his head. "I've got one, but I don't usually carry it around. We're not allowed to at school."

"What does it look like?" Elaine asked. Jan was glad she didn't bring out the one they'd found and show it to him.

"Black," Chris said. "With a Scout logo. Nick's is just like it."

"Their grandfather gave them to the twins," Des said. "Their initials are stamped on the biggest blade on each one.

But they have strict orders to leave them home except for camping and Scout meetings."

"Great," Elaine said. "Thank you very much, both of you. I think that's it, isn't it, Jan?"

"Yeah, I think it is," Jan said. "We appreciate it."

As they walked back to the house, Elaine said, "I'm glad we caught them outside. Jo probably would have been upset if she saw us."

"Maybe." Jan sighed. "Okay, what have we proven?"

"That it wasn't the twins."

"No. Well, we're pretty sure it wasn't Chris. Nick's shoes are different."

"They're the same size. You don't really think…"

"Different brands might vary," Jan insisted.

Elaine sighed. "Yes, they might. So how big were the footprints?"

"About the same as Chris's. Maybe a little larger, but not much," Jan said. "And the print in the powder was faint at the back. I'm just not sure. And if Nick's shoes are a different brand from Chris's, they could vary a little in the length, even if their feet are the same size."

"Well, this certainly isn't their knife." Elaine took it from her pocket and gazed at the pocketknife through the plastic bag. The casing was tortoiseshell, and the gold ornament on one side was the manufacturer's logo, not a Boy Scout trefoil. "So I guess I should give this to Dan."

"I guess so," Jan said reluctantly, but she couldn't think of a better course of action.

# CHAPTER FOUR

On Sunday morning between the Sunday school hour and the morning worship service, the church was buzzing with conversations about the break-in. Elaine and Jan didn't like to talk about their role in the discovery, but apparently others had already spread that news, and several people came to them to ask about it. More than once, Elaine found herself jumping to the defense of the Murphy boys, and yet she had no other suspects.

About five minutes before the service was to begin, Jan's daughter Tara came in. Elaine spotted her first and waved her to their pew.

"Hi!" Tara slid in beside Jan and kissed her on the cheek. "Happy Mother's Day."

"Well, thank you, honey," Jan said. "This is a nice surprise. I didn't expect to see you until later."

"Figured I might as well go to church with you this morning."

"I'm glad you did." Jan squeezed her hand.

Elaine reached past Jan and patted Tara's arm. "Good to see you." She felt a small pang of regret that her children couldn't be here with them. But her mother would be here, something Jan could never have again on this earth. And Sasha was coming in just two days, she reminded herself, and Jared and Corrie would certainly telephone her this afternoon. She sat back, content. She had so much to thank the Lord for.

Not the least of which were the two men who then slipped into their pew also and were greeted enthusiastically—Nathan Culver and Bob Claybrook. Bob was dating Jan of course, and Nathan was fast becoming the focus of Elaine's thoughts and dreams. He was a longstanding friend who owned an auction house in Waterville. She and Nathan had recently begun dating steadily. With them and Tara, they had filled out Jan and Elaine's row.

Mark and Bristol Payson and their tall, blond son, Greg, claimed the pew in front of them. Mark held the office of town clerk, and Bristol owned the Bookworm, next door to Tea for Two.

Elaine leaned forward and touched Bristol's shoulder. "Good morning."

Bristol turned around, smiling. "Hi! I guess you see who's home for the summer."

Greg also shifted in his seat and grinned. "Hey, Mrs. Cook." He held out his hand, and Elaine shook it.

"Welcome home, Greg."

"Thanks for the muffins. They were terrific," he said.

"Oh, that was all Jan," Elaine told him with a laugh. "She's the incredible baker at our house. What are you up to this summer?"

His expression sobered. "I'm not sure yet. I should have been putting in applications a month ago, but I got sort of caught up in the end-of-the-school-year activities."

Elaine nodded. "Well, we need to replace a few boards in the steps that go down to our back deck, if you want to pick up a day or two of work."

"That might be good," Bristol said, eyeing him expectantly.

"Sure," Greg replied. "I'd be happy to do that."

"Should I bring him with me when I open the store tomorrow morning, or is that too soon?" Bristol asked.

Elaine sensed that she was anxious for Greg to start something meaningful. Maybe she was afraid he would lie around the house all summer, though she couldn't imagine this athletically built young man sitting still for long.

"That would be great."

The women on the flower committee brought in boxes from a florist's shop, and the chatter quieted down. Mother's Day was celebrated in grand fashion at Lancaster Community Church. Every woman in the congregation received a corsage, and special prizes were awarded to those with the most children, the newest child, and the most family members present. A lot of counting went on before it was determined that Pearl Trexler had earned the third award. She and Will were delighted that their son, Billy, had flown in for the weekend, and of course she could count her granddaughter, Kit Edmonds, along with Kit's husband, Russell, their daughter, Marcella, and two cousins who also were members of the church. Sarah Ryder presented her with a beautiful photo album.

"Aren't these lovely?" Elaine whispered to Jan as she pinned on her pink rosebud corsage.

"Beautiful." Jan had chosen a white orchid posy, following the tradition of wearing white flowers in memory of her deceased mother.

After the service, the people were slow to leave the church, as nearly all had questions for Pastor Mike about the vandalism.

"I really don't know anything about it," the pastor said over and over. "It was a mess. We cleaned it up. Dan Benson is investigating."

Unfortunately for those who clamored for information, Dan was absent from church that morning. Elaine surmised that he was working on this case or another one. Dan worked hard and attended services whenever he could, but he was often on duty during the weekend. His absence meant she couldn't pass the pocketknife on to him as she had intended to do.

"I hope you two are joining us for dinner," Elaine said to Nathan and Bob, who had kept close to their sides as they moved toward the parking lot. "We're hosting my mom and all of Jan's kids and grandchildren. We'll have plenty of food."

"I'd love to, but I need to get back to town," Nathan said. "My son Jacob and his family asked me to have dinner with them."

"Go and enjoy yourself," Elaine said, disappointed but understanding that he needed to decline. She had strong feelings for Nathan, but she was glad he stayed close to his own family. "We'll miss you."

"Maybe next time." Nathan bent and kissed her cheek.

"I'll come today," Bob said. "I think I'll run home and change first though, if you don't mind."

"That's fine," Jan said. "Come when you're ready, and prepare to be mobbed."

Nathan swung toward his car, but turned back again. "We four ought to go out together again sometime."

"That would fun," Jan said. "What did you have in mind?"

"I hear the Friday night trivia tournaments get really competitive at the Pine Tree Grill," Bob suggested.

"That sounds like a great idea." Jan's eyes shone. "How about it, Elaine? Nathan?"

Elaine was beginning to see the method in Bob's madness. Jan loved puzzles of all sorts, and she would love the trivia tournament. She looked uncertainly at Nathan. "Well...what do you think?"

"You should go," Tara said to Elaine with an encouraging smile.

"I'll try anything once," Nathan said. "But I warn you, I know nothing about science. I'm more of a history person."

"Great," Bob said with his boyish grin. "We'll pick you ladies up at your house—when, Nathan? Six thirtyish?"

"Sounds good, if Elaine's up for it." Nathan said.

"I guess so," Elaine said.

Nathan grinned. "I'll see you then."

He was gone in seconds, and Elaine smiled. She was excited about the idea for Friday night.

"You don't mind, do you?" Jan asked as she fastened her seat belt in Elaine's car moments later.

"No, it will be fun." Elaine shot her a sidelong glance and added, "Fun, if you don't expect much. I'm with Nathan: we'll leave the math and science to you and Bob."

Jan waved a hand, as though dismissing her concerns. "Those two guys are so smart, we're sure to win. I think it will be a blast."

Tara followed them back to their house in her car. Elaine knew they had at least a half hour before the rest of Jan's family would arrive. Since her mother was coming, she decided to stay in her dress. Jan, however, dashed upstairs to change. No doubt she'd be chasing Amy's five-year-old twins around.

"Can I help you set the tables?" Tara asked.

"That would be great." Elaine found her an apron. "When there's this many of us, we usually set up in the east parlor. We tried putting the adults in the dining room and the kids in one of the parlors, but they like to be where we are. So we put everyone in the biggest room now."

"I don't blame them," Tara said. "When I had to sit at the kids' table, I always felt like I was missing something."

Tara helped her push small tables together in the roomy east parlor. They ended up with a large U-shaped table that would seat everyone.

"Now let's see if the plain tablecloths will cover all of this," Elaine said, heading for the cupboard in the dining room where she kept the cloths they used on special occasions.

Jan came down and took charge of making sure all the hot food would be ready at once, and Elaine left Tara with the silverware tray and went to the kitchen to oversee the salad, bread, and relish parts of the meal. Jan had baked a large ham and was preparing mashed potatoes and green beans amandine.

"Think we'll have enough food?" Elaine asked with a chuckle.

Jan said, "I hope so."

"I was kidding."

"Ha. Remember how much those kids eat? Not to mention Brian and Van."

"True. Okay, you got me. But don't forget, we have a freezer full of cookies if we get desperate."

Just as Brian drove in, Elaine set the ham out on the counter to cool for a few minutes before he carved it. Jan had her gravy ready and keeping warm on a back burner.

Tara poked her head in the kitchen door. "Looks like everyone's here."

"Great." Elaine took off her apron and smoothed her hair. She and Jan went out to the entry hall, where Tara was opening the front door to let the mob in.

Elaine loved these large family gatherings, even if they did make her miss her own loved ones more sharply.

Avery and Kelly bounced in first.

"Hi, Elaine. Hi, Grandma," Kelly said.

"Yay, Aunt Tara's here." Avery ran into Tara's arms.

Brian was holding Virginia's arm as she mounted the steps, and Paula came behind her, carrying two colorful bouquets.

"Mom!" Elaine stepped outside and met her on the porch. "I'm so glad you could come."

"Any excuse to get out," her mother said with a laugh.

She let Elaine engulf her in a hug. When they stepped back, Elaine eyed her mother's plum-colored ensemble and perfectly coiffed hair. "Don't you look lovely?"

"Thank you. Now, we've got to settle which day you're bringing Sasha for lunch."

Elaine smiled. "Okay, Mom." She and her mother and Sasha would have their own special day soon at her mother's apartment.

"Hi, Elaine." Paula kissed her cheek. "These are for you and Mom. Where should I put them?"

Elaine looked down at the bright bouquets and full, frothy ribbon bows. "Oh, those are lovely. You didn't have to get me anything though."

"We wanted to."

"Well, let's find vases and put them in the east parlor, where we can all enjoy them while we eat dinner."

"Look what they brought me," Elaine's mother said, touching the carnation and baby's breath corsage on her sweater.

"How nice." Elaine took her arm and drew her inside.

Van and Amy had unbuckled the twins by this time and turned them loose from their car seats. As the little boys ran up the walk, Bob's car pulled in at the curb and he climbed out.

Elaine greeted Amy and Van, and swiped a pat on the twins' heads as they dashed past her.

"Hello, Bob!" she called. "Come on in."

"Am I the dog's tail?" he asked.

"The last to arrive, if I'm not mistaken, but if someone else shows up, they're welcome."

As she entered with him and closed the door, Avery came to her side. "Elaine, may we go up to the tower room?"

"Oh, I think we're about ready to sit down, honey. Why don't you wait until after we eat?"

"Okay. I'm really hungry," Avery said with a grin.

Elaine went to the kitchen to help Amy find vases. Then she stood in the kitchen doorway and watched all the greetings among the different generations. All of the Blakes and Kincaids pulled Bob in as if he was a part of the family, which was as it should be. Elaine gave silent thanks for a wonderful day. If only every day could be this full of joy.

Thoughts of the vandalism at the church crowded in on her, and she shoved them aside. She would not spend this happy day worrying about someone else's hurtful actions.

# CHAPTER FIVE

Greg Payson rang the doorbell at the big Queen Anne house at quarter to nine on Monday morning. Elaine let him in.

"Well, hi." She glanced at the small toolbox he carried. "I see you came prepared."

"I wasn't sure what you had for tools," Greg said.

"That's great. If you need something you don't have, just ask. Jan and I have a pretty good collection." Elaine led him back through the kitchen, where Jan was removing a tray of cream puffs from the oven and Rose was filling a pastry bag with the filling.

"Hi, Greg," Rose said with a big smile.

"Greg, it's great to see you," Jan said.

"Thanks." Greg grinned at Jan. "Yesterday I scarfed down all the muffins Mom got, so I hope you have more I can take home today." He pulled a five-dollar bill from his pocket.

Jan laughed. "You bet we do, but put that away."

He hesitated, then smiled and put the money back in his pocket.

Elaine led him through the back porch to the offending steps. She pointed downward.

"See how the third step is cracked? That one and the next two should be replaced, I think. And there are a couple more that have some rot, down between the deck and the boat dock."

"Okay," Greg said. "If it's just the treads, that should be easy to fix. What if it's the stringers too?"

"Well, then we have a major job, don't we?" Elaine said. "Let's cross that bridge when we come to it. Now, you can take my car to the lumber store to get whatever you need. I'll call them and ask them to bill me. We'll want the pressure-treated lumber. I think we have some leftover stain in the garage, but you might want to make sure before you go to the store."

"Sounds good." Greg set the toolbox on the top step and hopped over the side to stand in the grass beside the stairway. He stooped and looked underneath and rapped on the side boards with his knuckles. "This side seems okay. I'll check both sides all the way down though."

"Thanks," Elaine said. "So when did you get out of school?"

"I finished my exams Friday."

"Was this your sophomore year?" Elaine had tried to remember, but it slipped her mind.

"Yeah, I'm halfway done."

"Before you know it, you'll have your degree. What's your major?" Elaine asked.

"Biology."

She nodded. "I'm impressed. What do you plan to do after you graduate?"

"Uh, I'm not sure yet." Greg put his foot on a step below the ones she had indicated and cautiously tried his weight on it. When it held firmly, he stood on it and reached up over the intervening steps to open the toolbox. "Maybe grad school. I might like to go into research. I don't really know."

Elaine smiled. He sounded like the typical twenty-year-old these days, she thought.

"Come on up and find me when you're ready to go to the store, and I'll get you the car keys," she said. "We'll check on that stain before you leave."

She went into the kitchen through the back door.

"Hey," Jan said, "got a minute?"

"Yeah. What's up?" Elaine sat down on a stool at the island.

Jan was taking hot scones from a baking sheet and she kept working until she had them all on cooling racks. "I was thinking about the fingerprint kit and how we should order more powder for that."

"Okay." Elaine was the one who bought the kit in the first place. "I can order some this morning. Is that quick enough?"

Jan smiled. "Thanks. You just never know when you'll need it."

GREG CAME IN the back door of the kitchen about eleven o'clock. Rose was loading the dishwasher, and Jan looked up from the cookbook she was studying and smiled at him.

"I'm finished," Greg said.

"Great. I'll tell Elaine." Jan got up and put a glass of milk and a plate of cookies in his hands. "Why don't you take these and have a seat in the tearoom?"

She found Elaine at her desk in the office next door.

Elaine followed her into the west parlor, where Greg was sitting at a corner table enjoying his cookies. Rose had a couple of other parties she was waiting on nearer the front of the room. Zale Atherton was among them with a middle-aged couple, probably guests at Green Grove Cottages, Jan surmised.

Elaine smiled at Greg. "You're finished already?"

"Yeah." Greg jumped up. "I replaced three treads on the top steps and two on the lower ones. I checked all the other boards, and I even looked over the deck and the dock, but I think they're sound."

"I'm glad of that," Elaine said.

"Me too," Jan said. "We use the deck a lot."

"I think you just had a few boards that had cracked in the cold and ice, and the water got in past the stain," Greg explained. "You should be good for the summer."

"Great," Elaine said.

"I put some muffins in a box for you to take home." Jan stood and hurried to the kitchen to get them. When she returned, Elaine had handed Greg a check.

"Thanks a lot for making time for us, Greg."

Jan set down the take-out box, and Greg looked at it.

"Are you sure I can't pay for those?"

"Nope," Jan said. "That's a bonus."

"Hey, thanks. That's really nice of you."

"You're welcome, Greg," Elaine said. "I know you want to get a full-time job, but if you don't find something right away, we might have more odd jobs you could do."

"Sure. Call anytime. But I really do need to get something steady. College isn't cheap."

"I'm sure," Elaine said.

"I did qualify for a couple of scholarships, and they help, but they don't cover the whole bill. Not by a long shot." Greg took a big bite of a coconut-oatmeal cookie.

They chatted for a few more minutes, and when Greg had finished his snack, he picked up his toolbox and the muffins. Jan and Elaine walked with him to the front door.

Rose was cashing up a customer's slip. She put her change on a tray with a copy of the receipt. "Nice-looking kid," she said.

"Yeah, but he comes by it honestly. Look at his parents."

Business in the tearoom was slow enough that afternoon that Elaine sat down in her office and made out supply orders and paid bills. The fingerprinting powder was high on her list, and she ordered it online with two-day shipping. Afterward, she walked over to the post office to mail the items that had to be sent the slow way. Jo Murphy was leaving the building as Elaine approached.

"Jo! Hi!" Elaine said.

"Oh, hello." Jo paused at the bottom of the steps and brushed her curly brown hair back out of her eyes.

"How are you doing?" Elaine noted worry lines on Jo's forehead, and her friend's reply reinforced the impression.

"Not great." Jo let out a big sigh. "Dan Benson came around again this morning."

"To talk to the boys?"

"No. They're in school. I think he stopped for gas and decided to come in and reassure Des and me."

"And that's bad?" Elaine asked.

"I guess not. It's just that I know everyone in town is looking at Chris and Nick now and wondering if they made the mess at the church."

"Surely not."

Jo shrugged. "Dan said he hasn't found any evidence saying they did it. That's all. And that's supposed to make us feel better."

"Well, that's something," Elaine said.

"No. I want evidence that they *didn't* do it."

"It's pretty hard to prove a negative."

Jo's face tightened. "Well, when he can show that someone else did it, I guess the boys will be in the clear, and then people will stop suspecting them. Not until."

Elaine thought of the clues she and Jan had found in the church—the pocketknife that didn't belong to the twins and the shoeprint that at least wasn't Chris's. Probably best not to bring those up now, since she realized she still had the pocketknife and Des had implied that Jo might be upset if she knew they'd been examining Chris's shoes. She decided just to express the sympathy she felt.

"Oh, Jo, I'm so sorry. This has been stressful for all of you."

"You bet it has." Jo let out a little sob. "I'm sorry, Elaine. I didn't mean to take out my frustration on you. But it's really hard having everyone think your kids are bad apples."

"I don't think that, and neither does Jan. In fact, a lot of people came through the tearoom this morning, and I didn't hear anyone saying that."

"Well, good. Thanks." Jo managed a lopsided smile. "And thanks for letting me blow off steam. Dan said he's still talking to the people who live near the church."

"Let me guess—he can't tell you if he's learned anything or not."

"Well...I think he could see how frazzled I was. And Des was pretty stern with him about what this is doing to us. The boys didn't want to go to school this morning. Dan did say that Dr. McInnis—Matt, that is—was late coming home from the hospital Friday night, and he saw someone walking across the church parking lot."

"Did Dan say who it was?"

Jo shook her head. "He didn't know. Matt apparently assumed it was Pastor Mike, but he says he wasn't out at that time of night. So Dan's asking around, trying to see if anyone else saw anything."

"The damage may have been done hours before the boys went over to do the yard work," Elaine said.

"That's what I think. And Sarah Ryder did say that she saw the boys out her window a couple of times Saturday morning, and they were working hard in the flower beds and the front yard. But people just don't want to believe they would work steadily for a couple of hours and not go into the church for anything. If they had, they would have seen the mess, and I'm sure they would have gone and told the pastor or Sarah."

"I think so too," Elaine assured her.

JAN WATCHED FOR Elaine to come back from the post office. When her cousin came in the front door, she met her in the hall.

"Hey, I'm getting cabin fever. What do you say we take a breather?"

"Did you have something special in mind?"

"Not really. Maybe the flea market?" Jan and Elaine loved to browse the booths at Mainely Bargains. Several of the teapots and cup-and-saucer sets they used to serve customers came from there, and they'd found various other items they loved in the barnlike building.

"Are you sure you want to go there?" Elaine asked.

"What? Are you thinking about the little misadventure we had there last year about this time?"

"I am."

"That was not my fault," Jan said with mock severity. "And as you know, that vendor is no longer selling things at Mainely Bargains. According to the *Morning Sentinel*, several new sellers have booths there this year, and they just opened for the season. I think we should go now, before the summer people come and pick everything over."

Elaine grinned. "I'm with you. But we'd better check with Rose and Archie first."

"It's slow today, so it should be fine," Jan said.

They peeked into the east parlor, where Archie had two parties seated—four women at one table and two at another. Across the hall, Rose had only one mother-and-daughter pair sipping tea near the window. She was clearing another table, near the corner display of special teapots and other china.

Jan and Elaine stepped toward her.

"Mind if we run into town?" Elaine asked.

"We're fine," Rose said. "Jan, your peanut cookies were a hit today."

"That makes me glad," Jan said. "I love those cookies."

"Macy does too . . . she took home two dozen of them," Rose said with a smile. "Now, go and enjoy yourselves."

Elaine spotted a crumpled napkin under an empty table. She stooped to pick it up. "What's this?"

"What's what?" Rose asked.

Elaine straightened with the napkin in one hand. She held out a white plastic disk with the other.

"It looks like a poker chip," Jan said.

Rose nodded. "It sure does."

Elaine frowned. "I guess someone dropped it."

Rose looked around. "Several people have sat at this table today. But I know the floor was clean when we opened."

"Well, we can leave it by the checkout, I suppose," Elaine said.

Jan shook her head. "Who would come looking for something like that? Come on, let's get moving."

"Okay, get your jacket. We'll take my car." Elaine put the chip in Rose's hand and headed for the garage. She pulled her red Malibu into the parking lot at the flea market twenty minutes later and found a space not far from the entrance.

"Good," Jan said. "It's not too crowded."

The flea market was one of their favorite summer outings. They could find all sorts of things here—handcrafts, antiques, yard sale leftovers—just about anything. One of Jan's favorite past purchases was a box of old cookbooks, from which she had culled several recipes the tearoom patrons now enjoyed.

When they got inside, they strolled through the aisles of tables at a leisurely pace. Elaine picked up two saucers off a linen-covered table.

"These match Corrie's china."

"Get them," Jan said. "You can give them to her the next time she's here."

Jan spent a whopping fifty cents for a battered, hardbound copy of Louisa May Alcott's *Eight Cousins*.

"Avery loved *Little Women*," she explained to Elaine. "I thought I'd put this up in the attic and let her discover it."

"I love it when kids read old books," Elaine said.

"Me too. E-books are good in a way, but they say there's something about turning actual pages that helps comprehension."

"Interesting."

"Yeah, I plan to stock some older picture books for the twins too. If you see a good buy on some of those, grab them, especially if the illustrations are nice. Max and Riley are wild about trucks and construction equipment right now, but I'll take fairy tales and cuddly bedtime stories too."

Elaine stopped walking and touched her arm. Jan looked up from the table of knickknacks she'd been scanning. "What?"

"Look at that painting." Elaine nodded toward the peg-board wall standing behind the vendor's booth, where several pieces of framed art hung.

"Which one?"

"The woman looking out the window."

Jan found it just as she spoke and nodded slowly. "That's beautiful."

"There's something about it..."

"Is it an oil painting?" Jan asked. "It doesn't really look like a print."

"I think so." Elaine caught the vendor's eye and leaned over the table toward the woman. "Could we have a closer look at that painting up there? The one with the woman at the table."

"Sure." The red-haired woman pushed up out of her lawn chair and looked at the piece Elaine indicated. "Why don't you come back here and look, if you don't mind? That would be a lot easier than taking it down."

"Okay." Elaine and Jan squeezed in between the woman's table and the one next to it and entered the space behind, where the vendor had two chairs, a tote bag, and several empty boxes.

"Sorry. Can you get through?" The woman shuffled a few boxes and put the tote under the table.

"You're fine," Elaine said. "Thanks for accommodating us."

The woman turned to wait on another customer.

Elaine peered closely at the canvas. "It's definitely oils. I can't see a signature though."

She studied the picture, and Jan's gaze lingered on it too. The painting portrayed a woman sitting at a table inside a house or apartment—apartment, Jan decided, as the view out the window was higher than ground level, but the room looked like the living room or main room of the residence. The woman's brown hair was fixed in a knot on the back of her head, and she faced slightly away from the viewer, as if she gazed out the window. Even though she couldn't see her full face, Jan could tell she was beautiful. On the table was a bouquet of flowers that varied from pink through lavender to purple, and a steaming cup of tea, which was probably one reason Elaine felt so drawn to the subject.

"Her teacup looks like bone china." Elaine's voice held a quiver of excitement. "And the vase those flowers are in is lovely."

Jan was searching the bottom of the canvas, trying to find a signature. "Maybe a local artist?"

"I don't know," Elaine said. "The landscape outside doesn't really look like New England to me. Does it to you?"

Jan frowned and focused on the part of the picture that lay outside the woman's window. "It could be a park."

"That's what I was thinking," Elaine said. "So green. What you can see of the architecture is lovely. The buildings look old. Classic, somehow. And there's a steeple showing above those trees, and another building over there."

"I like it," Jan said, "but it's not very realistic. Kind of dreamy."

"Yeah, it looks sort of Impressionistic," Elaine agreed. "The woman's clothes look newer than that period though. Maybe 1930s? Twenties, at least." She leaned back a little and swept her gaze over the entire painting. "It's really well done. See the brushwork in the flowers and leaves? It looks old though. A little grimy."

Jan shrugged. That shouldn't be a problem. "Heather Wells could clean it."

Elaine nodded. They had become friends with a restorer in Waterville, and Elaine knew she could do the job. She reached for the price tag.

"How much?" Jan asked.

"It says two hundred."

Jan winced. That seemed like a lot to her, but she'd seen Elaine spend more than that on art before. "What do you think?"

Before Elaine could answer, the red-haired woman was at her elbow.

"I could give you twenty-five percent off on that. I'd like to earn enough today to cover the cost of my booth for a month, and that would just about cap it off."

"*Hmm.* Thanks. I'll think about it while we browse the rest of the market, okay?" Elaine asked.

"Sure." The woman looked a little disappointed.

"I do like it," Elaine assured her. "It's just—you know—I wasn't planning to buy a painting today."

"I understand." The vendor sat down and unscrewed the top of a water bottle.

Jan and Elaine went back out into the aisle and moved away, slowly scanning the tables as they walked down the row.

"I hate to disappoint her," Elaine said, "but still. A hundred and fifty dollars. I don't need it." She looked wistfully back over her shoulder. "I do like it though. The colors would be great in the west parlor."

"Oh yes, between the windows," Jan said. "We have a blank spot there, and that really would go nicely with our old-fashioned tearoom décor."

Elaine paused at another table and picked up a saltshaker shaped like a skunk.

"Cute," Jan said, "but wouldn't it make you think the food smelled bad?"

Elaine laughed. "Silly. Oh, look, the vendor has a box of old picture books. Just what you wanted. I see some old Golden Books."

Half an hour later, they had looked over all the booths. Elaine and Jan both had made several purchases, but none of them were expensive items. Jan turned to her cousin. Time to talk turkey.

"Well? The painting? Are you going to take the plunge?"

"I think so," Elaine said soberly.

Jan wasn't surprised, really. "Then let's take another look at it."

They walked back to the booth where the woman had displayed the painting.

"Oh no." Elaine stopped walking. "It's gone!"

# CHAPTER SIX

Elaine stared toward the table, her eyes on the display board behind it. The place where the painting she loved had hung was now empty. Odd how putting a thing out of reach instantly made it more desirable.

"Maybe God didn't want you to buy it," Jan said feebly.

Elaine couldn't help it. Her lips quirked into a smile. "You could be right. And if that's so, then it's for the best. That lovely picture will grace someone else's home and bring them joy. I'm going to ask the vendor, just to be sure."

They reached the booth as another customer moved on with a smile and a bagged purchase. The bag was too small to hold the painting, however.

"Hi," Elaine said. "Remember us? We were interested in the painting..."

"I knew you'd come back." The woman smiled and stooped to pull something from beneath her table. The framed oil rested in a large cardboard box. "Still want it? I'll let you have it for one twenty-five."

Elaine managed to keep her jaw from dropping. "That's very nice of you."

The woman shrugged. "I made a couple of good sales after you left. And I just had a feeling I'd see you again. When my husband dropped by a few minutes ago, I asked him to take the painting down for me, so we wouldn't have to do it ourselves when you came to get it."

Elaine gazed down at the picture. Its colors and composition pleased her, but it was the woman's face that drew her most. The sweet sadness in her expression tugged at Elaine's heart.

"I'll take it."

"Great. I've got a roll of bubble wrap somewhere under here that I can wrap it in for you." The seller leaned down again and poked around under her table, straightening with triumph in her eyes and the packing material in her hand. Elaine wrote her a check and then helped steady the frame while she efficiently wrapped it.

"Now, do you need help out with that?" the vendor asked.

"I think I can carry it, if Jan can get my other bags."

"No problem." Jan slipped the handholds of the plastic sacks over her wrists. "What about your purse?" She consolidated a few of their purchases so that she only had three bags and two purses to lug.

At last they had everything under control and carried their bounty out to the car. Elaine laid the painting carefully on the backseat, and Jan stored the other items in the trunk.

"It's almost half past four," Jan said in surprise.

Elaine laughed. "I'm surprised it's not later. My stomach's growling. Do you want to go home or eat out?"

"I think I've spent enough money for one day," Jan said. "We'd better get home and have leftovers."

"Your wish is my command." Elaine turned her red Malibu toward Lancaster. The scenery became more and more rural as they left the small city. They passed a dairy farm and a sawmill, and rolled on through a stand of tall pine trees. When they passed Tyson and Claudia McInnis's apple orchard, she knew they were almost home.

"Look, the apples are budding out," Jan said.

Elaine smiled. "I love this time of year. In a week, that whole orchard will be pink and white. I hope I remember to take some pictures."

When they arrived at the house, they carried their bundles in through the garage. Jan carried the sewing supplies and books she had bought upstairs while Elaine set the wrapped painting on the dining room table. It would be safe there until she decided for sure what to do with it. She peeked into the east parlor. Archie was wiping down the tables. Every chair was in place, and the floor looked spotless.

"Hello!" she called.

Archie looked up and smiled. "Welcome home, madam."

Elaine smiled at his mock formality. "Everything go all right here?"

"We had a splendid day. A large party came in shortly after you left, and I think you'll be pleased with the receipts."

"Terrific. I hope we didn't leave you in the lurch though."

"Rose and I were able to serve everyone satisfactorily. And we sold two packages of loose tea and one of those brown teapots from the shelves in front of the cash register."

"Fantastic." Elaine went out the hall door. Sure enough, there were some gaps in the shelves where they displayed retail items. She would replace those this evening.

She went to the doorway of the west parlor. Rose was just coming out with a broom and dustpan in her hands.

"Oh, hi! Did you have a good time?"

"It was lots of fun, and we have treasures to show you later," Elaine said.

"*Ooh!*" Rose grinned. "That's always fun. Did you eat?"

"Not yet. We'll have a picnic supper on the back porch, I think. Do you and Archie need any help?"

"We're nearly done. Archie and I will be out of here in a few minutes. And I started the dishwasher."

"Thank you," Elaine said. "That's a big help."

"Good." Rose whisked past her to empty her dustpan in the trash can behind the checkout counter.

When she and Archie had hung up their aprons and left, Elaine went to the kitchen and opened the refrigerator. She found a plastic container of chicken salad and was making two sandwiches when Jan came into the room.

"Chicken salad okay?"

"Sure." Jan opened a cupboard and took out a pitcher. "I'll make some iced tea."

They were soon settled on the screened porch, where they could view their end of the lake. Boats put in and left from the marina docks nearby, and a motorboat pulling a water skier set out from the float at Green Glade Cottages.

"*Brrr.* It's early for water skiing," Elaine said in surprise.

"I know. That lake water is still ice-cold." Jan lifted her glass of iced tea. "But Zale was in the other day and told me she and Shane were having some friends over for a party, before they get too busy with the summer people."

That sounded reasonable to Elaine. The string of rental cottages would be full after Memorial Day. Macy Atherton and her son and daughter-in-law, Shane and Zale, would be busy all summer, catering to their paying guests.

"Even so, I'm not putting on my swimsuit until the end of the month."

Jan gave an exaggerated shiver. "Me neither, but you know young people. Do you want to have Brian hang that painting the next time he's over?"

"Maybe Greg could do it, unless you think Brian will stop in within a couple of days."

Jan picked up half her sandwich. "I'm not sure. He and Paula were here yesterday, so we might not see him again for a while."

"Well, I don't know if Greg has found a job or not, but we can ask," Elaine said. "I'll set the painting in the sewing room upstairs, out of the way, until someone can come do that."

A gray cat with a lush, long-haired coat slunk through the new grass on the slope and hopped up on the edge of the deck below. He looked up at them and meowed.

"Come on up, Earl." Jan sprang to her feet, setting her plate on the small table between her chair and Elaine's, and went to where they kept a canister of cat food. She filled his dish and let him on to the back porch. Earl Grey was strictly forbidden to enter the house, per state regulations for establishments that served food, but he was very happy to socialize with Jan and Elaine on the porches. Sometimes he even let some of the customers stroke him.

"I'll pat you after I finish eating," Jan told him, and Earl seemed content with that and his bowl of food. Jan resumed her seat and picked up her glass.

"Sasha's coming in tomorrow," Elaine said.

"That's right. What do we need to do?"

"Nothing, really. The guest room is all made up. I'll put some fresh flowers in there and check on the towels, but she's an easy keeper."

"You should drive over to Sugarloaf with her on Thursday."

Elaine shook her head. "I'd just be in the way. But I'll spend her free day with her, for sure." She looked suddenly at Jan, remembering their Saturday obligation. "I almost forgot about the Mother-Daughter Tea."

"I checked on the dishes and tablecloths Saturday, while we were cleaning things up at the church," Jan reminded her. "Annie took most of the kitchen linens home to wash, and we'll have Priscilla's good tablecloths."

"Right. We made a list of things to take over. Maybe we can do some preparations the day that Sasha's on her business trip. What happened to that list anyway?"

"It's on my desk," Jan said, "along with the lists of refreshments I'm making and the tea blends and punch recipe for you to prepare."

"Oh, good." Elaine sighed. "I'm glad one of us is thinking. I shouldn't have taken so much time off today. I've got the ads to prepare for the high tea for our season opening too. We can't ignore our first anniversary."

"No, it's too good a publicity opportunity," Jan said. She sat back with a sigh and looked out over the lake. "Today was fun. We needed a break."

"It was, but I'll be putting in the next three hours on the books or I'll get woefully behind."

"And I'll start making the four dozen cupcakes for tomorrow and do extras for the tea on Saturday. After I give Earl Grey a pat or two."

The cousins smiled at each other.

"I'm so glad we're in this together," Elaine said.

"Me too."

# CHAPTER SEVEN

The tearoom was abuzz on Tuesday morning. Elaine had fussed over the guest room and made sure everything was spotless. She picked a bouquet of wildflowers as soon as the dew was off and arranged it in a charming Rookwood pottery vase. After that, she was at loose ends and decided to help Rose and Archie out front to distract herself.

"When does Sasha's plane land?" Rose asked her when they crossed paths in the entrance hall.

Elaine glanced at her watch. "She should be on the ground about quarter past two."

"Only a couple more hours," Rose said with a grin.

"Yeah, but then she has to drive up here from Portland. I'm guessing she won't be here much before four. It takes a few minutes to get the luggage and the rental car sorted out, you know."

Rose nodded. "Maybe more than that. But she ought to be here for supper."

"Jan's planning on that." Elaine threw her hands up. "I can hardly stand it."

"So that's why you volunteered to wait on Macy," Rose said in a conspiratorial voice.

"You're right. I needed to think about something besides my daughter." Elaine picked up the tray she had fixed for Macy's party. "Did you know that those three women with Macy are ones she hired to clean the cottages before the summer guests arrive?"

Rose's eyebrows arched. "That's generous of her, to bring them here for an outing."

"Unusually so for Macy," Elaine agreed. "She told me they're having some work done in the kitchen, so I guess she couldn't make tea in there."

"Well, I'm glad they came to Tea for Two." Rose breezed into the parlor bearing her customers' order on a tray. Archie was manning the counter in the entry at the moment, cashing Pearl Trexler out, and Elaine went into the parlor opposite to where Rose had gone.

At noon, only a few patrons remained. After Rose and Archie had both eaten, Jan said to Elaine, "Grab the drinks and let's eat down on the deck. Then I'm going into turbo-baker mode."

"Greg did a good job on these steps," Elaine noted as she followed Jan down to the seating area. The breeze that came over the lake was not so cool as to make her uncomfortable, but Elaine was glad she had worn a sweater. Birds flitted about the nearby maple tree.

"A purple finch," Jan whispered.

Elaine followed her gaze and saw a bird colored all over in what she would call pink. "He looks like he took a bath in cherry Kool-Aid."

Jan laughed. "We ought to put some birdhouses out here. Don't know why we haven't thought of it."

"Because we've been busy every minute for the last year."

"Not really," Jan said. "We loll around out here fairly often, you know. Not through the winter, it's true."

"No, but I guess we did our share of lazing about on the deck last summer, and in front of the fireplace when it was cold."

"Exactly. I love lazing about."

Elaine smiled. "I like to be busy. I think it makes these pauses even better than they would be otherwise."

"I know what you mean."

Jack Weston, the game warden for the region, brought his cabin cruiser in slowly toward their dock.

Elaine waved, and Jack waved back.

"He's coming here," Jan said.

Sure enough, Jack nosed the boat in gently and tied up to one of the end posts, then hopped out on to the dock and walked swiftly its length and up the steps to the deck.

"Hello, ladies."

"How's the fishing today?" Elaine asked.

"Not bad. I've checked at least a dozen licenses on the lake. Saw some nice lake trout too, and a couple of bass."

"That's what we like to hear," Elaine said. "It brings the summer people back year after year."

"Yup, I wouldn't have a job without 'em. Do you mind if I moor here while I grab some lunch at Kate's Diner?"

"You're welcome anytime, Jack," Elaine told the handsome young man. Jack came by fairly often since he had befriended Jan's daughter, Tara. Both Elaine and Jan could tell there was a spark between them, but they also didn't mind that they seemed to be taking it slow.

"In fact, you can have lunch here if you'd like," Jan said. "We've got more leftovers than you could shake a stick at."

He laughed. "Thanks, but Lydia wanted to interview me for the *Wave*, so I said I'd have a late lunch there and she could ask me questions."

"Aha," Elaine said, as if that explained a mystery. Lydia Pierce worked with her mother and sister at the family-owned diner, but she also published a small weekly paper for the tourists who flooded Lancaster in the summer. They could pick it up in local businesses, and it had turned out to be good advertising for Tea for Two and the other shops and services in town.

"Well, come some other day," Jan said. "We've always got something here."

Jack grinned. "And the best cookies in town."

"Thanks." Jan chuckled. "You're a sweet-talker, in more ways than one. Come to the back door on your way to the boat after the interview, and I'll give you some dessert."

"You're on."

WHEN SASHA PULLED into the driveway and got out of the snazzy rental car, Elaine was out the door and down the porch steps before Jan could even get her apron off. She loved seeing Elaine with her daughter, laughing and hugging and talking over each other in their eagerness to catch up. Jan got to see her own kids often, but Elaine's lived far away and their time together was rare. Phone calls and e-mails were good, but they weren't the same.

The tearoom had been closed half an hour, and they were almost done with the daily routine of cleanup. As Elaine and Sasha entered with their arms around each other, Jan went to greet her, unable to tone down her grin.

"Sasha! You made good time."

"Thanks, Jan." Sasha gave her the firm, solid hug she expected from the athlete. "You look good."

"Thanks. Are you hungry?"

"That depends. How long until dinner?"

"About an hour and a half."

"In that case, I could use a snack," Sasha said. "And I know you've got 'em. What's the cookie of the day?"

Jan came back with, "I've got six varieties in the kitchen, and if you don't like those, we'll look in the freezer."

They all laughed, and Sasha said, "I've never met one of your cookies I didn't like."

Rose came out of the east parlor with a damp green cloth in her hand. "Sasha! Welcome."

"Nice to see you, Rose." Sasha looked around expectantly. "Okay, where's Archie?"

"He left as soon as we closed," Elaine said. "Had to pick up his car from the garage before five. But you'll see him tomorrow. Unless you're going to Sugarloaf then."

"No, that's Thursday, remember? Tomorrow I'm having fun with you!"

"Oh boy," Elaine said. "I was hoping you'd say that."

"I have a special outing in mind for us," Sasha said.

"What is it?"

"Not telling yet. I haven't set it up, and I don't want to disappoint you if we can't do it."

"Okay." Elaine walked with her into the kitchen. "What do you want to drink?"

Sasha made a guilty face. "Got any diet soda? I know it's a tearoom..."

Elaine laughed. "And I know you. I stocked up on your favorites." She opened the refrigerator door. "Take your pick."

"Oh, you're the best mom ever." Sasha chose a bottle of diet cola, and Elaine handed her a glass. "Want ice?"

"No, this is good."

"The cookies are over here."

Elaine opened several plastic containers that Jan had left neatly stacked on the counter. While Sasha was choosing her snack, Jan came to the doorway.

"Looks like you two are good for a while. I told Priscilla I'd pick her up when the library closes. She's got those lace tablecloths she offered for the tea, and we thought we'd take them over to the church."

"Oh, you don't have to do that now," Elaine said. Priscilla Gates was the town librarian, and she and Jan had become good friends.

"I know, but she called me and said she'd brought them along to the library today, so I figured we might as well go over for a few minutes. It will give us a chance to hash over what the book club is going to read next month too. But I won't be gone long." While she was talking, Jan went to the stove and turned on the oven. "I know you two will be gabbing a mile a minute, but when that's preheated, put the potato scallop in, okay?"

"Will do," Elaine promised. As soon as Jan left, she looked at Sasha. "Now, don't let me forget to do that."

Sasha laughed. "Okay, Mom. Getting forgetful, are you?"

"Not as a rule, but I'm so excited to have you here that it might slip my mind. Now, tell me how your training is going."

Sasha pulled out a chair at the small kitchen table and sat down with her soda and cookies. "It's good. My coach thinks I have a decent chance of making the Olympics."

"That would be *so* thrilling." Elaine gave an exaggerated shiver.

"Well, we won't know for sure until a month or two in advance, so I've got to keep on my game and enter every world-class competition I can. That's part of why I'm here. I'm sort of an ambassador to encourage the management at Sugarloaf to upgrade an event they're hosting next fall. And to set up training time for me and some of the others in my group before the meet." Sasha shrugged. "I could have arranged that by phone, but Terry—my coach—thought I could persuade them to beef up the event to world class. It wouldn't take that much from the owners, really. And we'd love to see them add another meet around February. We'll see."

"It's really important, I guess?"

"Yeah. We need more events big enough to draw the foreign competition in, so we can see what they've got and practice going up against the real elite."

"Would athletes come here from Scandinavia for an event like that?"

"Sure, if they knew it was top notch. They go to Vail and Sun Valley for them. And we fly over there to compete."

"I know. It seems like you're on the road all the time."

Sasha's phone beeped. "Oops, gotta take this. It may be confirmation for our outing tomorrow."

"Okay." Elaine glanced at the stove. "Oh, it's time to put that casserole in."

Sasha put her phone to her ear and meandered into the empty tearoom. Elaine put the scalloped potatoes in the oven and scanned the refrigerator to see what Jan was serving with them. London broil, apparently. Elaine decided to leave that to her cousin, but she could get the vegetables ready. She was hunting through the utensil drawer when Sasha returned, beaming.

"We're all set. Tomorrow at two, we'll be at the shooting range."

Elaine almost dropped the vegetable peeler. "Shooting range?" She gulped. "Okay, honey. If you're going, I'm going."

JAN AND PRISCILLA gathered the table linens Priscilla was loaning for the Mother-Daughter Tea and carried them to the parsonage door. Jan rang the bell, and Sarah Ryder opened the door.

"Hello."

"Hi," Jan said over her armful of tablecloths. "Just delivering stuff for the tea. Could we borrow the key please?"

"Oh, you don't need it," Sarah said. "Mike's over there in his office. Just go in the front door."

"Okay, thanks," Jan said.

They walked across the grass to the church parking lot and went up the front steps. Priscilla managed to open the big front door, and Jan ducked inside. With her friend following, she went down the steps to the fellowship hall. Just for a moment, Jan wondered if they would again find the hall in disarray, but that was silly. The vandals wouldn't return to trash the church all over again.

She turned on the lights and relaxed. Everything looked fine. She walked past the memorabilia case and lowered her load of tablecloths onto a table.

"Isn't this where they keep the Henry Knox letter?" Priscilla asked. She had stopped beside the case.

"Yeah, it is," Jan said.

Priscilla brought her load of linens over and laid them beside Jan's. "I'd love to see it again. The church loaned it to the library a couple of years ago so we could display it."

"Oh well, that's easy. I think there's a switch here for the spotlights."

Jan walked back to the case and located the light switch on the wall. "There we go." She flipped it up, and track lighting came on, illuminating the trophies and other items in the case. "I've heard about it a few times, but I never paid much attention to it." Her gaze bounced over the other items and landed on a framed letter, sitting on the center shelf. "That's it, isn't it?" Something seemed odd to her. Her friend was smoothing out a wrinkle in one of the tablecloths. "Priscilla, come look at this."

Priscilla came closer and stared into the case, frowning. "That can't be it. It doesn't look right."

"That's what I was thinking," Jan said.

"Although it does look like the frame Knox's letter was in when we displayed it."

Jan bent down and looked closer. She caught her breath as she realized what was wrong. The paper was too white, the script too dark. She and Priscilla looked at each other.

"You're right," Jan said. "That's not two hundred years old. It looks like...like a photocopy."

# CHAPTER EIGHT

W e have to tell Pastor Mike," Jan said. "I'll go upstairs and get him."

"Okay," Priscilla replied, looking at the letter again. "I'll stay right here."

Jan hurried up the way they had come and through the sanctuary. The door of the pastor's office was wide open, and Mike was sitting at his desk inside with a Bible, two heavy books, and a notebook open before him.

Jan knocked lightly on the door panel. "Pastor?"

He looked up, focused on her, and smiled. "Hello, Jan. May I help you?"

"I . . . well, I'm sorry to bother you, but there's something I'd like you to look at in the basement."

His expression sobered. "Not again."

"No, it's not that. Not vandals. It's just that Priscilla Gates and I brought some things over for the tea, and she wanted to see the general's letter. You know, in the trophy case."

Pastor Mike nodded.

"Well, it looks odd."

He eyed her for a moment. "Odd, how?"

"Can you take a look? I'm sure you've looked at it a lot more times than I have."

"All right. I needed a break anyway." He pushed his chair back and rose. Jan followed him to the nearer back stairway that came out on the other end of the fellowship hall. He walked briskly across the room toward Priscilla. "Hello, Miss Gates."

"Hi," Priscilla said. "I was just helping Jan with some things..." She stepped back a little.

"That's fine. Now, let's see that letter." Pastor Mike stood squarely in front of the case and zeroed in on the framed letter. He stood in silence so long that Jan began to grow concerned.

"Pastor?" she asked softly.

"That's a fake."

Jan exhaled. "We thought so."

"The ink looks black," he said. "It was brownish before. And the paper doesn't look old."

"That's what we thought. Priscilla and I noticed it right away."

Priscilla raised a hand and shrugged. "I see a lot of old documents when I'm researching at the State Archives. Genealogy, you know?"

"Well, this isn't the letter, at least not the *real* letter," Pastor Mike said.

Priscilla reached absently to smooth her glossy brown hair. "Wasn't it sent by General Henry Knox to the first pastor of this church in 1797? That date sticks in my head."

"Yes," Mike said. "He was thanking the reverend for his hospitality the previous week, and he mentioned his estate in Thomaston and several family members. The church has had it here on display in the building ever since. But that's not the real letter."

"What do you think happened?" Jan asked.

Pastor Mike sighed. "I don't know."

Priscilla leaned in. "I'd say someone made a photocopy and swapped it out for the genuine letter."

"That's awful." Jan pulled her phone from her pocket.

"Are you calling the police?" Pastor Mike asked.

"No, I was going to call Elaine." Jan felt her cheeks color.

"Oh, sure," the pastor said. "But I think I'd better call Dan Benson."

"Of course."

"I'll go up to my office and make the call. Please don't touch anything, okay, ladies?" Pastor Mike shook his head, discouragement etched on his features.

"We won't," Jan promised.

He went up the stairs. Before Jan could wake up her phone, it rang, startling her.

"It's Elaine," she said to Priscilla. She pushed the green button. "Hi, Elaine."

"Hi," her cousin said. "I just noticed that box of decorations for the tea. Did you want those over there now?"

"Uh...No, I don't think so, but thanks. We haven't even started with the tablecloths. Something new has come up over here."

"What kind of something?" Elaine asked. "Not another break-in, I hope."

"I don't think so. But we've just noticed that something valuable is missing. You know that handwritten letter from General Knox?"

"Yeah. In the glass case. You mean that's missing now?"

"Seems to be," Jan said, throwing Priscilla an apologetic look.

"I'm sure people looked at that case after the break-in and said everything was intact," Elaine said.

"Well, it's not exactly missing, but the one that's in there now is a fake, according to Pastor Mike. And Priscilla. And me."

After a moment's pause, Elaine said, "That is really weird."

"Yeah," Jan said. "I mean, if the vandals wanted to steal it, why didn't they just break the glass in the door and take it? Why bother to make a fake?"

"Very good question."

"The pastor is calling Dan," Jan told her. "It may be best if Priscilla and I leave the stuff here and come back another time."

Priscilla leaned toward her and said quietly, "Let's at least get the tablecloths on and make sure they're going to work."

Jan nodded and said to Elaine, "I guess we'll do a little, but you and I will have to come another day and decorate."

"Okay," Elaine replied, "but don't stay too long. Remember you've got the cupcakes here to decorate for Ella Richardson's party."

"Oh yeah," Jan said.

"Do you want Sasha and me to…"

"No, I'll have time. But you're right. I'll try to get home as soon as I can."

She heard men's voices and footsteps on the stairway and ended the phone call. If necessary, she would embellish the cupcakes during her early-morning baking session, but she would rather have Annie Richardson's special order done and boxed tonight.

"Hello, ladies," Trooper Benson said as he reached the alcove at the bottom of the stairwell.

Jan and Priscilla greeted him.

"You must have been close by," Jan said.

Dan grinned. "Over at Murphy's, shooting the breeze with Des, as a matter of fact." Dan glanced at the case and looked toward Pastor Mike. "This it?"

"Yes," Mike said. "The framed letter, there in the center."

Dan leaned in close to examine the item he indicated. "Oh yes. And how do you know it's been substituted for the real one?"

"I'm pretty sure that's a photocopy, in black and white, on modern paper. Somebody copied it, trimmed it to the right size, and slipped it into the frame. The old ink was brownish and faded, for one thing. And the paper just doesn't look old."

Priscilla went closer and bent to look closely. "I agree with Pastor Ryder. We had this on display at the library one time, a few years ago. It looks the same at a casual glance, but when you look closely and think about it, it's obviously not the real thing."

"Okay," Dan said, straightening. "Is the case locked?"

"No," Pastor Mike said.

"Why not, if you have valuable historical artifacts in it?"

Pastor Mike huffed out a breath. "I don't have a good answer for that, except that most of the things in there aren't worth much. Bible quiz trophies, the old key to the original building…just look at it. It's memorabilia, not antiques."

"Except this one letter."

"Well, yeah." Pastor Mike rubbed the back of his neck, looking a little embarrassed. "The case has never been locked since

I came here. I don't even know if there's a key to that lock. But the church is usually locked up, except during services or if I'm here working in my study."

"There might be fingerprints on the frame," Jan said. They all looked at her, and she felt a blush coming on. "Sorry."

"No, you're right," Dan said. "There could be some on the door as well, but we'd have to fingerprint the entire church to rule the members out."

"But the frame shouldn't have too many prints on it." Jan thought once more of the professional fingerprint kit Elaine had bought a few months ago and wished she and her cousin could have a go at that wooden frame.

"We can try." Dan first took some photographs of the case, then took out a handkerchief and opened the cabinet door. He unfolded it and reached in to bring out the framed letter. "I don't suppose you'd have a bag this would fit in, Jan? The evidence bags I have on me are too small."

"Hold on." Jan hurried to the kitchen and found a box of bags designed for roasting turkeys. She took it out to Dan.

"That ought to work," he said.

Jan opened one and held it out, and he slid the frame into it carefully.

"Thanks." He took it from her.

"I was wondering why the thief would make such a mess of the church and not break the cabinet glass," Jan said.

Dan frowned. "I don't know. But since the cabinet wasn't locked, perhaps he thought that would draw attention to the theft. I have another question though." He turned to the pastor. "How likely do you think it is that someone stole the letter, took it somewhere else, made the copy to substitute, then brought the framed fake back here?"

Pastor Ryder looked confused.

"That seems very unlikely to me," Jan said. "That is, if you want my opinion, which you probably don't."

Dan smiled at her. "On the contrary, your opinion is usually valuable."

"So you're thinking he had the copy with him when he came here?" Pastor Ryder asked.

"More likely that he made it here," Dan said.

"But..." Pastor Mike swallowed hard. "The copier's upstairs in my office."

"Do you keep the office locked?"

"No."

"Is there a counting device on the copy machine?" Dan asked. "Do you keep a log of the copies made?"

"There's a counter," Pastor Mike said, "but I hardly ever pay attention to it. If someone asks to make personal copies, we ask them to put a quarter for each copy in the jar on the shelf above it."

Jan doubted this person had left any quarters, but it didn't seem like a comforting thing to say at the moment, so she kept quiet.

"Mind if I take a look up there?"

"No," Pastor Mike said, "but you saw it on Saturday. My office was a mess, just like the fellowship room and the kitchen."

"And you didn't find anything odd when you cleaned it up?" Dan asked.

"No." Pastor Mike's chin rose suddenly, and he breathed sharply.

"Well?"

The pastor looked at Dan, a frown wrinkling his forehead. "There was one crumpled sheet of paper in the wastebasket, the kind we use in the copier. But my office had been cleaned the day before."

"Would it still be there?"

Pastor Mike shook his head. "I filled the wastebasket with trash and debris and took out the garbage bag. Asher and I made a run to the dump that afternoon with all the garbage we cleaned up. It never occurred to me that that piece of paper could be important. If I'd looked at it, I would have realized something was up."

"I can't imagine we'll get it back." Dan sighed. "It sounds like a lot of people were aware of the letter being here."

"Well, sure," the pastor said. "All of the church people, at least."

"Not to mention everyone who saw it when the library displayed it," Priscilla added.

"It seems like a lot of trouble to go to, messing everything up, when they could have just snatched the letter and run with it," Jan said.

Pastor Mike's frown deepened. "You don't think someone stole the letter and someone else vandalized the church, do you?"

Jan shrugged. "I'm just saying, we don't know that the letter was taken at the same time the church was trashed. If the letter had been switched before we discovered the vandalism, none of us noticed it."

"True," Pastor Mike said.

Dan turned a page in his notebook. "Okay, so when is the last time you were sure the real letter was here in the case?" He looked at Priscilla first.

"I haven't seen it since the library borrowed it," Priscilla said. "And that was two or three years ago."

Dan arched his eyebrows at Jan.

"I'm afraid I haven't paid much attention to it," she said. "I looked closely at it the first time I learned its history, but since then, I've pretty much ignored it."

Pastor Mike's brow furrowed. "Once in a while I stop and look at it, since I'm related to the recipient of the letter, but..."

"You are?" Jan stared at him. "I didn't know that."

"Oh yeah, it's well known in our family. And once in a while a distant relative will come by and ask to see it, and I'll show it to them. But not lately. It's probably been six months or so since that happened."

"So you have no idea when the real letter was switched out for the fake?" Dan asked.

"I'm afraid not. But..." Pastor Mike shook his head. "Surely I'd have noticed the ink fairly soon. I mean, I must have looked at that letter hundreds of times."

"*Hmm.*" Dan wrote something in his notebook.

"What?" Pastor Mike asked.

"Has anyone ever asked you what it was worth?"

"Not that I recall."

"Do you know what it's worth?" Dan held the pastor's gaze.

"Well, I did some online browsing once, out of curiosity."

"What did you find?"

Pastor Mike ran a hand through his hair. "I saw a few General Knox autographs in the five hundred to a thousand range. Letters he wrote pertaining to the military go for more."

"Okay. And how long ago did you do this research?"

"Maybe three or four months," Pastor Mike said.

"You must have looked at it closely then."

"You're right, I did. That was probably the last time for me. I even took it out of the case once and carried it up to my office so I could look at it and compare the signature to the ones I found online. It had been suggested by Alan Oakley and a few others that the letter be sold to help pay off the church mortgage." Jan remembered that too. It was more than a suggestion, if Jan remembered correctly. It actually caused some tension for a while between Alan and Pastor Mike. "I thought the congregation ought to know what they had here."

Dan just looked at him.

"What?" Pastor Mike asked again.

"Just thinking, Pastor."

"Wait a second, you don't think I took the letter, do you?" Pastor Mike threw a somewhat panicky glance Jan and Priscilla's way. "Dan, I wouldn't."

"I'm sure."

But Dan's neutral tone didn't comfort Jan, and she could tell by the pastor's uneasy expression that he didn't like it either.

# CHAPTER NINE

J an still wasn't home, and Elaine was afraid the potato scallop would be overdone, so she took it out of the oven and
started cooking the London broil. Sasha pitched in to toss the
salad, and they set the table together.

At last Jan came in from the garage and set down her purse.

"About time," Elaine said.

"Sorry. We stayed while Dan talked to the pastor about the
letter, and then I had to take Priscilla home."

"Well, we've just about caught up on all the family news,"
Elaine said. "I hope the scallop's not too dry. You're going to
have to tell us every detail about this letter business over dinner."

Jan was happy to oblige, and Elaine soon picked up on a
slight misgiving in her tone.

"What's the matter?" she asked. "Besides what you've
already told me."

"Did you know that Pastor Mike was related to the first pastor of the church?" Jan asked. "The one who got the letter from
General Henry Knox, I mean."

"I had no idea," Elaine replied.

"Well, Dan seemed to find it significant."

Sasha's eyebrows arched. "That's pretty interesting. I remember how Grandma used to do all that family history research about our ancestors. Wasn't she in the DAR?"

"Yeah, she still is," Elaine said. "By the way, she wants to see you. Do you think we could stop at her place before we go to the shooting range tomorrow? She'd like us to eat lunch with her."

"What?" Jan cried. "You're going to a shooting range?"

"Sasha needs to practice, and I'm going with her," Elaine said, with more confidence than she felt.

"I want to check out a new sight for one of my competition rifles at the gun shop too," Sasha said. "I thought it would be a fun outing for Mom and me."

Jan eyed Elaine doubtfully, and she tried to pull out a cheerful smile. "We'll have a great time. And we'll see Grandma beforehand."

"Okay," Jan said. "Just be careful. Now, about the Knox letter…"

"Yes." Elaine sobered at once. This was serious business. "Do you really suppose Dan would think Pastor Mike stole it?"

"I would have said absolutely not, but he looked so noncommittal this afternoon. Like he was keeping all his options open."

"Detectives have to do that," Sasha said. "You can't rule someone out just because you know them. Or like them."

"Or trust them?" Elaine asked. "I mean, he's the pastor! And he's a wonderful man."

"Yes, he is," Jan said. "It seems ridiculous to even think he might be involved."

Sasha held up one hand in protest. "I'm not saying he swiped the letter. But he is there every day, so he had plenty of opportunity, and he's related to the family. Some people might see that as motive."

"I just don't know," Elaine said. "Pastor Mike probably thought it was cool that the church had the letter, but would he really steal it?"

"I have to say, I'm with Elaine," Jan said. "I know it's possible, but it's very hard for me to believe that Mike is our culprit. Oh, and I asked about fingerprints, and Dan did take the frame the letter was in away with him. But I'm not sure he'll have the state lab test it. If they do, it will probably take forever."

"Too bad," Elaine said. "We might have been able to find something if we had it here."

"That's what I thought," Jan said.

"What, you two are into fingerprinting now?" Sasha asked with a skeptical glance between them.

"Don't laugh," Elaine said. "It's a useful science."

"Dan said we'd have to fingerprint the whole congregation if we wanted to rule everyone out." Jan pursed her lips in disapproval.

They continued to discuss the theft while they finished supper and loaded the dishwasher. Elaine was hanging up her apron when the doorbell rang.

"I'll get it." She was planning on a quiet evening with Sasha, so she hoped whoever was on the front porch wouldn't have other plans for her. She swung the door open and, to her surprise, found the Ryders waiting.

"Hi, Elaine," Sarah said. "I hope we're not interrupting anything."

"Not at all," Elaine replied. "Come on in. Jan told me about what happened this afternoon. I'm so sorry."

Pastor Mike's mouth skewed into a frown. "That's why we're here. It doesn't make sense to me. Sarah and I have been racking our brains, trying to think who would do this."

"Well, come right in." Elaine threw a glance down the entrance hall as Jan and Sasha walked out of the kitchen. "My daughter Sasha arrived today. She flew in from Colorado, and she's going to visit for a few days."

The Ryders greeted Sasha, and they all decided to move upstairs to Elaine and Jan's cozy sitting room.

"Can I fix tea or coffee?" Jan asked.

"No, we're good," Pastor Mike said.

"We just ate supper." Sarah grimaced. "Not that Mike would eat anything. This thing's got him all tensed up."

Sasha hesitated at the doorway of the sitting room. "Do you mind if I sit in? I'm intrigued by this mystery, but I don't want to intrude."

"Don't worry about that," Sarah said. "The whole town knows about it, and it might be good to have someone more removed from it to reason through all this chaos."

"You mean, someone outside the church?" Jan asked as she guided them all to comfortable seats.

Pastor Mike settled on the sofa next to Sarah. "It's so crazy. I mean, who would do this?"

"Somebody who knew the letter was there," Elaine said.

"Well, yeah. And that includes a lot of people—more than we might realize. But Dan Benson seemed to think I was the most likely person to take the letter."

"Oh, honey, he doesn't think that." Sarah rubbed his shoulder. "Just because you're related…"

"Can you please explain to me about the letter, and how the church came to have it?" Sasha asked.

"General Knox's family owned land up here before the Revolution," Pastor Mike said. "Or rather, his wife's family did. They were loyalists, and they fled the country. Some of their land in Maine was part of the old Waldo Patent."

"Of course, it was all part of Massachusetts then," Elaine mused.

"That's right. After the war, when the federal government was in place, General Knox became the second secretary of war. He was still a fairly young man, in his forties, I think, when he retired to Maine and built up his estate. From what I've read, he was in charge of the disposition of land confiscated from loyalists, and I suppose that helped him acquire some of the tracts of land that he did."

"Really!" Jan seemed quite indignant at this.

Pastor Mike shrugged. "I'm just telling you what I've read. You can study up on it yourself and tell me what you think. Anyway, at some point after he retired, he got to be quite friendly with the first pastor of this church. That was probably in the 1790s. I'd have to look it up to be sure when Knox moved up here."

"That pastor was Mike's ancestor," Sarah put in.

"Right. His name was George Rider, with an *i*. Someone changed the *i* to *y* later, I guess, and we spell it R-y-d-e-r. But it's the same family. I hear I have distant cousins who still spell it the old way. Anyway, George Rider lived near General Knox, over Thomaston way, but he was asked to start a church over here on Chickadee Lake, so he moved here, but he kept up a correspondence with the general."

"Fascinating," Elaine said. "Are there other surviving letters?"

"I'm not sure," Pastor Mike replied. "Supposedly the Massachusetts Historical Society has preserved a lot of his papers, but I've never had a chance to go down to Boston and look at them. I don't know of any in the family."

"Did you know about the letter the church had when you came here?" Elaine asked.

"Not until I was interviewed as a candidate. I was really surprised when they showed it to me. I'd known George Rider was in the family tree, but I had no idea that a letter addressed to him was here, and from one of the Founding Fathers."

"That's not why you decided to take the job, is it?" Jan asked with a straight face.

They all laughed.

"Seriously, though, Pastor," Elaine said, "Do you feel Dan really thinks you had anything to do with what's happened at the church? I know he can't rule out suspects without evidence, but he knows you well enough to realize how improbable that would be. You wouldn't mess up the church."

Jan cleared her throat, and they all turned their attention to her.

"As I mentioned this afternoon to Dan, we have no way of knowing whether the same person vandalized the church and stole the letter."

"You're right," Sasha said.

Pastor Mike nodded reluctantly. "And as I told Dan, I'm not sure that the genuine letter was in there the week before the vandals hit—or even the month before. I like to think I'd have noticed, but the truth is, the last time I looked at it closely was when I did some research on General Knox, and that was at least three months ago."

"Wow," Elaine said. "I was assuming that the thief did the other mischief to distract everyone from his crime."

"That's what I thought too," Jan said. "When Pastor Mike first told me the letter was missing, I had no doubt it was taken by the same person."

Sarah laid a hand on her husband's sleeve. "Now, wait a minute. I looked at that letter pretty closely a couple of weeks ago, and I didn't notice anything odd about it."

"You did?" Mike's eyebrows shot up. "What were you doing, dusting the stuff in the case?"

"No, I was showing it to a guest at church. One of the cottagers from Green Glade."

"When was this?" Mike asked.

"Oh dear. You don't think..." Sarah brushed back a strand of her dark-auburn hair and frowned. "I certainly hope I didn't show the thief where it was. Now let me think. Last Sunday was Mother's Day. It wasn't then. It must have been the Sunday before."

"That was the Sunday before the vandalism," Elaine said. "Are you sure it was that week? It might be important to tell Dan about it."

"Yeah," Mike said. "Exactly what did this person say?"

"Well, he asked me about it after the service. You had gone out back for a Sunday school teachers' meeting…"

"That was last week all right," Mike said. "The one before Mother's Day, I mean."

"Most of the people had left, but a few were lingering," Sarah said. "Most of them were waiting for people who were in the meeting, I guess. But this man was a stranger to me. I went up to him and said hello and introduced myself. I just wanted to welcome him to the church."

Mike nodded soberly. Sarah made it a point, as he did, to greet all visitors to their church.

"Did you get his name?" Jan asked.

"*Hmm.* I think he did tell me. You didn't have any visitor cards turned in that day, did you, Mike?"

"I don't think so. Was this guy alone?"

"Yes, and he was wearing a Tommy Hilfiger shirt."

Mike stared at her blankly. "Huh?"

"The designer," Sasha said.

"Oh." Pastor Mike still looked a little confused, but he looked back to his wife. "What color was it?"

"Pale blue with a fine windowpane check," Sarah replied without hesitation.

"Oh, I think I saw him!" Elaine cried.

Mike shook his head. "What did the man look like? Honestly, I can't believe you two recognized him from his shirt, but you have no idea what he looked like."

"He was pleasant-looking," Elaine said.

Sarah nodded. "Around fifty, I'd say. Not as tall as you, Mike, and he carried a few extra pounds. Short brown hair. I can't remember what color his eyes were."

"I guess I missed him," Jan said.

"I do remember a visitor," Mike said slowly. "Did he sit near the back on the right? My right, I mean."

"I don't know," Sarah said. "I didn't notice him until afterward. He was probably sitting somewhere behind me during the service."

"Pale-blue shirt," Mike mused.

"Okay, so how did the subject of the letter come up?" Jan asked.

"Yeah, I want to know that too," Mike said.

"He asked me about it. He..." Sarah snapped her fingers. "Prior. He said his name was Prior. I can't remember the first name, but I thought it was slightly interesting because a prior is sort of like a clergyman. But he said he works at a college in the Boston area. He'd just finished up classes for the semester, and he was up here for a week of fishing and relaxation."

"That's great," Elaine said. "We can ask Macy about him and see if he's still at the cottages."

"No, he's not." Sarah pulled a face. "He said he was leaving the next day."

"I can't believe you had this long conversation with the guy and didn't tell me about it," Mike said.

"I'm sorry. It really wasn't much of a conversation. If he'd been staying longer, I surely would have told you so that you could have called on him."

"Well, it was nice that he visited," Jan said.

"Yes, but now I wonder if he just came to see the letter," Sarah said. "After we'd done the chitchat thing, he told me he'd heard the church owned an original letter written by Henry Knox. I said, 'Yes we do,' and he asked if he could see it."

"I wish I'd known that when Dan was giving me the third degree this afternoon," Mike said.

"Well, we can tell him, honey." Sarah patted his shoulder.

"I think you should," Jan said. "I'm ready for a cup of tea. How about you, Sarah? Pastor? Feeling a little better now?"

"Yes, thanks," Mike said. "I feel like we came up with something that really might be helpful. And I'm hungry now."

Elaine laughed. "That's good. Why don't we all go downstairs? If you want, we'll heat you a plate of leftovers, and I know we have tons of cookies in the freezer."

They all trooped down to the dining room, and Elaine and Jan soon had refreshments on the table.

"You know," Sasha said with an air of confession as she slid two cookies onto her plate, "All this sleuthing you've been doing has me intrigued, Mom. I almost feel as though I'd like to see the scene of the crime."

Elaine laughed. "You've been to our church before."

"Yeah, but I didn't notice the fateful case with the memorabilia in it."

"You can see it any time you want," Pastor Mike said, reaching for a triple chocolate brownie.

"Mom and I are going to the shooting range in the morning." Sasha threw Elaine a questioning look.

"We could stop by the church first if you want," Elaine said.

"Why don't you just come over tonight when we go home?" Sarah asked.

"That sounds like a great idea," Sasha said, grinning.

"Aren't you tired?" Elaine eyed her critically. "You were traveling all day."

"Nope. I've got my second wind." Sasha took a bite of a cranberry-white-chocolate oatmeal cookie and made a little sound of approval, almost like a cat's contented purr.

"It's the resilience of youth," Jan said.

Somehow, they all ended up descending the stairs at the church a half hour later. Pastor Mike went first and turned the lights on.

"There it is." He walked with Sasha to the display case, and the others followed. Mike turned on the lights inside the case, spotlighting the items inside.

Sasha leaned close. "That is so cool. I take it the letter was right in the middle, where the gap is?"

"Yes, it's in an eight-by-ten walnut frame, and it was standing on the shelf there."

"What are the trophies for?"

Pastor Mike smiled. "Our youth are very good at Bible quizzes, especially Dori Richardson and the Murphy twins."

"And our Asher," Sarah added.

"Well, yeah." Pastor Mike seemed to be trying not to look too proud. "And that old one on the bottom is from a decade or two ago, when some of our men played in a church basket-ball league with... Hey!"

"Hey, what?" Sarah asked.

"I just noticed..." Pastor Mike stooped down and put his face close to the glass. "Where's the old medal?"

"Will Trexler's medal?" Sarah leaned in to look.

"Yeah," Pastor Mike said. "It's supposed to be right there, between the trophies. But it's not."

# CHAPTER TEN

O h, wow, you mean something else is missing?" Sasha asked, her blue eyes sparkling with excitement.

"I'm not sure I remember the medal you're talking about," Jan said.

"Will won it way back when he was young, in a Bible quiz tournament," Sarah told her.

"I think he's prouder of that than he is of Trapper Will's Fly Dope," Pastor Mike added.

"Really?" Elaine asked. "Isn't the bug repellant what he made his fortune on?"

Pastor Mike nodded. "That's right, but he told me once that the Bible verses he memorized when he was young are a better treasure than all the money he got for his patent on the bug dope."

Elaine smiled. "That sounds like something Will would say."

"I'll bet he meant it too," Jan added.

Sasha turned to the pastor. "How old was the medal?"

His brow furrowed. Before he could answer, Sarah said, "We're talking 1950s, I think. Will's eighty now, and he probably won it while he was a teenager."

"Was it there Saturday?" Elaine asked.

"I don't know," the pastor said after a moment. "I'm not even sure if it was there today when we realized the real letter was missing."

"Dan Benson took pictures of the case," Jan reminded him. "We could ask him to look at those."

Pastor Mike nodded. "And I've got some older pictures up in my office of the display the way it was a few months ago. I saw them again when I was cleaning up Saturday."

"Why don't you run up and get them?" Sarah suggested. "We'll stay here."

He hurried through the fellowship hall, toward the back stairs that came up near his office.

"How could we miss that, if it was gone earlier?" Sarah wailed.

"None of us were thinking about the medal," Elaine said, patting her arm.

A moment later, Pastor Mike was back with a photo album.

"Are the pictures predigital?" Sasha asked.

"Some are." He opened the book and flipped a couple of pages. "One of our members made this as a scrapbook for a church anniversary celebration. She put all the pictures in here so the members could look at it anytime."

He laid it open to a double-page spread of views taken on the lower level of the church building, including the kitchen, the decorated fellowship hall, and the display case.

"There it is." Sarah pointed to a close-up of the newer Bible quiz trophies. Nestled between them was a round, silver-colored medal on a red-and-blue striped ribbon. Beside it was a neatly lettered card that read, "Central Maine Pastors' Association, Bible Quiz Champion 1952, Won by Wilton Trexler." The medal itself pictured a little lamp that Elaine thought of as an Aladdin's lamp, and the words, "Thy word is a lamp unto my feet."

"Oh yeah," Jan said. "I think I remember seeing that before."

"I called Dan," Pastor Mike said. "He's helping out with a car accident on I-95, but he said he'll come by tomorrow about this, or he could send someone else. I told him I didn't think it was urgent."

"I guess there's nothing more we can do tonight," Jan said, a little disappointed that the sleuthing session was apparently over.

"We'd better get home," Elaine said. "You've got four dozen cupcakes to decorate."

"I'll help," Sasha said brightly. "I'm very good with frosting."

Elaine laughed. "She really is. You'd better take her up on that, Jan."

JAN LOADED HER boxes of cupcakes and got in her Camry Wednesday morning. When she arrived at the Richardsons' farmhouse, it was barely nine o'clock. Annie greeted her at the door and took her into the kitchen, where her husband, Gavin, and his dad, Ethan, were enjoying a cup of coffee at the thick pine table.

"Oh, I'm interrupting your breakfast," Jan said.

"Breakfast? Hardly!" Ethan, who lived with Gavin and Annie and their children, winked at her. "We had breakfast hours ago."

"This is their coffee break," Annie said, smiling as she went to the cupboard. "They have it every morning after they finish the milking. Would you like a cup?"

"No, thanks," Jan said. "I've got Ella's cupcakes with me. Where would you like them?"

"Right here on the counter, I guess," Annie said. "There's no room in the fridge."

Gavin pushed back his chair. "Need some help?"

"Thanks, that would be nice." Jan led him out to her old blue sedan. "It's those two boxes on the backseat. If you want to get one, I'll get the other. Just try to keep it level, okay?"

"Got it." Gavin leaned in and took the first box. Jan opened the door on the other side and lifted out the second. They carried them in through the kitchen door, and Annie waved them to the spot she had cleared on the counter.

"Fabulous. Thanks so much, Jan." Annie opened her purse. "Is there tax or anything?"

"That's just right." She accepted the bills Annie held out and gave her the slip she had made out before leaving home.

Ethan finished his coffee and set down his mug. "Nice weather we're havin'."

"Yes, it is," Jan said with a smile. "I hope it lasts."

"Oh, I expect we'll get some rain before tomorrow night."

"Really?" Jan asked. "Too bad. Elaine's daughter is here, and she's driving to Sugarloaf tomorrow."

"That's nice," Annie said. "That she's here, I mean, not that she's going to drive clear over there in the rain."

"She's here on business," Jan said. "For the biathlon team, you know."

"Now, what's that?" Gavin asked, resuming his place at the table.

"Something to do with guns, isn't it?" his father asked.

Jan nodded. "They ski and then they shoot. They carry their rifles on their backs while they ski."

Ethan shook his head. "Crazy sport, if you ask me."

"I think it started in Scandinavia," Jan said. "Their soldiers do it for training."

"Is she going to be in the next Olympics?" Annie asked.

"That's what Sasha's hoping for."

"Annie was telling us about the mess at the church on Saturday," Ethan said.

Jan just nodded.

"Said the Murphy boys were working outside all morning."

"I don't know about *all* morning," Jan said, remembering Jo's distress. "They said they didn't go inside while they were working."

"And now we hear the General Knox letter's been stolen," Gavin said.

Word traveled fast, Jan thought. But Gavin was on the board of trustees for the church this year. She supposed it made sense that Pastor Mike had informed him.

"Yes, unfortunately," she said. "But we don't know that the same person who took it messed up the church."

"Huh." Ethan sipped his coffee and then looked up at her. "Dori was saying she was talking about the stuff in the trophy case with some of the other kids after their last youth group meeting."

Jan didn't like the sound of that. She wanted to believe Chris and Nick Murphy had nothing to do with the vandalism. She hadn't totally ruled them out yet, but she wanted to.

"Really? Did she say what brought it up, or what they were particularly interested in?"

"They were talking mostly about the Bible quiz team," Annie said. "Dori's been practicing, and Pastor Mike quizzes them every week."

"When does the competition take place?" Jan asked.

"Not for a month or two. I think they were just looking at the trophies and speculating that they could win one."

Jan nodded, thinking back over the last few days. "Annie, you were there on Saturday when we were cleaning up. You didn't notice anything missing from that case, did you?"

Annie shook her head. "I remember us remarking on what a blessing it was the vandals didn't break the glass in the front. But then last night we heard about the famous Knox letter being stolen."

"So do you think that was done at the same time?" Gavin asked.

"If it was, we didn't notice it had been switched," Jan said. "It's odd, because the mess in the fellowship hall and the kitchen and the classrooms looked like it was done in a hurry.

But it would take time to remove that letter, make a copy, and put the copy in the frame. So was the thief in a hurry or not?"

"You got me," Gavin said.

"And there's something else." Jan glanced around at the three of them. "I guess it's okay to tell you. Yesterday, Pastor Mike noticed that another item was missing."

"What was it?" Annie asked.

"An old medal Will Trexler won sixty years or so ago for Bible quizzing. It was in the case near the trophies, but it's gone now."

Annie's lips parted.

"Was it there Saturday?" Ethan asked.

"That's what we're trying to figure out," Jan said.

"Maybe the kids noticed it last week after the youth meeting." Gavin stood and carried his mug to the sink. "Well, it's nice chatting with you, Jan, but I've got work to do. Come on, Dad."

"Oh, you're always cracking the whip on me." Ethan smiled at Jan as he made a show of slowly getting up and taking his cup to the drainboard. "Someday this old body's going to give out on me, and you'll have to get a new hired hand."

Annie made a face at him. "You know you can work circles around me. Stop complaining. Sixty's not that old."

"I sure hope not," Jan said, figuring how few years she had left until reaching that milestone. "I'd better get going too."

"See you," Annie said cheerfully as Jan moved toward the door. "Thanks again."

Jan drove home mulling over their conversation. Did the kids in the youth group have anything to do with the missing medal—or the letter, or both?

# CHAPTER ELEVEN

Elaine pulled out of the driveway before Jan arrived home from delivering the cupcakes. The tearoom was quite busy, but Rose had assured her things would be fine. Elaine was glad, because she and Sasha had a firm luncheon date with her mother before their outing to the gun shop and shooting range. When she had called to set up a time, Virginia had told her the menu was all set, and she urged Elaine to come as early as she could.

"I hope she doesn't go to a lot of trouble," Sasha said. She wore khaki pants and a white shirt printed with green palm fronds—very safari, Elaine thought. Her own outfit was a coordinated light-blue set—pants and a shell, with a short-sleeved jacket over it.

"She won't do anything too strenuous, but she loves to entertain," she assured Sasha. "Just let her fuss a little and enjoy having you here."

They did a bit of shopping after arriving in Augusta. About half past eleven, Elaine pulled up before her mom's small, well-landscaped bungalow in the Millpond Senior Community.

The management kept up the lawns and shrubbery, but Virginia liked to putter in the flowerbeds herself.

They walked up the path to the front door, and Sasha shifted her shopping bag to her other hand and pushed the doorbell. Before it stopped ringing inside, Virginia flung the door open.

"Sasha, baby! You look wonderful!" Virginia engulfed her granddaughter in a fervent embrace.

Sasha chuckled, hugging her back. "You look pretty good yourself, Grandma." She stood back a little and looked the hostess up and down. As usual, Virginia's hair was coiffed to perfection. She wore white slacks, a silky mauve blouse, and matching necklace and earrings in a deeper shade of purple.

"Come in, come in."

Elaine kissed her mother's cheek.

"Hello, honey." Virginia led them down the short entry hall, into the open kitchen that flowed into the dining area.

"This is cute," Sasha said, looking around at the hardwood floors and tasteful decorations.

"It's small, but it's about all I want to take care of," her grandmother said. "I'm past running up and down stairs, thank you."

She had lunch all ready, and the table was set for three. Elaine helped her take fruit salad and iced tea from the refrigerator, and her mom pulled a small meatloaf and potato wedges from the oven. They talked mostly about the family and Virginia's social life at the senior community while eating the delicious meal. Afterward, Elaine and Sasha loaded the dishwasher, and the three of them sat down in the living room to continue the conversation.

The subject of the gun shop didn't come up until Sasha caught Elaine's eye and raised her eyebrows. Elaine glanced at her watch.

"Oh, I'm sorry, but we need to get going."

"Do you have to go so soon?" Virginia wailed as Elaine looked around to see where she had set down her purse.

"Yes, Mom. We have a two o'clock appointment. And don't you have bridge this afternoon?"

"Not until three."

"Well, you'll have plenty of time to get ready," Elaine said.

"Where are you going?" Virginia asked.

Elaine hesitated, but Sasha smiled and said, "To a shooting range, Grandma. I have to keep up my shooting practice."

"Heavens, I don't know what the attraction is," Virginia said. "You'll lose your hearing for sure."

"I always wear ear protectors," Sasha assured her. She reached for the shopping bag she'd brought in. "Look here, I brought you something from Colorado."

"Really?" Virginia's face flushed with pleasure as she took the bag from Sasha and sat down on the couch to open it. She pushed back the silver tissue paper in the bag and pulled out a pink zipper-front sweatshirt.

"For when you go out walking," Sasha said.

"Oh my. Look at that." The logo of Sasha's biathlon team, a small target seen through a gunsight, was printed in navy blue on the left side.

"That's my team, the Aspen Sharpshooters. You can tell your friends."

"Thank you, dear. It will be a real conversation starter." Virginia slipped off her jacket and pulled the sweatshirt on.

"Do you like it?" Sasha asked.

"I love it. It's nice and warm. Do I look athletic?"

"You sure do. I'll call you before I leave on Friday." Sasha gave her a kiss and headed for the door.

"Nice change of subject," Elaine admitted when they got to the car. "I thought she was going to fuss about the shooting range."

"Eh, Grandma's okay with it," Sasha said.

"She's proud of you, even though she's a little timid about firearms." Elaine laughed. "The sweatshirt was the perfect gift. Her favorite color, your favorite sport." She buckled her seat belt. "Ready?"

"Drive on," Sasha said.

When they arrived at the gun shop, Elaine's watch showed ten minutes to two. She was surprised at the attractive façade of the large building. They entered into a showroom with weapons displayed on walls, racks, and in locked cases. A section behind the counter held ammunition boxes of all sorts. A couple of art prints featured Civil War battle scenes, and some old ammunition ads were framed and hung on the walls. It wasn't what she'd hang in her living room, but Elaine could see something like that in her husband's study. A pang of regret hit her that Ben wasn't here to see what a beautiful and poised woman their daughter had become.

Sasha at once struck up a conversation with the middle-aged man behind the counter.

"Hi. I'm Sasha Cook, and this is my mother, Elaine. We're scheduled to shoot at two."

"Great. I'm Ron Eames, the owner. We have a couple of parties on the range now. Would you like to start now, or wait until two? You're the only ones scheduled for the next hour."

"We can wait," Sasha said. "I'm a member of the US biathlon team, and I'd like to see what you have for competition rifles."

Ron came from behind the counter. "Really? I love to watch biathlon when the winter Olympics are on TV. I wish it came more often." He nodded toward a rack on the left wall. "I've got a used Fortner 1827. Don't usually stock new ones. We don't have that many folks in the area who do sport shooting."

"Too bad," Sasha said. "It's a great hobby."

She followed him to one of the gun cases, where he took out a rifle with a sling and handed it to her. It looked all business to Elaine. She wandered around the shop, examining the framed prints while Sasha and Ron talked about ballistics and sights with snow covers.

Three people came through a door at the back of the shop and went to the counter. A young man followed them out and went to wait on them.

"Looks like the range is free," Ron said. "As soon as Tony's done with those customers, he'll take you back there. He's our firearms instructor." He looked at Sasha. "Do you want to try the Fortner?"

"Sure," Sasha said. "And my mom might like to try a small Glock pistol."

"Oh no, not me," Elaine said. "I'm just along for the ride."

"Come on, Mom. Don't you ever think about getting a gun for protection?"

"Never. I'm pretty good with blunt instruments."

"Ha! You told me that story." Sasha shook her head and said to Ron, "My mom laid out a burglar with a knickknack once."

Ron gave a low whistle.

"But if you'd had a gun," Sasha said sternly to her mother, "he would never have gotten close enough to put his hands on you."

"I'm fine," Elaine said. But Sasha continued to cajole her until she finally admitted she was curious about the rifles Sasha used in her sport and how the competitors kept steady enough to hit multiple targets when they'd just skied a distance and their hearts were pounding.

"Well, I've got a nice little target rifle you can try out. Don't have any skis, I'm afraid." Ron winked at her. "But you can get the feel of the pressure and the rapid firing at several targets in a row. We can set you up against Sasha, and you can have your own little shooting match."

Elaine protested, but Ron and his helper Tony quickly set up the targets and brought the rifles, ammunition, and ear protection the women needed. Tony began by showing Elaine how to safely handle and load her weapon. She was not a total stranger to guns, as Ben had always kept a few in their residence, and thirty years earlier he had even taken her hunting a few times, but Elaine hadn't especially enjoyed it. She had given Ben's guns to Jared and Sasha after he died. She hadn't fired one for at least two decades.

By the time she was ready, Sasha had already gone through two targets, and Ron was praising her with remarks like, "Nice tight group," and "That's the way to do it."

"No fair," Elaine said. "You're all practiced up."

"You can take a few minutes to practice, Mom." Sasha leaned on the barrier between the shooters and the target area. "Go ahead."

Elaine wished she hadn't said anything because now Sasha and Tony apparently had nothing to do but watch her make a fool of herself. They heard a bell ring faintly, summoning Ron out into the shop to wait on a customer, but Elaine shot her first few rounds with Tony and her daughter staring at her.

"Not bad," Tony said, moving a lever to slide her target in. "See, you hit it four out of six rounds."

"Well, those four are all over the place." Elaine grimaced at the widespread holes in the paper.

"You'll get the hang of it," Sasha said. "Come on, Tony. Set us up. Five targets each."

It was the usual for a round in a biathlon competition. Elaine had studied up on the rules of the sport since Sasha had taken an interest in it and begun competing. She carefully loaded her rifle with the .22 caliber ammunition.

"Remember Salt Lake?" she called to Sasha.

Sasha grinned. "Do I ever."

"You were what, twelve?" Elaine asked.

"Yeah. I'll never forget that January."

Elaine and Ben had been stateside that year, and Ben's assignment that winter had put them within driving distance of the Olympic Games, hosted in Salt Lake City. He had an opportunity to get tickets to some of the skiing events at a good price, and they had decided to take the kids and make a family vacation of it.

That was the first time Sasha had become aware of biathlon. She had clamored for skiing lessons right away, and before long asked to learn to shoot. Elaine was hesitant at first, fearing her little girl would be injured on the slopes or in a gun accident, but Ben had encouraged Sasha to go for it.

"There's lots worse things she could be interested in," he'd told Elaine. Whenever Ben could, he took Sasha skiing or somewhere she could shoot. The next year, she'd attended a school that had a ski team. At an interscholastic competition in Nordic skiing, a professional coach had noticed her. From then on, there was no looking back for Sasha. After high school, she took jobs at ski lodges and continued her training, rising in the ranks of biathletes until now her eyes were on the Olympics.

She had narrowly missed making the team once before, and she went as an alternate. The experience fired her passion for the sport. Then, as the next Olympic Games approached, unfortunately, a badly sprained ankle had kept her from competing. She had told her mom she was determined—nothing would hold her back this time.

"All set?" Tony asked as she closed the bolt on her rifle.

Elaine nodded.

"Okay. When the light goes on, fire as soon as you feel ready. Just go from one target to the next."

"Is there a time limit?" she asked.

"We won't give you one on this round."

She nodded and got into position. The light came on, and she held her breath and squeezed the trigger. Sasha's shots popped off quickly, and she was finished before Elaine had fired her third shot. That was all right, she told herself. She took a slow breath and held it, adjusted her aim, and fired again.

When she had finished her round, she didn't feel too bad. She had hit two of her five targets, not a total disgrace. Tony praised her, and Sasha egged her on to do another round. They finished half an hour later, after their sixth round. Elaine had finally managed to hit four of her targets in one round.

"You'll be ready for the team before you know it," Sasha said with a grin.

They turned their equipment over to Tony and walked out into the store.

"How'd it go?" Ron called from behind the counter, where he was doing some paperwork.

"Great," Sasha said. "Mom's a natural."

"I don't know about that," Elaine said. "I think I'm better at bookkeeping and brewing tea."

Sasha grinned and walked over to the case where the sights were displayed. "I'll take that Anschutz sight you showed me before, Ron."

"Good choice." He walked over to unlock the case and get it out.

Elaine leaned on the counter. Ron had left the loose-leaf notebook he'd been working on open, and a form lay on top of it. Elaine didn't mean to snoop, but a name printed boldly at the top of the form caught her eye. She had read a couple more lines before she made herself look away. None of her business, after all.

Sasha soon concluded her purchase, and they went to the car and drove home, cheerfully discussing their shooting practice and their visit with Virginia.

As they passed through Penzance, Elaine braked suddenly. Three teenagers on bicycles swooped out of the road that led to the town beach. They curved on to the pavement and rode on, yelling to each other and hardly looking at the car.

"Whew!" Elaine drew in a shaky breath. "You okay?"

"Yeah, but one of them almost hit the side mirror," Sasha said. "Are *you* all right, Mom?"

"I think so." Elaine put the car in motion again. She had almost caught up to the cyclists when they ducked off the pavement on to a dirt side road. At least she didn't have to pass them again.

The tearoom was nearly full when they got home. Sasha excused herself and went upstairs. Elaine donned an apron and took over the cash register to relieve Rose of that duty so she and Archie could give more attention to their customers. Only thirty minutes remained before closing time, but thirsty patrons and special orders kept coming. Archie turned the sign to Closed at four o'clock, but several parties lingered over their pots of tea and conversation.

"Thanks for your help," Rose told her. "We're fine now. I'll start cleaning tables until the rest are ready to check out."

Elaine went out to the kitchen. Jan was packaging the leftover pastries. Elaine went to the counter and automatically started loading the stacked dishes into the dishwasher.

"Hi," Jan said. "I heard you out front, but you were pretty busy. How was your day?"

"Good," Elaine said. "Mom was in her usual form."

"How about the shooting range?" Jan asked.

Elaine chuckled. "I didn't think I'd say this, but I actually had fun." She frowned. "There was one thing there that bothered me a little."

"What was that?"

Elaine fitted several saucers into the rack and straightened. "I saw an application lying on the counter at the shop. I shouldn't have seen it, but the owner was distracted and he left it there. I didn't mean to peek."

"What did you see?"

Jan was taking her seriously, so Elaine got right to the point. "It was paperwork for the purchase of a handgun. You know how you have to wait a few days while they do a background check?"

Jan nodded. "So?"

Elaine swallowed hard. "It was for Alan Oakley."

# CHAPTER TWELVE

A lan is buying a gun?" Jan frowned. "I wouldn't have expected that, but still, he has a perfect right."

"Oh, I know," Elaine said, "and it's none of my business. I just..."

"Just what?" Jan tried to read her cousin's expression. "You think Alan has some sinister reason for wanting a gun?"

"No, not really." Elaine turned back to loading the dishwasher. "I know we've had some wrong ideas about Alan in the past, and I'm sorry about that, but I can't help remembering how he fought against Pastor Mike last fall at the business meeting."

Jan nodded slowly, trying to figure out where Elaine was going with this. Alan Oakley was not only a member of Lancaster's board of selectmen, he was also a prominent member of their church. "I remember too. Pastor Mike mentioned it to Dan Benson when Priscilla and I found that the letter was a fake. It was the quarterly meeting. Alan wanted to pay off the church mortgage, but the pastor said we couldn't afford to, and we should just wait and see how much money we could raise before the balloon payment is due—Hey! That's coming right up, isn't it?"

"In June, I think." Elaine's blue eyes held that troubled look again. "Do you remember what Alan suggested we do to raise the money?"

Jan shook her head.

"Well, maybe he didn't say it in the meeting, but I think Maureen mentioned it to me later. She said Alan thought we ought to sell General Knox's letter."

Jan stared at her. "Yeah, he did say that to Dan, that someone had mentioned the possibility of selling it."

"Yes. Pastor Mike told the board members they shouldn't consider that, so it was dropped," Elaine said.

"But a few months later, Pastor Mike researched it online, to find out how much the letter is worth," Jan mused.

"Maybe he was starting to doubt that the money would come in," said Elaine.

Sasha had been following their conversation and looking puzzled. "So what does that have to do with one of your board members licensing a handgun? I mean, lots of people buy guns for their own protection, or for sports."

Elaine sighed. "Nothing, I'm sure. I suppose I was just upset about Dan treating Pastor Mike like he's a suspect in all of this. When I saw Alan's name on that application—well, all the negative things I've ever heard about Alan started to surface, I guess."

Jan took off her glasses and rubbed the bridge of her nose. She was tired, but there might be something in all this. She looked up at Elaine. "What if Pastor Mike thinks Alan took the letter so he can sell it and pay off the mortgage?"

Elaine's eyes widened. "No...what if Pastor Mike thought Alan would insist on selling the letter, since six months have passed and we still haven't come up with the mortgage payment? What if he replaced it with a phony so that Alan couldn't get his hands on the real letter? Maybe Pastor Mike just wants to keep that letter safe."

Jan shook her head. "I don't know. It's hard for me to imagine he'd do it this way."

"But it's possible," Elaine said. "His office has a copier right there in it. He'd researched its value."

"I know. But if Pastor Mike did hide it somewhere for safety, why would he admit to having researched it?"

"True," Elaine said. "I feel like we're going in circles with this."

"I don't know these people," Sasha said, "but do you really think any of them would steal something out of your church?"

Elaine let out a big breath. "Not really. Especially not Pastor Mike. But we do know that he's a direct descendant of the minister who received the letter from General Knox. That's a point against him. He'd want to keep such a family letter close rather than letting it go to the highest bidder."

"True," Jan said. "Like it or not, that gives him a motive for not wanting to see it sold. But he wouldn't steal it. And I don't think he'd hide it and lie about it either. And...well, there's more."

"More what?" Elaine looked truly stressed now, and Jan hastened to calm her.

"It's nothing really. It's just that when I went to the Richardsons' this morning, to deliver the cupcakes, Annie said the youth group had been talking about the trophies in the case Sunday night. I wondered if maybe they'd noticed the medal was missing."

"Do you think that's worth telling Dan about?" Elaine asked.

"I don't know. Maybe we could just ask Dori and the other kids about it. It was probably an innocent conversation. Annie says they've been drilling a lot lately for the Bible quiz competition. I wouldn't want to bother Dori today—it's her sister's birthday party."

Elaine's head jerked up. "What about Asher? He wouldn't be at the party, would he?"

"No, I think it's all girls," Jan said.

"Well, he's not one of the kids who's under suspicion, like the Murphy twins are. Maybe Asher could tell us what the teens were talking about."

"Maybe," Jan said. "Or he might have missed that huddle completely. Worth a shot, I guess."

"I'm in," Sasha said.

Jan caught her breath. "I'm sorry. This wasn't how you planned to spend your limited time with your mom."

Sasha shrugged. "It's okay. I have to admit, I've been curious about how you two have solved all these mysteries I keep hearing about. You even found out where that gorgeous sapphire ring in your wall came from."

Archie came in from the tearoom carrying a tray laden with dirty dishes.

"Put 'er right here, Archie," Elaine said, patting the counter over the dishwasher. "I'm in the loading business."

Rose came in behind him. "I think we got everything cleaned up. Mind if I take off now? I've got class tonight."

"No, go right ahead," Jan said. "We'll see you in the morning."

Archie was soon out the door as well, and Sasha eyed Elaine and Jan. "Still going to talk to the pastor's boy?"

"Well, if you're game," Elaine said. "But let's go after we eat supper. The Ryders will probably sit down to their meal soon, and we don't want to interrupt them."

"That's the sanest thing I've heard all day," Jan said. "I can have something ready in twenty minutes. I put together a nice stromboli this afternoon."

"Yum! I'll help you with the rest of it," Sasha offered.

While they were preparing the food, the smell of the cooking bread-wrapped sausage and cheese wafted through the kitchen. Bits and pieces of conversations from the last few days floated through Jan's mind. She paused with a paring knife in her hand.

"Elaine, didn't Pastor Mike say Dan Benson would check the photos he took yesterday?"

"Yeah, and he said Dan would stop by the church today. Do you want me to call him?"

Jan glanced around at the food and dishes spread over the counter. "Do you mind? Maybe check in with him while Sasha and I finish up here."

"No problem. I still haven't given him the pocketknife I found in the restroom at the church either. I'd better tell him about that." Elaine went out the door, and soon they could hear her muted voice as she spoke on the phone in her office next door.

When she came back, Jan had finished the salad and the stromboli was browning nicely in the oven. Sasha was setting the kitchen table for three.

"Well?" Sasha asked eagerly.

Elaine's face was sober. "Dan says the medal wasn't in the pictures he took Tuesday morning."

Jan wiped her hands on a dish towel. "So that means it was gone when we realized the letter was missing."

"Yeah," Elaine said. "None of us noticed, but it was already gone."

Jan nodded slowly. Maybe the youth group members would remember something.

ELAINE WAS HAVING second thoughts by the time they set out for the Ryders' house an hour later.

"I hate to stir things up again in a way," she said. "Sarah was pretty upset yesterday."

"I don't think they'll mind," Jan assured her as she turned into the church parking lot. "Pastor Mike wants this thing solved and forgotten as soon as possible."

"I guess you're right. Sarah does too."

Elaine and Sasha climbed out and followed Jan's determined figure to the parsonage door. Jan rang the bell, and Pastor Mike opened the door a moment later.

"Hello, ladies."

At least he didn't look disappointed or upset at the sight of them, Elaine thought.

"Hi, Pastor," she said. "A couple of things came up today that might have a bearing on the Knox letter business. If you don't want to talk about it, it's okay, but…"

"Come on in." He opened the door wide and called over his shoulder, "Honey, it's Elaine and Jan and Sasha. Do we have plenty of ice cream?"

"Oh, none for me, thanks," Elaine said. "We just ate."

Jan also declined, but Sasha accepted a serving of Rocky Road, and they all joined the family at the dining table, where the children were finishing their dessert. Pastor Mike carried in an extra chair from the kitchen to give them all a seat. He introduced Sasha to the kids.

"Nice to see you all," Sarah said. "I've got coffee made, or tea by the cup via the microwave."

It didn't take Sarah long to see everyone settled with a beverage, and then Elaine turned to the pastor with a smile. "We really came to talk to Asher, if you don't mind."

The fifteen-year-old blinked at her with gray eyes much like his father's. "Me?"

Elaine nodded.

"Is this about the vandalism?" Pastor Mike asked.

"Only indirectly," Elaine said.

"I don't know anything about it," Asher said.

Jan cleared her throat. "Maybe you know something but you don't realize it. The Richardsons told me that Dori and the other teens were talking about the items in the display case after the last youth meeting."

"Oh, I see." Pastor Mike nodded.

"I don't," Sarah said.

Jan smiled apologetically. "I'm sorry to keep harping on this thing…"

"Don't be," Sarah said quickly. "If you have any insight into what's going on, we'd be happy to help you."

"Okay." Jan turned her gaze on Asher and smiled, hoping she wasn't making him too nervous. "It seems the teens had been drilling for the next Bible quiz."

"We do that a lot lately," Asher said, his voice cracking a little. "We really want to bring home the trophy at the end of the season."

Jan nodded. "I know you're all working hard. Did you go over to the case and look at the trophies?"

"Yeah."

"What night was that?" Elaine asked.

"Sunday," Pastor Mike said. "We had the meeting at six o'clock. The kids had refreshments afterward."

"So it was after the vandalism," Elaine said slowly.

"Yeah," Asher replied.

"But I hadn't noticed the phony letter yet," Pastor Mike said.

"Did anyone notice the letter?" Sarah asked, looking at Asher. "Did anyone say anything about it at all?"

He shook his head. "We were just reading the names and the years on the trophies."

Jan said, "What about the old medal that was lying between two of the trophies? Did you see that?"

"Yeah. We were trying to figure out how old Mr. Trexler was when he won it."

"I think the medal is cool," said twelve-year-old Leanne. "They should give those instead of trophies."

"So Will's medal was there on Sunday evening." Jan's forehead puckered.

Pastor Mike looked at her and then at Elaine. "Okay, that's something. The medal was still in the case after the vandalism happened on Saturday. That makes me wonder if the genuine letter was too."

"Pastor, did you look at the trophies when the kids did?" Elaine asked.

"No, but I heard them talking about them and wondering how big this year's trophy would be, and if there would be room in the case for another one."

Elaine was disappointed. She had hoped that Mike had looked at the case at that time too. Then he might remember looking at the letter. Surely if he'd done so, he would have noticed the fake, if it was in place then.

"But who could have taken the medal out after that?" she asked.

"I guess anyone who was there Sunday night, and a Bible study group met downstairs Monday afternoon. One of the Sunday school teachers came by earlier on Monday to get some materials while I was in my office." Pastor Mike shrugged. "A lot of people were in the church between the youth meeting and when I noticed that the medal was gone."

"Maybe you should make a list and give it to Officer Benson," Leanne suggested.

"You're thinking like a detective," Jan said with a smile. Leanne grinned back at her.

Jan looked at Pastor Mike. "So just for a drill, would you mind if I ask the kids where they were Saturday morning, and also if I take a look at their shoes?"

Sarah's eyes widened, and she looked at her husband, as though waiting for Mike to make that decision.

# CHAPTER THIRTEEN

Mike seemed to consider Jan's request for a moment. He sat back in his chair. "I don't see any harm in that, just to rule things out."

Jan nodded. "Not that I think they had anything to do with it." She smiled at Asher. "So were you here Saturday morning?"

"Yeah. Mom let me sleep in."

"Did you see Nick and Chris when they were out here working?"

"Yeah. I waved at them when we—oh, that's right. Mom, we drove over to the Old Grange, remember?"

"You're right. I'd forgotten all about it," Sarah said. "Lydia Pierce had asked me to drop off a couple of items for the play the theater group is starting on. I let Asher drive, so he could log a little practice time on his permit. After the Old Grange, we went around to Main Street. I wanted to pop into Sugar Plum for a minute, and Asher walked over to the post office for me while I was in there."

"I only got, like, fifteen minutes of driving in." Asher scowled at his father. "You should take me out for an hour tomorrow, Dad."

Mike sighed. "I'll try. I know you need to get your time in."

Jan turned to Leanne. "So did you go with them?"

"No, Caleb and I stayed here. They weren't gone very long."

"Did you see Chris and Nick?"

Leanne shrugged. "I think I saw them out the window once when they were working in the flower beds. I didn't talk to them."

"I saw them," Caleb said.

"You did?" Jan turned her attention to the young boy. "Tell me about it."

"I was upstairs in my room. They were breaking up branches out under the trees by the road."

"So you didn't talk to them either," Jan said.

"Nope. But I saw them talking to other kids."

"What other kids?" Pastor Mike straightened and eyed Caleb sharply.

"I dunno." Caleb squirmed in his chair. "Just kids on bikes."

"Did you recognize them?" Sarah asked sternly.

"Huh-uh. But they stopped and talked to Nick and Chris."

"Which way did they come from?" his father asked.

"I dunno."

"Okay," Jan said slowly, "did you see where they went after they talked to the twins?"

Caleb shook his head. "Leanne yelled at me to come down-stairs because we were going to watch a cartoon."

Leanne's face flushed, as though she was embarrassed that she had watched a cartoon at the mature age of twelve. "It was *Frozen*," she said, as if that would explain it.

"Oh, I love that movie," Sasha said, smiling at Leanne.

"But you didn't see those other kids Caleb saw?" Jan asked.

Leanne shook her head. "Sorry."

Sarah let out a pent-up breath. "Well, you kids had better get at your homework."

"Show the bottoms of your shoes to Mrs. Blake before you go," Pastor Mike said.

Asher eyed her curiously, but pushed back his chair and held one foot out before him.

Jan glanced at the smooth sole. "Is that what you wore Saturday, or did you wear sneakers?"

"These. Do you want to see my sneakers?"

"If you don't mind."

Asher got up and left the room.

Leanne was wearing her tennis shoes, and she lifted one foot obligingly.

"You pass," Jan said after a quick look at the tread.

"Okay, Caleb, you're next," Mike said, and Caleb stood with his back to Jan and lifted one foot behind him, so she could see the bottom.

"You're good," she said. "Your tread is similar, but your feet are too small."

"Don't tell him that," Sarah said. "He'll outgrow them soon enough!"

"Go do your homework," Mike told the boy.

"I don't have any," Caleb said.

"What about that poem you were working on for Mrs. Edmonds?" his mother asked.

Caleb's face fell. "Oh yeah. What rhymes with turtle anyway?"

"Girdle," Leanne said, and they all laughed.

"How about hurtle?" Asher asked as he came back carrying a pair of high-top sneakers and another of hiking boots. He held them out to Jan.

She checked them both quickly and smiled up at him. "Thanks, Asher. I didn't think they'd match what I'm looking for, but I appreciate your willingness to indulge me."

Asher gave her the ghost of a smile. "No problem. Come on, Caleb. I'll help you with your poem."

"Myrtle," Sasha called after the kids as they left the kitchen. "Rhymes with turtle."

"What's myrtle?" Caleb asked.

"It's a lady's name," Leanne told him.

"And a kind of tree." Asher's voice faded as the kids went up the stairs.

Sarah looked at Jan, Elaine, and Sasha. "Do you think Dan would take us seriously if we did make a list for him?"

"Of people who had been in the church last weekend? Why wouldn't he?" Elaine asked.

Pastor Mike sighed. "He came by today to tell me that he wasn't able to get any fingerprints off the letter's frame."

"Really?" Jan looked at Elaine, but she shook her head. Apparently Dan hadn't mentioned that in their phone conversation. "Do you think the thief wiped it clean?"

"Could be. Because my prints should have been on it. They were all over the door to the case. There were some more there that probably belong to other people in the church. Dan's not sure it's worth printing everyone."

"We'll be first in line when he does," Elaine said. Dan hadn't seemed very eager to get the pocketknife from her when she'd phoned him and suggested it might have prints on it. She thought back over her own amateur efforts at lifting fingerprints. "I wonder if he tried to get some off the paper. I've read that you can't always, but sometimes they can get partials."

"He didn't say." Pastor Mike ran a hand through his hair.

"This must all be very bothersome for you," Sasha said.

"It is," Sarah admitted. "We can't help thinking about it. Of course, we're praying that it will all be solved, but…"

"Dan also apparently looked into our bank records," Pastor Mike said, a pained expression crossing his face.

"Is that a problem?" Elaine asked. "I don't want to probe where I shouldn't, but…"

Pastor Mike shrugged. "I did tell him earlier that we had nothing to hide and that he could see whatever he wanted, if he thought it would be helpful."

"He was looking for motive," Sarah said. "We owe a large amount in medical bills. It's from when I had surgery a few years ago. We're paying it off slowly, but we still owe about six thousand dollars."

Jan shook her head in disbelief. "He actually thinks you would steal the Knox letter to sell it and pay off your medical bills?"

"I'm not saying he thinks that," Pastor Mike replied. "He did ask us about it."

"We pay a hundred dollars a month," Sarah said. "It's all we can afford right now."

Elaine reached over and squeezed Sarah's hand. "Well, it's great that you've been able to keep paying on it. Does the church know about this need?"

"We haven't told anyone," Pastor Mike said. "We don't want the trustees to think we're asking for money."

"And we don't want them to think we're unhappy with what Mike is paid," Sarah added. "I mean, it would be nice if it was more, but we know what comes in every week in the offering. The church is doing okay, but nothing out of the ordinary. We couldn't ask for more right now."

Especially with the mortgage coming due, Elaine thought. She nodded soberly. She would never have imagined the Ryders had an outstanding debt they had been paying down for years. There ought to be something she and Jan could do to help them, without broadcasting their private affairs to the world.

"There are other things Dan doesn't like," Sarah said.

"Like what?" Jan asked.

"Well, for instance, Mike can't account for every minute of his whereabouts during the time Dan says the vandalism could have happened. He was here in the house most of that time, but he ran over to Murphy's store for a minute in the morning, about an hour before he headed out on visitation, and he walked out in the cemetery the night before."

"The cemetery?" Sasha asked in surprise.

Mike nodded. "I was just thinking about my sermon and clearing my mind. I walk out there a lot, and I pray for the families who've lost loved ones. It was only for twenty minutes or so, around nine o'clock, but it doesn't make a very good alibi."

"That may be true technically," Elaine said, "but the fact remains that you wouldn't do what those vandals did. And why make a big production of stealing an item you're in the same building with every day? Why point out the theft of the letter a few days later?"

"Yeah," Jan said. "In my book, you make a lousy suspect. I'm sure there's an explanation for the letter being switched out, and for Will Trexler's medal going missing. But I highly doubt it includes you."

"What time did Matt McInnis see someone out in the parking lot?" Elaine asked.

"I think that was closer to midnight," Pastor Mike said.

Sarah sat back in her chair with a little moan. "I just want this all to go away."

Sasha's eyes darted back and forth between her mother and Jan. "Maybe this isn't a good time to bring it up, but what about the guy with the handgun application?"

"What?" Pastor Mike's eyes widened. "Did I miss something?"

"It's nothing," Elaine said quickly. "I saw something I shouldn't have seen."

"No, I think we should talk about it," Jan said. "Pastor, you remember the business meeting last fall, when we talked about the mortgage?"

Pastor Mike's mouth tightened. "Yeah. That was one of our less cordial meetings."

"Somebody mentioned using the Knox letter as an asset that the church could sell to raise the money for the mortgage."

"I remember," Pastor Mike said.

Sarah said bleakly, "I think we all remember. Alan implied that we were stupid not to sell it. I could take it if he said we weren't good stewards, but…"

"It's okay," Pastor Mike said. "That's just Alan. He gets excited about things, not always in a good way. And once he gets something in his mind, he doesn't want to let go of it. But we get along all right. Once he saw that the rest of the board was against it, he quit insisting."

"He's probably still thinking about it," Jan said.

"He did mention it to me again a few weeks ago," the pastor admitted. "We're still about ten thousand short for the big mortgage payment. But I reminded him we all agreed to pray for another way to pay it off. He didn't seem upset, really. He was just reminding me that maybe we had a way to get the payment right under our noses."

Sarah looked at Elaine and made a little face. "The mortgage payment is still due. And it's more than our medical bills. The church people will have to dig deep to meet that payment."

"There's still another six weeks or so," Pastor Mike said. "It's not due until the end of June."

"So how *will* the church pay it?" Elaine asked softly. "You must have thought about it."

"I don't know. We've prayed about it all this time, and it's true, I think about it a lot. The treasurer and I have an appointment with the bank to talk about it next week. So…" He looked around at all of them. "Sasha, you said something about a gun?"

"That's my fault," Elaine said. She explained about how she had seen the paperwork lying on the counter at the gun shop. "It was none of my business, and I shouldn't even have seen that paper. It just reminded me of how bitter Alan was at that meeting when the church voted against selling the letter."

"He almost resigned from the board over that incident," Sarah said.

Pastor Mike pulled in a deep breath. "I was glad he didn't. Alan has a good head on his shoulders, and he's an asset to the board. But when he gets a bee in his bonnet, it can be a little challenging for the rest of us to calm him down."

"What was that mortgage for anyway?" Jan asked.

"The church took it out years ago, when we needed a new roof. That's when they plumbed in the extra bathrooms downstairs too."

"So how does this Alan guy feel about it now?" Sasha asked.

"He might be a little smug," the pastor said. "You have to understand, he doesn't want the church to have problems, but so far he's been right about this one. We haven't found another way to pay off the debt."

"I don't think he'd steal the letter," Sarah said.

"No, and I don't think the gun he's buying has any relevance at all," Elaine put in.

Pastor Mike shook his head. "No, I'm sure it doesn't. Knowing Alan, there's probably a perfectly sensible explanation for it."

"I still don't think we can rule him out completely," Jan said. When they all stared at her, she went on, "I'm just saying, it makes more sense to me that Alan would take the letter and try to sell it to pay off the mortgage than it does that you would take it, Pastor Mike. He might figure that if we church members are too stubborn to know what's good for us, he needs to give us a shove."

Elaine pondered that for a moment. "Do you think he might see it as taking care of business for the church when the rest of us won't?"

"I encouraged people to give more for the mortgage last fall, but only a couple of thousand has come in for it." Pastor Mike shook his head. "I don't like to think he would do that, Jan, but he can be a bit of a curmudgeon when he thinks he's right and everyone else is wrong."

They sat in silence for a moment, and then Elaine said. "Should we mention this to Dan?"

"I don't know," Pastor Mike said. "That might just stir up more trouble with the church folks. And if Alan had nothing to do with it..."

Sarah said what the others were thinking. "He might find it hard to forgive."

# CHAPTER FOURTEEN

Jan was surprised when she left her room at five thirty on Thursday morning to find Sasha also creeping out into the hall.

"Hi," Sasha whispered with a grin. She looked great in slim black pants, a striped T-shirt, and a navy zipper hoodie with the Aspen Sharpshooters logo.

"Good morning. Ready for breakfast?" Jan asked.

"Almost." Sasha held up her cosmetic bag. "I'll be down in ten minutes."

Jan and Elaine were blessed with private bathrooms in the remodeled Queen Anne house, but anyone else staying over usually had to go down to either the full bath by the office or the powder room off the entrance hall that the tearoom guests could access.

In the kitchen, Jan immediately put the teakettle on. She had watched Sasha yesterday and learned what she liked. It would be green tea this morning, with a dab of honey, orange juice, eggs, and muffins. Jan would have prepared all but the eggs anyway, and the muffins would be yesterday's leftovers, but she knew Sasha liked to eat protein with every meal, as did a lot of athletes.

When Sasha entered a few minutes later, she looked ready for anything. Jan couldn't detect whatever makeup she'd applied, but her skin glowed, and her shoulder-length hair was pulled back with a tortoiseshell clip.

"Hi," Jan called. "I made an omelet with a little chopped ham and onions in it. And cheese, of course. That okay?"

Sasha walked over to the stove, sniffing the air. "*Mmm*, that smells and looks wonderful, but I hope it's for both of us. Especially if you expect me to eat one of those yummy muffins you put out."

Jan smiled. "I guess I could eat a little bit of it." She carried the pan to the table, sliced through the omelet with her spatula, and slid two-thirds of it onto Sasha's plate, the rest onto her own.

"Are you always the early bird?" Sasha sat down and unfolded her napkin.

"Pretty much." Jan took the pan to the sink and came back to pour the tea. "I get a jump on the baking, and it gives me a little time alone to plan my day and have my quiet time. Your mom will probably be down in an hour. It works for us."

"I'm so glad you've got each other now." Sasha looked up at her. "I was a little worried about Mom after Dad died. I wasn't sure what she'd do with herself. For a while I thought she might find a place near Jared and his family."

Jan took her seat. "I know she misses you and Jared and Corrie and the kids, but I think she's happy here."

"Oh, me too," Sasha said. "She seems to love this new life. Shall I ask the blessing?"

"That would be great." Jan bowed her head. Hearing any of her children or grandchildren pray always blessed her heart, and now she was sharing a short time of prayer with Elaine's daughter. At Sasha's amen, she opened her eyes and smiled. "I suppose you're off to Sugarloaf this morning."

"Yeah. I didn't want to wake Mom up, but I probably won't make it back until this evening, and I have to leave tomorrow."

Jan nodded, imagining Elaine's disappointment if she didn't see Sasha all day. "Just go up to her room right before you're ready to leave. She'll appreciate it if you pop in to say good-bye."

A faint meowing came from the back door.

"Oh, there's Earl Grey." Jan pushed her chair back.

"I want to see him," Sasha said. "I think I've only seen him once."

"He's still a little shy," Jan said, "but not as bad as the last time you were here. Do you want to feed him? If you've got cat food in your hand, he probably won't run away from you."

Jan got the food from a cupboard and measured it out for Sasha. "There. Just open the back door quietly and let him on to the porch. His bowl is on a mat near the outside door, with his water dish. You'll see it."

Sasha grinned like a child as she took the container of cat food and tiptoed on to the back porch. Jan followed her and closed the door to the kitchen firmly behind them so that Earl Grey would have no chance of getting into the kitchen. He meowed again on the steps outside. Sasha poured the cat food into the bowl on the mat and gingerly opened the screen door.

The long-haired gray cat looked up at her with his wide-set green eyes and sniffed.

"Oops. I poured the food out first," Sasha whispered.

"It's okay," Jan assured her. "Just step back a little and give him his space."

Sasha followed instructions, and Earl Grey minced over the threshold and to his mat. Sasha crouched down and watched the cat make short work of his breakfast.

"He might let you pet him when he's done," Jan said. "He's even getting pretty good with my grandchildren. Well, not the twins yet. They're too rough-and-tumble."

Sasha inched closer and held out a hand. Earl Grey turned and looked over his shoulder at her, and she froze. He padded over to his water bowl and took a few licks, then turned and lifted his regal head. He sniffed Sasha's hand. A moment later, Sasha was patting his thick, silky coat.

Earl Grey oozed over to the screen door and meowed.

"Guess he's had enough attention for now," Jan said.

Sasha sighed and rose. "Guess so." She opened the door and watched the cat walk smoothly down the steps to the back deck and hop over the side.

"Show's over." Jan shut the door.

"So what are you and Mom going to do today?" Sasha asked as they went back to the table.

"We've still got a lot to do before the Mother-Daughter Tea on Saturday," Jan said. "I have some special baking to do, and we haven't really had a chance to decorate and set up the napkins and tea service."

"I wish I could be here." Sasha picked up her fork and took a generous bite of the omelet.

"I wish you could too," Jan said. She glanced toward the window. "I heard it was going to rain today. I hope you don't have to drive in it the whole way over to Sugarloaf and back."

Sasha followed her gaze and frowned, considering. "It hasn't started yet. Maybe I'll beat the storm." She lifted her fork and shook it playfully at Jan. "And if you do any sleuthing, you'd better fill me in tonight. I feel like I'll be missing out on something."

"We'll tell you every little clue we uncover," Jan promised.

"Great. Well, thanks for the breakfast. I'd better get a move on. I'll run up and see Mom—or should I say, wake up Mom."

"She'll be glad you did." Jan smiled as she watched Sasha jog out to the stairway and on up the steps. "I'd better get a move on too," she told herself with a glance at the clock. "I've got a lot of muffins and cookies to turn out this morning."

She had another solid hour to herself before Elaine showed up. If not for her yawning, she would have looked perky and energetic.

"I meant to get up after Sasha woke me, but I guess I drifted off again."

"It's okay," Jan said. Soft rain was pattering against the windows now. "She got off before the rain started."

"Let's hope it blows out to sea." Elaine got herself a small plate, sat down, and reached for a blueberry muffin. "Well, I'm prepared to work hard today."

"We need to." Jan began spooning blobs of cream puff batter onto a baking sheet.

"Just tell me what to do."

"Don't worry, I will. But eat first."

The cousins kept busy in the kitchen until Rose and Archie showed up about half past nine.

"Oh, can I fill the cream puffs?" Rose asked when she saw several cooling racks covered with them. She reached for her apron.

Jan laughed. "You're the expert on that. I'm sure Elaine won't mind."

"I'll do the setup," Archie said. Every morning he and Rose made sure they had plenty of teacups, trays, creamers, and other necessities ready, along with extra spoons and napkins near the checkout and full bowls of assorted sweeteners on every table.

"Well, if you think you can handle the last bit of baking and cleanup," Elaine said, arching her eyebrows at Jan.

"Sure we can," Jan replied. "What are you up to?"

"I wanted to run my laptop over to Computer Gal and see if Diane can tell me how to change my default settings for the purchase order form. I had some trouble with it earlier in the week, when I was ordering a lot of things."

Jan waved her away with a shake of her head. "Just tell me when you're back."

ELAINE WENT TO the small office beside the kitchen to pack her laptop, power pack, and mouse into her padded computer bag. It was as small as a lightweight briefcase, and she decided to walk down the street and around the corner to the computer repair shop.

Traffic was light, so she crossed the street toward the library and turned to her right, passing a gray Cape Cod and then Murphy's General Store. Burk King, who owned the Hearthside Restaurant, was filling his tank at the gas pumps outside Murphy's, and Elaine waved to him.

Around the corner, the small building that housed Computer Gal was the first business on the street. Diane Blanchett, the owner, was standing outside the door of the shop, with a basketweave purse and a covered coffee mug on the ground beside her. She wore jeans and a baggy beige boy-friend sweater and low-top Nikes. She must be opening late this morning—the shop was usually ready for business by nine.

"Morning," Elaine called.

Diane looked up at her. "Hi. Maybe you can give me some advice."

"I'll try." Elaine walked nearer. "What's the trouble?"

"I've locked myself out." Diane blew out a breath in exasperation, making her short bangs fly up. "I went in, and I had left my coffee in the car, so I went back to get it, and I didn't realize I had flipped the lock. And my keys are inside on my workbench."

"Oh boy. Are you sure they aren't in your purse?" Elaine looked pointedly at the bag on the step.

"I'm sure, but I looked, just in case. I know exactly where I left them. I don't know why I went out with my purse on my arm and left my keys behind. Well, yes, I do. My mind was on something else."

"I've done things like that before," Elaine said. "Let's think. Do you have an extra key?"

"The landlord does."

"Well, that's good. Can you call him?"

Diane's mouth skewed. "He's out of state for a week."

"Okay, that won't work then."

"I knew I should have made an extra." Diane picked up her travel mug and took a sip. Then she smiled wryly. "This is gold-plated coffee. It's already cost me ten minutes' work, and who knows how long it will be before I get in there."

Elaine eyed the door. There was no window in it. If there had been glass, they might have been able to break a pane and reach in to unlock the door.

"Is there a back door?"

"Yeah, but it's got a deadbolt on it, locked from inside."

"Okay." Elaine drummed her fingers on her jawbone. "I don't guess you want to break a window and climb in?"

"I'd rather not," Diane said.

"Thought so."

"I'll probably have to call a locksmith."

"Eldon Carter is a locksmith," Elaine said, thinking of the chairman of the town's board of selectmen.

"Oh, that's right. Do you have his number?"

Elaine scrunched up her face. "Afraid not. But we're not far from Murphy's store. We could walk over there and use their phone book."

"Why not? It's close." Diane pocketed her phone and picked up her purse. "Shall we?"

They walked around the corner on to Main Street. The sun sparkled off the water between the buildings on the other side. A phoebe fluttered past them and winged toward Kate's Diner.

Elaine pulled in a deep breath. Spring was her favorite time of year. Everything was so alive.

"Oh, look. There's Greg Payson." Burk King was gone from the gas pumps in front of Murphy's, but Elaine spotted Greg, putting gas into the tank of his mother's red Toyota.

"Morning, ladies!" he called.

"Hi, Greg," Diane said.

"How's the job hunt going?" Elaine asked as they came closer.

"Working on it. I have a couple of prospects."

"That's great."

They went into the store, where Jo was at the counter. Diane explained her predicament, and Jo pulled her phone book from beneath the counter.

"Here you go. Sorry you're having a bad morning."

Elaine browsed the greeting cards while Diane looked up the Carters' number and tried to place the call. She walked over to Elaine a short time later.

"No answer."

"Maybe Des can help you," Elaine said. "He's really good with tools and things."

"I asked Jo, and he's gone to Augusta this morning." Diane frowned. They stepped outside. "I sure hope I don't have to call someone all the way from Waterville."

Greg had finished pumping his gas and walked toward them. He looked them over, his gaze lingering on Elaine's computer bag. "What's up?"

"Oh, I locked myself out of my shop," Diane said. "We can't get hold of Eldon Carter, and Des isn't around."

"Maybe I can help you," Greg said.

Elaine smiled. "Are you good with locks?"

"Well, I've had my moments." Greg wiggled his eyebrows at her, and Elaine and Diane laughed.

"I'd be happy to have you take a look," Diane said.

"Sure. Just let me pay for my gas, and I'll be right over."

Elaine and Diane turned back for the short walk to Computer Gal.

"Going to be warm today." Diane unbuttoned her bulky sweater.

"I love May," Elaine said. "Our tulips are getting ready to bloom."

"You and Jan have done a fantastic job with that house, inside and out."

"Thanks. So where do you live? I don't think I ever knew."

Diane shrugged. "I rent a little place down Cottage Road."

"On the water?" Elaine asked.

"No, on the other side. It's set back into the woods. If I lean out my bedroom window and squint, I can see water. Sometimes."

Elaine laughed.

"It fits my budget at the moment," Diane explained.

"Nothing wrong with that."

They had barely reached the front of the shop when Greg drove up in the Toyota. He got out and opened the trunk, then approached with a small toolbox in one hand.

"Let's see whatcha got."

He eyeballed the lock Diane indicated, then opened the toolbox on the step. He removed a small, thin piece of metal and another tool. He began to tinker with the lock. Elaine watched in amazement as he bit his lower lip and concentrated on the job. Greg certainly looked as though he knew what he was doing.

She and Diane exchanged a look over his head. Diane seemed to agree with her that silence was the best work atmosphere, though Elaine had no idea whether Greg was listening to the lock or not She had some vague memory of reading about "tumblers turning" or some similar phrase in a mystery novel that featured a cat burglar.

In less than two minutes, he stood with a grin on his face and turned the knob.

"Ta-da!" The door swung inward.

"Oh! Thank you so much," Diane said. "What do I owe you?"

"Aw, it's on the house."

Diane gave him a mock scowl. "You know that if I'd had to call the locksmith in Waterville, he'd have charged me eighty bucks just to come all the way out here, right?"

Greg laughed. "Tell you what, next time my computer crashes, you can run diagnostics on it for free."

"You've got a deal." Diane smiled at Elaine. "Now that that's settled, please come in, Elaine. How may I help you this morning?"

# CHAPTER FIFTEEN

Jan spent two hours after lunch preparing petits fours and sandwich cream cookies for the church tea. She was meticulous about her petits fours. Each one of the little square, layered cakes was iced just so and then, when the icing had set, decorated. The main colors of icing were pastels, and the decorations were done in chocolate, white, and pink.

"Oh, those are so beautiful," Rose said when she came out to the kitchen for a tea order. "Will you show me how to do it?"

"I'll save a couple of dozen to decorate after closing if you want," Jan said.

"Really? I'd love that."

"Sure. I'll just put a crumb coating of icing on them so they don't dry out."

Rose looked lovely in her pink top and white pants, with her serving apron over them. Her long wheat-colored braid swung behind her back as she poured water over the tea blend her customer requested.

"Are there any blueberry scones left?" she asked.

"A few, I think. Check the red container." Jan covered the bowl of chocolate icing and set it in the refrigerator. "There, that will keep for later." She covered two containers of completed petits fours.

"Do you have to refrigerate those?" Rose asked.

"Not necessarily, but they're for the tea on Saturday, and I want them to be perfect. I'm putting them in airtight containers, and I'll slide them into the fridge to make sure they stay fresh."

As Rose left the kitchen with her tray, Elaine came in.

"There! I've finally caught up on my purchase orders, since Diane helped me with the program this morning. That woman is a whiz!"

"Did you order the extra take-out boxes?" Jan asked.

"Yes, and the doilies you suggested, and the international tea blends from the supplier in Boston."

Jan nodded. "That sounds like everything."

"Well, everything we couldn't find locally." Elaine stood still, frowning.

"What's wrong?" Jan asked.

"Nothing, really. I just keep thinking about that application of Alan Oakley's that I saw. He was out walking Dot and Dash when I came home from the computer shop this morning, and I wanted to rush right over and ask him about it."

"Maybe you should have." Jan started gathering up the utensils she had used in her baking. "That would be the easiest way to put it to rest."

"I'm sure it's nothing." Elaine sank down on one of the chairs at the round table. "I don't want Alan to think I'm nosy."

Jan gave a little snort. "He already thinks we're nosy. Remember when we found out he was mixed up with those crossword puzzles of Katelyn's?"

"Oh yes, I remember." Elaine grimaced. "That's part of why I hesitate to ask. You know it doesn't take much to get Alan in a dither."

"Yeah, I do. Julie Yeaton came in this morning for tea with a friend of hers." Jan loaded dishes and utensils into the dishwasher as she talked. "She said that at the last selectmen's meeting, Alan wouldn't quit harping at Darby Clement about the potholes on Pine Ridge Road."

Elaine chuckled. "Isn't it traditional for the road commissioner to butt heads with the selectmen over things like that?"

"Probably, but I think it's always Alan that Darby wrangles with."

"I guess you're right—I should talk to him about it if I want to know."

"And you know it will keep eating at you until you do," Jan said.

Archie entered the room holding a tray of used dishes before him. "Jan, there's someone in the east parlor I think you'd like to see."

"Oh!" Jan fumbled to untie her apron strings.

"Is it Bob?" Elaine asked, smiling at Archie.

"No, it's your daughter."

"Tara?" Jan's voice rose and octave. She hadn't talked to Tara since Mother's Day. This was one of her busiest times of year, getting her jewelry ready and delivered to all the gift shops that carried it during the summer rush, and Jan was indeed surprised that she had stopped in unexpectedly.

"That's correct," Archie said. "I'm getting her a peppermint iced tea and some date-filled cookies. Would you like me to add some for you as well?"

"Just the tea," Jan said. "Thank you!" She hurried out into the entrance hall and through to the east parlor.

Tara sat near the bay window at the front of the room, and Jan walked over to her table.

"Hi, stranger!"

Tara rose and hugged her. "Hi! I took some inventory into A Little Something, and I thought I'd stop in here and see you and get 'a little something' else."

Jan laughed. "I guess we could have used that name for this establishment, if it wasn't already taken by Faith Lanier for the gift shop."

"Yeah. She's really sweet," Tara said, resuming her seat. "She not only took everything I brought her today, but she asked for two dozen bracelets, as soon as I can make them up for her."

"Oh, wow. That's great." Jan sat down beside her. "Now, are these the mineral ones you showed me?"

"Yeah. I've sold quite a few earrings and necklaces, but I think the bracelets are catching on. She wanted lots of chunky quartz, and she asked me if I could do tourmaline."

Jan arched her eyebrows. "Pretty ritzy. Can you afford to order the materials?"

"I sure can. Six of the necklace and earring sets I brought her today were tourmaline. I may even start doing some other semiprecious stones."

"I'm impressed." Jan looked up and smiled as Archie brought their frosty glasses of iced tea and a plate of the date-filled cookies she'd made that morning.

"That looks great," Tara said. "Just what I need. Want a cookie, Mom?"

"No, thanks. Those are for you. I've been indulging too much lately, and Elaine and I have a dinner date tomorrow."

"Oh, that's right—trivia night at the Grill! Let me know what you win, Mom."

Jan laughed. "I'm sure there will be lots of people there who know more than I do."

"I doubt that. I expect to hear great things."

Archie had moved away, but Elaine entered the parlor, striding quickly between the tables.

"Hi, Tara."

"Hi, Elaine. Great to see you."

"Likewise." Elaine leaned close and lowered her voice. "I just wanted to give you a heads-up. Jack Weston is pulling his cabin cruiser up at our dock as we speak."

For a moment, Jan had wondered if Tara had arranged to meet Jack here, but it was obvious from her expression that she'd had no clue she would see him.

"Jack?" Tara hissed. "Oh, Mom, my hair must be awful. Can I run up to your bathroom for a minute?"

"Of course," Jan said, but Elaine looked over her shoulder toward the side windows.

"Too late. Here he is."

Jack walked into the room and grinned when he spotted Tara.

"Well, hey! Didn't expect to see you here."

"Back at ya," Tara said. "Have a seat."

"Thanks." Jack took the chair Jan had vacated and looked sheepishly up at the cousins. "I know you don't serve meals, but I also know you make little sandwiches. I've been out on the water all morning, and I didn't want a hot meal. I wondered..."

"Jack, for you, we'll make a couple of man-size sandwiches," Elaine said. He looked very dashing in his summer uniform, and he carried his wide-brimmed hat in one hand.

Jan added, "We've got ham and cheese, or chicken salad. Or peanut butter and jelly."

"Uh...one ham and one chicken?" Jack asked tentatively.

"You got it," Jan said.

Jack turned his attention to Tara. "What are you doing here?"

Tara pretended to be offended. "I need a reason to visit my mom?" Then she smiled. "No, I've been making my rounds delivering jewelry today, and I couldn't pass by the house without stopping. So what are you up to today? Checking fishing licenses?" she asked him.

Jan turned to Elaine and seized her hand, and the pair had to suppress their giggles as they walked toward the kitchen.

SAYING GOOD-BYE TO Sasha the next morning was harder than Elaine had bargained for. She hugged her daughter tight as they stood beside Sasha's rental car, which was already packed to go.

"It seems like you just got here."

"I know," Sasha said with a sniff. "I have to get back though."

"Can you try to plan a few more days when you come in the fall?" Elaine asked.

"I'll try. It depends on whether things work out for the event they're planning. It's scheduled for a week before Thanksgiving. If the timing works out right, I'll see if I can stretch my stay to include the holiday."

"That would be great," Elaine said.

"Well, Thanksgiving is usually a big weekend on the ski slopes—the start of the new season, you know. My boss at the lodge will probably want me to give lessons every day. And I need to work when I can."

"I suppose you do," Elaine agreed reluctantly. "Maybe you could give lessons here."

Sasha pursed her lips. "The idea of me giving a workshop that weekend is not out of the question. I'll make some calls after I get back to Colorado."

"Wonderful!"

"Don't count on it too heavily," Sasha said softly. "And Sugarloaf agreed to host an event next year, probably in February or March. I hope to get to that one too."

"That would be great," Elaine said. "But come anytime you can."

"I will. Thanks for everything, Mom. It was great to see you again."

"Same here. Call me when you get home, okay?"

Sasha nodded. "You bet. And if you can sneak a weekend and fly out to see me, do it!" She opened the car door and got in. After starting the engine, she waved and smiled at Elaine through the window.

Jan came out the garage door and stood beside her. Together, she and Elaine watched the car roll down Main Street and disappear toward Augusta.

"Their visits are never long enough, are they?" Jan asked.

"Nope. I had one full day and a couple of evenings with her." Elaine wiped away a tear and laughed. "Isn't she something?"

"She sure is." Jan put her arm around Elaine. "Are you going to help me with the baking? Because the sooner I finish, the sooner we can go over to the church and get set up for the tea."

"Right." Elaine glanced at her watch. "Only thirty hours from now. We'd better get busy."

Elaine spent the next couple of hours with Jan, preparing the favors for the tea party while Jan baked. They'd decided on small collections of wrapped candy in colorful netting. Each would go in a teacup on the tables, along with a couple of tea bags of exotic blends.

When she had finished, Elaine scurried up the stairs to change her blouse. Rose and Archie were putting on their aprons, and Jan was still running baking sheets through the oven. A ping on Elaine's cell phone brought a smile to her face. Sasha had reached Portland and was about to board her plane.

Archie had opened the front door when she went downstairs again. Several customers came in and he greeted them cheerfully, his lilting accent seeming to make each customer happy. How many places in Central Maine could you be served tea by a cultured Englishman?

Rose smiled as she greeted a trio of women, offering to seat them in the west parlor. Elaine scanned the checkout counter to be sure all their supplies were in place. They could use some change in the cash register. She went to her office for that. When she was certain all was in place for whoever cashed up the first customer, she wended through the two parlors, saying hello to old acquaintances and welcoming a couple of newcomers.

Business had slowed down over the winter, but it was picking up again. The number of patrons who entered in the first hour was proof of that. Elaine thrived on the busy season, and it was coming at them full tilt.

When she carried a tray out to Archie in the east parlor, Pearl Trexler called her over to a table near the fieldstone fireplace's empty hearth.

"Elaine, I wanted you to meet my friends. These two gals are in my crochet club. This is Vivian Rowe and Lora Spencer."

Elaine smiled at the two women. Vivian looked about Pearl's age, with tightly curled white hair and a wrinkled face, but Lora looked two decades younger. She wore her hair in a shoulder-length straight cut and had liberally applied eyeliner and shadow.

"Welcome," Elaine said. "Crochet? What do you do—get together and work on your latest projects?"

"Yes," Vivian said, "and we swap patterns and yarn. Sometimes we go visit a yarn shop together."

"That sounds like fun."

"It is," Lora assured her. She glanced at Pearl and Vivian. "I've learned so much from these two!"

"I'll bet," Elaine said. "What are you working on now?"

"I'm making scarves to sell at a craft fair," Vivian said.

Pearl pulled a skein of pale-green yarn and a partly finished item from a tote bag. "I'm making baby afghans for the NICU at the hospital."

"Wonderful," Elaine said.

Lora chuckled "I'm just trying to figure out a pattern for an octopus."

Elaine had to laugh. "An octopus?"

"Yeah, it's for my granddaughter," Lora said.

"That's darling. I hope you all enjoy your tea." Elaine started to move away but turned back when she remembered something. "Oh, Pearl, did you hear about Will's medal being missing from the display case at church?"

Pearl's mouth opened in an expression of surprise. "Will's medal? You mean the one he won for Bible quizzing when he was a kid?"

Elaine nodded. "We're not sure how long it's been gone. Pastor Mike noticed it a couple of days ago."

Pearl shook her head, frowning. "I'll have to ask my husband."

"Do you think he decided to take it home after the vandalism?" Elaine asked.

"I have no idea. He hasn't mentioned it to me, but you can be sure I'll ask him about it."

"Okay. Sorry. I'm sure it will turn up." Elaine almost wished she hadn't mentioned it. She hoped Will had removed it from the display for safekeeping.

"These lemon squares are delicious," Vivian said. "Any chance I can get half a dozen to take home?"

"You sure can," Elaine said. "I'll get you a box."

When the influx of customers slowed down around noon, Elaine went out to the kitchen.

"Do you think we can get away and go over to the church?" she asked Jan. "Rose thinks she and Archie will be all right without us."

"Yeah, but I was surprised how busy it was this morning," Jan said. "I made a short list of last-minute grocery items—like lemonade concentrate for the punch. Do you think Murphy's would have that, or do we need to run into town?"

"Why didn't I buy that last weekend when I shopped?"

"Neither of us thought of it, I guess," Jan sighed.

Elaine gave an exaggerated shrug. "Let's try Murphy's first. I don't think we'll have time to drive to Waterville."

"That's right—we've got a date tonight," Jan said.

"I almost forgot. I'm not so confident about this trivia business."

"You'll do great," Jan said. "You know all sorts of random things."

Elaine laughed. "Let's hope Mel and Bianca ask about those things. Have you been studying up for this?"

"I'm not sure it's possible to study for that," Jan said.

"Well, sure. You could go over lists of things. Like presidents, and Oscar winners, and Renaissance painters—you know, stuff they ask at events like this."

"I've never been to a trivia tournament."

"Well, neither have I," Elaine conceded, "but I've played a lot of trivia games with the kids and at informal parties."

"Huh. I like to watch *Jeopardy* when I have a chance. I suppose that's similar. And I used to be able to list all the presidents."

"Me too. Remember, we had to learn them when we were in sixth grade?"

"Yeah," Jan said without cracking a smile, "but there are a lot more of them now."

"Oh, you! Come on! Let's get moving."

Jan drove to Murphy's and parked outside the general store. Elaine hopped out of the car and hurried inside. One of the twins was unloading a box of bananas onto a display counter at the front of the store.

"Those look good," Elaine said. "I'll take a few." She smiled at the boy. "Let's see... Nick, right?"

He smiled. "Yup. You're good, Mrs. Cook."

Elaine was satisfied she had learned to tell the Murphy twins apart. It was easy for her when they wore short sleeves. Chris had a small scar on the back of his left wrist from a childhood accident, and this boy didn't have it. "Do you know if you have any frozen lemonade concentrate?"

"Yeah, I'm pretty sure. Check the freezer case, near the orange juice."

"Thank you." She grabbed a shopping basket, put her bananas in it, and breezed down the aisle on the wall, past the dairy case, to the freezers at the back. Vegetables, frozen dinners, pizza, ice cream, fruit juice. "Aha." She put four cans of lemonade concentrate in the basket and walked to the front counter.

"Wait a minute." She glanced over her shoulder. Nick was still stocking the produce. "Sorry. I thought you were Nick. And you're even wearing different T-shirts."

Chris laughed. "No problem, Mrs. Cook." He rang up her purchases. "Got a hankering for lemonade?"

Elaine chuckled. "This is for the Mother-Daughter Tea at the church tomorrow."

"Oh, right." Chris sobered. "You know we didn't trash the church, don't you? We never even went inside that day."

"I believe you," Elaine said. She wasn't sure why, but she did. It wasn't logical to eliminate suspects based on how she felt about them, but she truly had faith in these two boys, and she could tell they were deeply hurt by people's suspicions.

"Thanks." Chris smiled wryly and double-bagged her lemonade. He put the bananas gently into a separate bag. "We wouldn't do anything like that. And we sure wouldn't steal the general's letter."

Elaine nodded. "I hope Trooper Benson finds out who did it soon, so you don't have to keep thinking about it."

"Me too."

"Say, Chris, somebody mentioned to Jan and me that some other kids came by Saturday, while you were doing the yard work at the church."

His eyes widened. "Oh yeah. Just some kids from school."

"Friends of yours?"

"Not friends, really. Just...kids. Guys. They were out riding around, and they stopped for a minute and said hi."

"I see. Well, thanks again." She wanted to ask more about the guys, but a long line had formed behind her, so she took her bags and went out to the car with a heavier heart. Just thinking about the theft and vandalism made her sad, and she couldn't imagine how awful it made the twins feel.

Sarah Ryder and Annie Richardson had agreed to meet them at the church to help get ready for the tea, and Ethan came along with his daughter-in-law.

"Well, hi, Ethan," Elaine said. "Glad to have you, but this is quite a surprise."

"The tractor's broken down," Ethan said. "Gavin went to get parts, and I was footloose. Annie thought I might be able to tack up crepe paper for you or something."

"We'll put you right to work," Jan said. "How did Ella's party go?"

Annie looked up from the grocery bag she was unpacking. "It was great. The girls really liked the cupcakes too. Ella asked me if you were making them for the tea."

"Not the cupcakes," Jan said with a laugh, "but you can tell her we'll have plenty of goodies."

They chatted as they went about decorating and arranging the napkins and dishes.

"I'll bring the flowers over first thing in the morning," Sarah said.

"Great," Elaine told her. "We're going to come over around noon so that we're sure we've got everything under control before people start coming in."

"Anything new from Trooper Benson?" Jan asked.

Sarah shook her head. "Mike's trying not to think about it. He's not usually one to brood, but this thing about the Knox letter really has him down."

"That's too bad," Elaine said. "I keep hoping Dan will turn up some clues that will show him someone else stole the letter."

"We're praying really hard for that," Sarah said.

"Let's take a break right now and pray about it," Elaine suggested.

"Great idea," Annie said. "There's got to be a way to prove Pastor Mike is innocent."

"And the Murphy boys," Elaine added. "They're still feeling some pressure because people threw their names out there in connection with the vandalism."

"I don't think they did it," Jan said staunchly.

"Me either," Ethan said. "They're good kids."

"But still," Jan said, "Dan Benson does have a point. We can't totally rule out anyone until we have more evidence."

Elaine felt a twinge of guilt, but she shook it off. Why should she feel guilty for thinking someone was innocent? Evidence or no evidence, she wanted to believe in people.

As they sat down to pray together, Elaine added a special petition for Dan Benson, that he would view the case clearly and impartially. That he would find some new evidence, and that maybe she and Jan would be able to help too.

# CHAPTER SIXTEEN

When the cousins got back to their house and went in through the garage door, Rose met them in the hallway.

"Elaine, Jan. I'm so glad you're back. I almost called you."

One look at Rose's strained face told Jan that something was wrong.

"What's happened?"

"It's Pearl and Will Trexler. They insisted on talking to you two. I figured you'd be back soon, so I sat them down with a pot of tea on the house and told them if you weren't back in ten minutes, I'd call you. That was nine minutes ago."

"Okay, thanks," Elaine said.

"They're in the west parlor," Rose called after them.

Jan detoured through the dining room and in the back door of the west parlor. Only the Trexlers and one other party were seated there, and Jan suspected Rose had steered any latecomers into the other room to give them a little privacy.

"Pearl, Will, how nice to see you." Elaine's smile was as sincere as ever. The couple was seated opposite each other at a square table, and she slid into a chair on the side. Jan sat down across from her.

"Thank goodness you're here." Pearl glanced at her watch. "I need to get home and start supper, but we just had to see you."

"What's wrong?" Jan asked. Will's face was even more sober than Rose's.

"Pearl says my medal's gone missing from the church," he said. "Did the thief who took the general's letter take that too?"

"I don't know," Elaine said.

"Well, someone should have told us," Pearl said.

"There now, honey, don't fuss," Will told her. "It's just an old hunk of steel."

"But it's a family heirloom."

Will laughed. "I wouldn't go that far. It's not worth anything but the sentiment attached. Besides, we're not supposed to be proud. Maybe the Good Lord let this happen to teach me some humility."

"Let someone steal your medal?" Pearl frowned at him. "That's a funny way to teach a lesson."

Elaine cleared her throat. "I'm sorry, Pearl. I didn't mean to upset you when I mentioned that it was missing from the display case at the church."

Pearl sighed. "Well, I didn't know about it, and neither did Will."

"We learned it was missing Tuesday night," Jan said, "but it was gone before that. Dan Benson had taken pictures of the case Tuesday afternoon, and it wasn't in there then, but no one noticed. Everyone was concentrating on the Knox letter."

"But we know it was still in there Sunday night," Elaine added. "The kids in the youth group saw it then, after their meeting."

"That's odd," Will said. "Didn't the thief break in on Saturday?"

"Friday night or Saturday," Jan said. "But we don't know if that was the same person who took the Knox letter."

"And we don't think your medal went out the door when the letter did," Elaine added. "We just know they both went missing about the same time."

Pearl shook her head. "Strange goings-on at the church lately."

Jan jumped up. "Let me go and get us all a fresh pot of tea and some cookies."

Neither Will nor Pearl refused, so Jan bustled out to the kitchen. As she heated the tea water, Rose poked her head in the doorway.

"Everything okay out there?"

"Yeah," Jan said. "It's a little wrinkle, but nothing Elaine and the Lord can't smooth out."

"I'm glad to hear it." Rose walked to the counter and began arranging scones on a plate for them. "Not long until closing. It will be quiet here, if they want to talk for a while."

"I don't think they're staying long," Jan said. She fixed a small box of cookies and put loose Scottish breakfast tea leaves in a tea ball.

When she got to the table with the tray, Pearl was smiling, and Jan took that as a good sign. Jan set the teapot, extra cups, and treats on the table.

"Those look good." Will reached for a scone.

"Now, don't eat too many," Pearl said. "You'll spoil your supper."

Jan picked up the small box she had prepared. "I put half a dozen cookies in here for you, if you want to take them home."

Pearl looked up at her. "That's sweet of you, Jan. Thank you." She glared at Will. "I'll save them until after supper."

They all laughed. Jan topped off everyone's tea and sat down, but everything important seemed to have been aired. Conversation turned to family news and the preparations for the Mother-Daughter Tea, which Pearl said she would attend with Kit and Marcella, her granddaughter and great-granddaughter. The Trexlers rose a few minutes later.

"Best get home," Will said.

Pearl picked up her tote bag. Will snagged the cookie box before she could take it.

"I'll keep track of these," he said.

Jan smiled and walked them to the door. When she returned to the parlor, Elaine was still in her chair. She sat back and huffed out a big breath.

"I really put my foot in it that time."

Jan sat down and picked up her teacup. "I don't know. They seemed okay when they left. It could have been a whole lot worse. Now, tell me, who is the secretary of agriculture right now?"

"What?" Elaine blinked at her. "What has that got to do with anything?"

"The guys are picking us up in two hours for trivia night, remember?"

Elaine moaned. "I don't suppose there's any chance of getting out of that?"

"No, there's not."

"Okay, so who *is* the secretary of agriculture?"

"You got me." Jan reached for a scone.

MACY ATHERTON HURRIED up the tearoom steps just as Jan was flipping the sign to Closed. Jan opened the door.

"Hi, Macy."

"Am I too late?"

"Well," Jan said, "it *is* closing time. Archie and Rose are cleaning up."

"I don't need to sit down," Macy said. "I just wondered if I could get a cookie assortment. We've got some of our most important clients coming in tonight. They come every year, but usually not until Memorial Day weekend. When she called this afternoon and asked if they could come early for a week, of course I said yes. Zale and I have been working to get their favorite cabin ready. But I'd like to have a nice little spread ready for them when they check in—cookies, coffee, you know." She stopped for breath.

"Of course," Jan said. "Come on back to the kitchen door, and I'll tell you what we've got handy." She was never one to turn down a special order, especially if it meant selling whatever pastries they had left at the end of the day. Besides, Macy was a very loyal customer and Jan had no problem showing her special privileges once in a while.

"I figured you could help me," Macy said, puffing a little as she followed Jan through the entrance hall. Archie came to the door of the east parlor with a tray of dishes, but waited for them to pass.

"Hello, Macy," he said smoothly.

"Hello." Macy sounded distracted. She was focused on the clients, no doubt about it. She paused just inside the kitchen while Jan surveyed the pastry racks and cookie containers.

"*Hmm.* We have three kinds of cookies, some blueberry and cranberry scones, carrot cake squares, and..."

"What kind of cookies?" Macy asked.

Jan smiled. Macy was a known cookie lover, though she seldom voiced her appreciation. "Looks like triple chocolate, salted peanut, and date-filled."

Macy's face fell. "I hoped you'd have some of those ginger chews."

"Let me look in the freezer." Jan opened the door where they kept a stash of cookies prepared in case they ran out during the day. "Yes, I have a dozen."

"I'll take those. What else?"

"Cinnamon snaps, shortbread, and oatmeal raisin."

"Okay, a dozen of the oatmeal and the triple chocolate," Macy said. "Shortbread should be outlawed."

"Some people like it."

Macy gave a little snort.

Jan got out the take-out boxes. Nothing Macy said ever surprised her. Something they had talked about with Sarah Ryder came to her just as Archie came in with his tray and began unloading it.

"Oh, Macy," Jan said, "I was wondering about a guest you had a couple of weeks ago. A Mr. Prior, I believe." She continued putting cookies in the boxes as she spoke.

"Felix Prior? Yes, he came to do a little fishing."

"Early, wasn't he?"

"Yes," Macy said, "but some people like to beat the crowds. And the mosquitoes. Why do you ask?"

"Oh, he came up in conversation when we were talking about the General Knox letter," Jan said.

"*Hmm.* Dan Benson came by a few days ago and asked me about him too. Felix did ask me about that letter the day after he got here. I didn't know much about it. I told him to ask over at the church, and I think he went to the service over there."

"Yes, he did. Where's he from, just out of curiosity?" Jan asked.

"Boxborough, I think. Boston area anyway." Macy shrugged. "I've probably got his address at my office, but I never give out private information like that."

"Oh, I know. Sorry." Jan smiled and handed her the cookie boxes. "Here you go, and thanks for your business." She looked over at Archie. "Could you ring up Macy, Archie?"

"Surely. This way, Macy. How are things over at Green Glade?"

Macy gave Jan a curt nod and followed Archie out toward the checkout counter.

Elaine gazed into her bathroom mirror and fussed with the collar of her yellow blouse. It just didn't want to lie flat tonight. After a few unsuccessful attempts, she peeled it off and took an embroidered red top from her closet.

Jan knocked briskly on her open door. "Hey. You ready? They'll be here any minute."

Elaine frowned at the red top. "Does this go with these pants?"

"Sure, but what's wrong with the yellow one?" Jan eyed the discarded blouse that lay on the bed.

"The collar isn't right."

"Oh. You look so good in pastels."

"Do I?" Elaine looked in the closet again and pulled out a green print tunic. "My light-blue top is in the wash."

"Not that one," Jan said in a tone that made Elaine wonder if the green tunic made her look sallow—or fat. "Go with the red. It looks nice on you too. And take deep breaths."

Elaine scowled at her but put on the red top and quickly chose a necklace that complimented it. She sighed and faced the mirror again. Not bad. At least she and Jan, who wore olive pants and a striped blouse, didn't clash and wore about the same level of casual style.

When the doorbell rang at quarter to seven, she found she was still a little nervous. As much as she had been around

Nathan this past year, she shouldn't be on edge, but the fact that they were now officially dating, like Jan and Bob, made the occasion seem more serious than a good friends' outing.

"Are you sure I look okay?" she asked Jan, her pulse fluttering as they went down the stairs to the entry. She put a hand up to the back of her hair and immediately felt silly.

"You're gorgeous." Jan hurried to the front door and opened it.

"Hi," Bob said. "You look great."

"Thanks! Come on in." Jan swung the door wide, and Bob walked a few steps inside. Elaine noted that even in his casual clothes, Bob always looked terrific. He stooped to kiss Jan's cheek before turning toward Elaine.

"Hi, Elaine."

"Hello, Bob." She advanced toward him, smiling.

Jan was shutting the door, but stopped and reopened it. "And here's Nathan, just driving in."

"Oh, good," Elaine said. When her cousin had ushered him in and they'd all greeted each other, she felt just a bit awkward. "Would you guys like something to drink?"

Bob glanced at Nathan and shrugged. "I figured we'll be getting something at the Grill."

"Of course." Elaine felt more flustered than ever. That was Mel and Bianca Stadler's point of holding the trivia contests, after all—to entice customers to sit there all evening and order food and beverages.

"Do you want to walk?" Bob asked.

"It hardly seems worth taking a car," Jan replied. The Pine Tree Grill wasn't far from the tearoom—just past the

Bookworm. She picked up the ivory sweater she had left on the checkout counter.

"Oh, I've got to get my jacket from the office." Elaine strode quickly across the entrance hall and into the small room next to the kitchen. She paused and took two of those deep breaths Jan recommended before picking up her light jacket and purse. Putting a hand to her cheek, she decided that, though it was warm, her face wasn't bright-red hot. "Relax," she told herself.

When she walked out into the hall, Nathan gave her the smile that always reminded her of childhood times. While their fathers talked business, they had formed a friendship that had lasted more than forty years. He took her jacket and held it for her, making her feel clumsy again as she groped for the sleeves. Finally they were ready and stepped out on to the porch together.

On the short walk, Elaine shivered and zipped the jacket.

"The nights are still cold," Nathan observed, slipping an arm around her.

"The weatherman said we might even get a frost tonight," Jan put in.

"Really?" Elaine wondered when her cousin had found time to listen to the weather forecast. "I hope it doesn't kill the tulips. They're just opening up."

A dozen cars filled the small parking lot in front of the log building that housed the Pine Tree Grill.

"Looks like it's a good thing we walked," Bob said. "These trivia nights seem to be pretty popular."

"I think so," Jan replied. "But they have more parking out back too."

When they walked in, country music was playing in the background, but not too loud for comfortable conversation. Bianca Stadler, who owned the business with her brother Mel, greeted them almost at once.

"Well, howdy folks! Welcome!" Bianca was at her finest when interacting with customers. Her bright smile and easy chatter made Elaine feel at home.

"Hi, Bianca," Jan said. "I love your boots. What are they made of?"

"Why, thank you." Bianca grinned and extended her left foot, displaying a two-tone blue-and-gray high-heeled boot with a natural design in the soft leather upper. "That's the finest ostrich leather, if you don't mind."

"I don't," Jan said.

Bob laughed. "Good to see you, Bianca. There are four of us tonight."

"I see that." Bianca looked Elaine and Nathan over. "Now, are you folks going to take part in the trivia tournament?"

"That's what we're here for," Bob said genially.

"Great. I'll seat you right in the thick of things. People who don't want to play the game like to sit over on the other side of the room. But I can see you're all set to put on a good show for us."

"I don't know about the show part," Jan said.

"Honey, you're going to love it. We're going to get started any minute, so come right this way. Mel's setting up the scoreboard."

They followed her to a round table, and Elaine saw several familiar faces in the crowd. Most had burgers, fried clams, or other fare in front of them, and everyone had a glass of something handy.

"What can I bring you all to get you started?" Bianca asked as they sat down. She took out a sales pad and poised her pen over it.

"Diet cola please," Elaine replied.

"And I'll have coffee." Nathan looked at Elaine and arched his eyebrows. "You want something to eat? Maybe a burger or something?"

"Maybe." She looked up at Bianca, knowing her calorie count was blown for the week anyway. "You know, I haven't had clams for a while."

"Clam plate?" Bianca asked. "It's really good. Comes with fries and coleslaw."

"Oh, but I'll skip the fries," Elaine said.

"Well, I won't," Nathan said. "I'll take the clam plate, and some onion rings on the side."

Elaine said nothing about the grease or the calorie intake. Nathan kept fit, and she knew he worked out at a gym near his office several times a week, not to mention the golf he loved in summer. As for herself, if she ate that much fried food in one sitting, she would suffer for it, she was certain.

As Jan and Bob put in their orders for burgers and fries, Mel Stadler stepped to the middle of the room carrying a portable microphone. His build was more slender than Bianca's, and he was a couple of inches shorter. His graying beard and mustache covered the lower part of his face. Elaine knew he was somewhat shy, and she was glad to see that he pushed himself to be outgoing when hosting the trivia games. Tonight he wore a flashy navy blue western shirt with a white yoke embellished with embroidery and fringe, along with worn jeans, cowboy boots that actually looked as though they'd been worked in, and a wide belt with a large, fancy buckle. He might have stepped right out of the rodeo pens.

"Good evening, folks! It's that time again, and we've got some great questions ready for you. My sister must have spent half her waking hours this week researching these, and I hope y'all appreciate that."

Everyone clapped.

Mel grinned. "That's for you, sis!"

Bianca turned around from where she was taking another order. She wiggled her fingers in a little wave and gave a half bow, smiling from ear to ear.

"Oh yeah," Mel said, glancing at a sheet of paper in his hand. "Great categories. Let me give you the list for round one. We've got one called Main Ingredients, where we'll give you the things that go into it, and you tell us what dish we're cookin'."

People clapped and whistled.

"And then we've got Maine Bigwigs, which is about famous people from the great state of Maine."

More applause.

Mel went on, listing off categories about birds, physics, baseball, and geography. Elaine was busy looking around at the people occupying the other tables. These would be their competitors. She noticed a few she knew—Julie Yeaton and her husband, Chuck, old schoolmates of hers and Jan's, and Katelyn Grande, who was Bristol Payson's assistant at the Bookworm. She was seated with music teacher Frank Conrad, who apparently was spending the evening with Katelyn. Elaine didn't recognize the other couple with them.

"We've got eight tables competing tonight," Mel said. "Each table can have from two to six people at it. We ask any singletons who want to play to join another table, and if you get more than six, you have to split into two teams. You're allowed to discuss the question among your team at your table, but we ask that you designate one person to give the official answers for each question, just to avoid confusion. Bianca and I are the judges, and our decisions on whether you're right or not are final. If you don't like the rules, you can leave now."

The room was quiet for about two seconds. Elaine was surprised at how serious Mel looked. Then he laughed, and the crowd joined him.

"All right. The winning table gets all the glory and a gift certificate for twenty-five dollars' worth of whatever at this establishment. Tonight we also have a bonus—the Gift Me shop is donating a T-shirt with canoes and the slogan 'Maine: The way life should be.' Want to hold that up, Bianca?"

Bianca had gone to the hostess station and obliged by holding up a forest-green T-shirt.

"Nice," said a man at the table behind them.

Bianca reached for the microphone. "And remember, absolutely no cell phones, tablets, or other devices or resources during this contest. Please turn off all devices now, and we'll be watching for crib sheets." She grinned and gave the mic back to her brother.

Elaine fished in her purse for her phone so she could turn it off. All around her, other contestants did the same.

"All right," Mel said. "Let's get started. For round one, each table can pick their category, and you'll be given a question in that category. You'll have thirty seconds to give your answer."

Bob leaned forward and looked at the others. "Okay, so what category do we go for?"

"Maybe the cooking?" Elaine asked.

"Yeah, and you're good at geography," Jan said. "I can live with physics."

Nathan eyed her keenly. "Really? I'm impressed."

"I'm okay with Maine people and maybe baseball," Bob said. "How about you, Nathan?"

"*Hmm*, history's my main thing, but maybe we'll get that in the next round. Geography, I guess, unless the ladies want to stake it all on cooking."

"Well, the Maine Bigwigs are probably historical figures," Elaine reasoned. "You all would probably do well with that. I've been away so long, I don't know if I would."

"It's okay by me," Nathan said.

During this discussion, Elaine gathered that Table 1 answered a baseball question correctly, but Table 2 missed their bird question. Mel and Bianca arrived at their table, each holding a clipboard.

"All right, Table 3," Mel said, "it's your turn. Have you folks played our game before?"

They all shook their heads.

"You choose your category, I ask the question, and Bianca keeps score. But first, who's your answer person?"

"I think Jan should be," Elaine said immediately.

"So do I," Bob agreed.

Nathan nodded. "Sounds good."

"All right, Jan, you give us the team's answer within thirty seconds after I start reading the question, okay?"

"Got it," Jan said.

"What's your category?"

"We'll try Maine Bigwigs," Jan said.

"Okay," Mel said, flipping a couple of pages on his clipboard. "Here's your question." He spoke clearly into the mic, so that everyone in the Grill could hear him. "This statesman was a professor of mathematics and ancient languages and a teacher of the blind before he served as both congressman and senator for the state of Maine, and was secretary of state under three presidents, but couldn't get to the White House himself."

"Wow," Elaine said. "That's quite a résumé." She had a vague memory of General Joshua Chamberlain being a professor before he joined the army, and later governor of Maine, but she didn't think he'd served in Congress.

Bob leaned in. "Is it Hannibal Hamlin?"

"I think it's Blaine," Nathan whispered.

"Oh, I'll bet you're right," Jan said. "Because Hamlin was vice president for Lincoln, wasn't he? They would have mentioned that."

Bob nodded. "Okay, let's go with Blaine then."

"Do you have an answer?" Mel asked.

Jan sat up straight and met his gaze. "Yes. Our answer is James G. Blaine."

Mel nodded. "That's correct. Ten points for Table 3."

"Way to go, rookies." Bianca made a notation on her clipboard and grinned at them. "Keep it up." She and Mel moved on to Table 4.

"Whew." Jan collapsed against the back of the chair. "Maybe somebody else should be the spokesperson. I'm exhausted."

"You're doing great," Bob said. "Let me get you more iced tea." He flagged down a waitress, and she came over to the table.

"We need a refill," Bob told her.

"Sure thing." She hurried off to get the drinks.

When the Stadlers came to them for their second question, they had to choose a different category, so they chose Main Ingredients.

Mel flipped a few pages, his eyes dancing. "Here you go. Bacon, onions, red wine vinegar or wine, rabbit m—"

"Hasenpfeffer!" Elaine startled even herself with her outburst. They all stared at her for a moment.

Jan's lips quirked. "Yeah. That's our final answer, from the lady who used to live in Germany."

"Hasenpfeffer is correct," Mel said.

"Congratulations," Bianca said, grinning. "Folks, that's ten more points for Table 3." She and Mel moved on to the next table.

"Whew," Elaine said. "Sorry about that. I should have consulted with you all."

"No, you knew it," Bob said. "I've never had hasenpfeffer myself."

"Folks around here would probably just say rabbit stew," Nathan added with a chuckle.

Unfortunately, their question in the bird category stumped them, which surprised and disappointed all four of them.

"I thought I knew my birds," Jan said, shaking her head. "Whoever heard of a harlequin duck?"

"That seemed pretty obscure to me too," Bob said, shaking his head.

Soon Mel and Bianca announced the tally for round one. "Only one table got all three of their questions right, for thirty points," Bianca said. That's Table 8." Everyone clapped. Elaine noted that Katelyn and Frank were at that table.

"And they didn't even have a music category," Elaine muttered, stabbing a juicy fried clam with her fork.

"Three tables got two questions right," Bianca continued. She read them off, including their own Table 3 and also Table 7, where Julie and Chuck Yeaton were sitting.

Mel took the microphone. "For round two, everyone gets the same questions," he said. "We'll give you a list of five questions, and each team will write down their answers. You'll have ten minutes to complete it. We'll collect and score them while you enjoy another round of drinks."

"I can see how they make their money on trivia nights," Jan said.

Bob laughed. "It's okay by me. We can get some ice cream if you want."

Elaine skipped the ice cream. The fried clams had tasted great, and she figured she would be ahead if she didn't overdo it.

Soon Mel and Bianca had distributed the list of questions to each table.

"When I say 'go,' you can turn over your paper and begin," Bianca said, grinning around at the people. "I'd advise everyone to keep their voices low while they discuss things."

On Bianca's go, Jan flipped over the paper, and they all huddled in to view the questions.

1. *Who is Hercule Poirot's friend and sometime sidekick?*
2. *What body of water does the Danube River empty into?*
3. *The first Nobel Prize in Physics was awarded in 1901 to the German physicist who discovered a shortwave ray called the X-ray. Who was he?*
4. *What composer penned* The Minute Waltz *and* The Funeral March?
5. *Britain's Queen Victoria belonged to what dynasty?*

Elaine gave a little groan. "Those are hard."

# CHAPTER SEVENTEEN

W ell, the third one's easy," Jan said.

Nathan chuckled. "I'm glad you think so."

Jan quickly wrote *Wilhelm Röntgen* below the third question.

"Makes sense to me," Elaine said. "Of course, I would have had no idea."

"That's what I like about her. She's a smart lady." Bob put his arm around Jan's shoulders and gave her a squeeze.

Jan flushed. "Thanks. Now, it's up to the rest of you to fill in the rest."

"I think number 5 might be the House of Windsor," Nathan said softly. "Isn't Elizabeth II a direct descendant of Victoria? And I know she's part of the Windsors."

"Okay, I'll put that down as a tentative answer," Jan said.

Elaine frowned, trying to pull an elusive name from her memory. "Poirot's sidekick was in several of Agatha Christie's books. He'd gotten married in one of them. I'm thinking... Captain Hastings?"

"Oh yeah, that's right. I liked him." Jan quickly wrote it under the first question. "Now, the body of water..."

"The Danube goes through Germany, doesn't it?" Nathan cocked an eyebrow at Elaine.

"It does, but it goes through a lot of countries. I've seen it several times. But where does it end?"

"Does it go up to the Baltic Sea?" Jan asked.

Elaine shook her head. "No, I think it flows east. I know it goes through Budapest."

"Hungary?" Nathan guessed.

Bob nodded. "I think she's right. It's really long. But Hungary is landlocked, isn't it?"

"I almost think it flows into the Black Sea," Elaine said.

"*Shh!*" Jan put a finger to her lips and looked around to make sure no one else was listening.

"Really?" Nathan looked a little skeptical.

"Yes. Through Romania," Elaine whispered.

"How sure are you?" Bob asked.

Elaine considered for a moment. "Eighty-nine-point-five percent."

Bob and Nathan laughed.

"I thought Jan was the number person," Nathan said.

"Well, I think she's right." Jan wrote *Black Sea* under the second question. "Okay, that just leaves the composer."

"Which, of course, is simple for Frank Conrad," Elaine said.

"Who's he?" Bob asked.

"Sitting over there with Katelyn Grande." Elaine glanced Frank's way. "Table 8. Green shirt. He teaches music in Augusta."

"That's not good," Nathan said. "Not good for us, I mean."

"So who could it be?" Bob asked. "Beethoven? Mozart?"

Nathan leaned back in his chair and closed his eyes. "No, that doesn't sound right. *The Minute Waltz.* I can't even think how that goes."

"At least we all know *The Funeral March*," Jan said. "Dum dum da-dum, dum da-dum da-dum da-dum," she intoned solemnly.

Elaine laughed. "But is that the one they're talking about? Maybe this is a totally separate thing."

Bob cocked his head to one side. "*The Minute Waltz*—is that a piano thing?"

"I think so," Elaine replied.

Nathan held up both hands. "Don't look at me."

Bob nodded, his expression growing more confident. He leaned forward. "I say Chopin. What do you think?" His eyebrows rose as he looked around at them.

"Good enough for me," Jan said.

Nathan nodded. "Sure."

"Go for it," Elaine whispered, and Jan wrote it down.

Elaine sat back in her chair and let out a big sigh. "Glad that's over, and we have two minutes left."

Jan smiled. "It was kind of fun, and we all contributed."

Bianca, Mel, and a waitress were ambling about the room, keeping an eye on the players.

"Everybody ready for another round of drinks?" Nathan asked.

"I'd take another diet cola," Elaine said.

"I'll have more coffee," Bob told him. "The waitress looks busy. Maybe we can just walk up to the bar and get refills."

"And I'm heading for the ladies' room." Jan pushed her chair back.

While the others were away from the table, Elaine looked over at the other side of the room. Two men sat together at a corner table, deep in conversation. One of them was Greg Payson, sitting with another young man she didn't know. A couple of tables away, Sylvia Flood sat opposite a distinguished-looking man with a neatly trimmed mustache. Sylvia looked great, in a retro-look pants suit with a bright pink-and-maroon scarf at her neck. She had really mastered the retro-chic style. Elaine reminded herself to walk over to Sylvia's Closet and browse some afternoon.

"Here we go." Nathan set two glasses on the table. Elaine's fresh cola had a straw and a paper umbrella in it.

"What's this?" she asked.

"Just whimsy."

"Okay." She eyed his glass. "You switched from coffee?"

"Yeah, it's a little late for more caffeine, so I went with root beer this time."

At that moment, Mel stood in the center of the playing area with his clipboard and microphone. Jan scurried back to the table as Bob set down his cup and Mel began to speak.

"All right, folks, I have some exciting news. We have one table that got every answer right on the second round." He swung around and looked right at Jan. "Congratulations, Table 3."

Everyone clapped, and Mel read down the list, telling how many answers each table got right. Surprisingly, Table 8, the leaders in the first round, had slipped and only got four of the answers right in the written round.

"And this means," Bianca said, stepping up with a chalkboard, "that Tables 3 and 8 are tied, with Table 7 right behind them. Now, you other folks, don't give up. You can still catch up and pass them in the lightning round."

Mel raised the mic and ran through the special rules for the upcoming round. "We'll go to each table and ask you a quick ten questions. You'll have two minutes to answer as many as you can. If you don't know an answer, you can pass on that question and come back to it after you've heard all the others."

He handed the mic back to Bianca, who said, "At the end of this round, the winner will be declared. If there's a tie, we'll have tiebreaker questions until we get a winner." She walked over to the first table.

Elaine enjoyed listening as Tables 1 and 2 ran through their questions. Bianca read the questions this time, while Mel kept the time and score. The players at Table 1 spent more time laughing and joking than seriously considering their answers and wound up with only three correct. Table 2 did better, coming up with six right answers. Bianca used the microphone when she asked the questions, so that everyone in the Grill could hear their answers.

"All right, Table 3." Bianca stood before them. "This is the final round. If you do well on this one, you'll be either the winners or headed for a tie breaker. If you stumble, you're opening the door for somebody else. And I won't mention any names, but you know who you are." She turned and winked broadly at Katelyn, Frank, and their companions at Table 8, and everybody laughed.

Jan grabbed Elaine's hand and gave it a squeeze. "We can do this."

Bianca nodded. "Just feed your answers to Jan, and she'll tell me. Time begins on Mel's count."

Mel gave them a quick smile. "Ready? One, two, three."

Bianca said, "Who was the first person to break the sound barrier?"

"Chuck Yeager," Jan said, before the men could even open their mouths.

"Right." Bianca went on, "Who was the Triple Crown–winning jockey in 2015?"

Elaine looked at Jan in dismay.

"The horse was American Pharoah," Jan said, frowning.

"Victor something," Nathan said, pounding the table with his fist.

"Espinoza," Jan yelled.

"Yes!" Bianca was grinning as she went to the third question. "Who was the oldest person in the Bible?"

"Methuselah," the four cried together.

Bianca laughed, and Mel made a checkmark on his scoresheet.

"What river runs through the Grand Canyon?"

Bob poked Jan. "The Colorado."

"The Colorado," she repeated.

"Right. What was the final battle of the American Revolution?"

"Yorktown," Nathan said, and Jan relayed it.

"Question six: Who was Great Britain's monarch just before Elizabeth II?"

Elaine squeezed her eyes shut. She never seemed able to keep all those Edwards and Georges straight.

Nathan apparently didn't have that problem.

"George VI," he hissed, and Jan said it out loud.

"Right. What bird flies the farthest in its migration?"

There was a pause and Elaine looked at the others.

"The arctic tern?" Jan didn't sound at all certain.

"Yes! The two highest mountains in Africa are...?"

"Kilimanjaro," Bob said to Jan.

"We need both?" Nathan asked Bianca, and she nodded.

"I know this," Elaine said, dredging the deepest recesses of her memory. "Ben went there once..."

"Should we pass?" Jan whispered.

Elaine smiled. "Mount Kenya."

Jan hauled in a breath and faced Bianca. "Kilimanjaro and Kenya."

"Correct."

Elaine almost collapsed.

"Which state has the most counties?"

Again they looked at each other.

"Well, we know it's not Maine," Jan said with a straight face.

The song they had learned in eighth grade immediately started playing through Elaine's mind: *Sixteen counties has our state, Aroostook and Penobscot...* She gave herself a little shake. She needed to concentrate.

"It's got to be Texas," Bob said.

"Or California," Jan added uncertainly.

"Should we go with Texas?" Jan looked at Elaine.

"Whatever you think."

"Texas," Jan said, looking Bianca in the eye.

"Correct."

"Thanks, Bob," Elaine said with a smile.

He made a formal little bow.

"And your last question."

"Ten seconds," Mel said.

Bianca said hurriedly, "What is it called when a binary star system explodes?"

Jan almost jumped out of her chair. "A supernova!"

"Yes!"

"Hooray!" Bob hugged Jan and planted a kiss on her cheek.

"Time," Mel deadpanned.

All of the customers applauded and whistled for several seconds. Bianca held up a hand. "Ladies and gents, that is going to be a hard act to follow. Table 3 just aced their lightning round. That means there's only one other team who can catch them."

Bianca and Mel made the rounds to each table. Chuck and Julie made a valiant effort, coming up with seven correct answers. Finally Mel and Bianca arrived at Table 8.

Katelyn, Frank, and the other couple sat forward, alert and ready to seize the prize. Mel counted down to the start, and Bianca gave the first question. The questions and answers went back and forth rapid-fire.

"What country's capital is Montevideo?"

"Uruguay."

"Right. Who wrote, 'In Xanadu did Kubla Khan/A stately pleasure-dome decree'?"

"Samuel Taylor Coleridge."

"Right. What two elements make up table salt?"

"Sodium and chlorine."

"Correct. What general oversaw the moving of the cannons from Fort Ticonderoga to Boston during the Revolution?"

Silence. Katelyn, Frank, and their two friends looked at each other blankly.

"Pass," Frank said.

Elaine was startled, since she had just read about that event while reading up on the missing letter's writer. She whispered to Nathan, "Henry Knox, right?"

He nodded, grinning.

"What author wrote *Ben Hur* while governor of New Mexico?" Bianca asked.

The players discussed it for a few moments and then Frank said, "Uris?"

"Incorrect."

The team at Table 8 ran quickly through four more questions, giving correct answers.

"Last question," Bianca said. "What is the longest side of a…"

"Time," Mel said, poker-faced.

Katelyn's team groaned.

Bianca's smile skewed. "Sorry, Table 8. You answered seven questions correctly. And that means…" She stepped back into the center. "The winner is Table 3!" She whipped off her cowboy hat and swept a deep bow with it in her hand.

Elaine gave a little squeal and immediately blushed because she sounded so childish. Everyone around them applauded, whistled, and cheered.

"All right," Nathan said heartily.

"You were great on those science questions, Jan," Elaine said.

"Well, we couldn't have done it without your Mount Kenya."

Bob clasped his hands together on the table, smiling. "It was a team effort."

Mel and Bianca brought them an envelope.

"Your prize is in here." Bianca held it out. "Who gets it?"

"I think our captain should take charge of that." Nathan nodded toward Jan.

"Oh! Well…" Jan looked around at them in confusion.

"Sure," Elaine said. "You and Bob are the most likely to use it."

Mel handed Jan the green T-shirt. "You can all fight over this."

"You gave us some exciting moments. We hope you'll all come back next week to defend your title," Bianca said.

"Oh, I don't know," Jan looked around at them. "It was fun though."

"Lots of fun," Nathan said. "We'll discuss it."

"That's all we can ask," Bianca said. "And here comes a plate of nachos and a round of whatever you're drinking, on the house, for our winners."

Elaine enjoyed the clapping and foot-stomping that followed. It was nice to have won something with her friends. Several people stopped by their table to congratulate them.

Julie stooped to give Elaine a hug. "Great job."

"Thanks. It was a good game," Elaine said.

Katelyn and Frank were also among their well-wishers.

"You people were incredible," Katelyn said. "Jan, I was so impressed!"

"Well, everyone helped," Jan said.

"You guys were pretty good too," Elaine added. "Do you do this often?"

Frank, who was holding Katelyn's hand, said, "We've been to three or four of them. It's fun. Maybe we'll go up against you again sometime."

"I think I want you on my team next time for musical questions," Jan said. "Katelyn, you were a whiz on anything book-related, but that's understandable."

Elaine glanced across the room as they talked.

Greg Payson was talking earnestly with the man he'd been eating with. The other young man passed him something. Money. Must be splitting the check, she thought. Greg shoved the bills into his pocket and got up. Elaine wondered if she should go speak to him, but Greg went quickly out the door.

The man he'd been with finished his coffee and rose. He went to the checkout, carrying a sales slip.

Jan elbowed her. "Want some nachos?"

"Huh? Oh, no thanks." Elaine frowned. Something was odd about what she had seen.

Bob went to settle their tab, and they went out into the cool evening air. The moonlight shone on the lake as they walked toward the tearoom.

"So, Bob, did I hear you've got a job offer out of state?" Nathan asked.

"Yeah, I do," Bob said. "In Baltimore."

"Are you going to take it?"

Bob looked at Jan. "I'm thinking about it. I'd be working with an old friend—my best friend in law school, actually. Bruce and I talked about going into the practice together when we graduated, but it didn't happen. Now he's top dog in a prestigious firm down there."

"Sounds like a good opportunity," Nathan said.

Elaine noted that Jan kept silent during this exchange.

"It's been a dream of mine for quite a while, but…" Bob let it trail off, then said, "Well, I'm still thinking about it."

"Best of luck," Nathan said. "Whatever you decide."

"Thanks."

They turned in at their driveway. By the time they were inside the well-lit house, Jan looked perfectly at ease.

# CHAPTER EIGHTEEN

Jan and Elaine ate an early lunch on Saturday and arrived at the church at noon, two hours before the Mother-Daughter Tea was slated to begin. They wanted to make sure every detail was perfect, so they had left the tearoom in Rose and Archie's capable hands.

The first thing they did when they came down the stairs to the fellowship hall was to stop at the display case.

"I don't think I can ever walk by this case again without stopping," Elaine said.

Jan flipped on the track lighting, and Elaine gasped.

"Look!" She pointed to the bottom shelf.

Jan stepped over beside her and looked where she had indicated. "Well, what do you know? Will Trexler's medal is back."

They looked at each other. "What do you make of that?" Elaine asked.

"I don't know. The Knox letter is still missing." Jan looked thoughtfully at the empty space on the middle shelf.

Elaine grasped her arm. "I know what we can do!"

"What?"

"The fingerprinting supplies. The package came, but we were so busy, I just stuck it in the cupboard in the office."

As the plan sank in, a smile worked its way over Jan's face. "Now?"

"What do you think? We could slip it into a bag and take it home with us."

Jan shook her head. "Someone at the tea might ask about it."

"True." Elaine pressed her lips together.

"I've got to start working on the food," Jan said. "But you could run home for the kit. It wouldn't take you long to check it here and lift the prints if there are any. Then we can put the medal back in the case and take the prints home and deal with them there."

Elaine exhaled slowly, nodding as she talked. "Okay, that may be best. I hope I can do it before anyone else gets here."

Jan looked around the fellowship hall. "Well, Sarah brought the flower vases this morning, like she said she would, so that's done. She and Kit said they'll be here at one. I think there's time. Go!"

Elaine hurried up the stairs, and Jan went to the kitchen. She tried to keep her mind on the tasks at hand, but she couldn't help wondering exactly where Elaine was at the moment and how quickly she could retrieve the fingerprint kit and get back to the church. Her hands flew as she put the cream they had brought into the refrigerator and began to arrange the petits fours on decorative plates.

In less than fifteen minutes, she heard the front door of the church slam and hurried footsteps on the staircase. She met Elaine, who was puffing for breath, near the display case.

"Quick, set it on that table, and give me the brush," Jan said. "I want to check the door to the case while you do the medal."

"Dan took prints on the door on Tuesday, remember?"

Jan nodded. "Yeah, but someone had to clean it afterward, or there'd be magnetic powder all over it. Any new prints since it was cleaned might tell us something." Since Elaine had bought the kit months ago, Jan had played with it herself. It was totally up her alley—literal and scientific, and legitimately helpful.

"Right."

Jan pulled a pair of white cotton gloves from the box.

She put them on, and Elaine passed her a jar of the powder she needed and a brush. Jan applied the material carefully to the edge of the door nearest the latch. Several fingerprints stood out under the powder. She didn't know if they belonged to the person who put the medal back or not, but she lifted them with the clear cellophane tape from the kit and fixed the tape to cards.

Meanwhile, Elaine had brought a long cooking spoon from the kitchen. She stuck it in through the open door of the display and slid the end of the handle through the blue-and-red ribbon that held the medal. Lifting it out carefully, she was able to get the medal from the case to a table without touching it.

"Don't do it on the tablecloth," Jan said. "It will make a mess."

"Yeah, I'd better take it in the kitchen and do it on the counter." Elaine carefully carried the medal, dangling from the spoon handle, and the printing supplies she needed. Jan finished her task and packed up the rest of the things from the kit. She took the whole thing to the kitchen.

"I think there's something here." Elaine's eyes shone with excitement as she dusted the medal. "Wow, maybe we're going to get to the bottom of this!"

By the time Sarah arrived, they had put away all traces of the fingerprinting activity. Elaine had stashed the kit in her car, and they had returned the medal to the display case. Elaine was measuring out the tea leaves to brew and Jan was arranging napkins in a fancy array.

As promised, Jan and Elaine had agreed to come a bit early to help with last-minute tasks. Kit Edmonds soon appeared at the bottom of the stairs. She paused by the display case.

"Hello," Jan called after a moment and walked out to meet her.

Kit jumped. "Oh, hi."

Sarah reached the bottom of the steps and joined her. "Hey, your grandfather's medal is back."

There was a moment's pause, and Kit said, "Yeah, it is. That's great."

"It seems kind of funny to me," Sarah said. "Jan, did you and Elaine see this?"

"Yeah, we did." Jan hoped she had succeeded in wiping away every bit of the fingerprinting powder.

They chatted for a few more minutes and then got to work.

"Where's Marcella?" Elaine asked.

"She's coming with Grandma, and she was wound up when I left."

"Is she excited about the tea?" Jan asked.

"More like hyper." Kit rolled her eyes.

"Is Leanne coming over?" Jan asked Sarah.

"Definitely. I told her she could come at ten minutes to two."

The four of them bustled about the kitchen and fellowship hall. At quarter to two, other women and girls began arriving, all dressed up for the special event.

Jan spotted Marcella, Kit's six-year-old daughter, coming in with Great-Grandma Pearl. The little girl wore a full-skirted pink-and-white dress. Jan hurried over to greet them.

"Hello, Pearl. Glad you could come." She bent closer to Marcella. "You look very pretty, Marcella. I love your dress. It's awesome."

Marcella fingered the pink satin ribbon tied around the end of her long, blonde braid. "Thank you, Mrs. Blake. I hope you have hot chocolate."

Jan smiled. "We do. We also have cold punch for those who don't want a hot drink."

"And cookies?"

Jan stepped aside and waved toward the serving tables. "What do you see?"

Marcella's eyes widened. "Yum!" She tugged on Pearl's hand. "Grandma Pearl, can we get some now?"

"Hold on a bit," Pearl said. "I'm sure the ladies will tell us when it's time to eat." She was looking toward the display case. Frowning, she walked closer to it. "Oh my goodness!"

Elaine shot Jan a glance and stepped over to stand beside her.

"Look!" Pearl pointed. "That's Will's medal. It's right where it's supposed to be."

"You're right," Elaine said. "I'm glad that story had a happy ending!"

"But how . . . ?" Pearl eyed her suspiciously. "You know something, don't you?"

"I don't," Elaine said calmly. "Jan and I had nothing to do with that medal reappearing, but when we got here to set up, it was there in the case."

"*Hmpf,*" Pearl said.

"Can we eat now?" Marcella asked.

"Mrs. Ryder's going to talk to us first," Jan said, "but it won't be too long, and we'll eat right after that." She straightened and smiled as her daughter-in-law, Paula, arrived at the bottom of the stairs, holding out a hand to steady Elaine's mother. Paula and Brian's two girls were close behind them.

Jan hurried to them. "Hi! Aunt Virginia, so nice to see you again."

"Thank you," Virginia said. "I wouldn't miss it. I just wish Sasha could have stayed and been here for Elaine."

"Grandma!" Avery rushed over to kiss Jan, and Kelly followed.

"I'm going to the karate tournament, Grandma," Kelly said, excitement shining in her eyes.

"Fantastic," Jan said. "Where is it?"

"At the Civic Center in Augusta."

"I should be able to come. I'll get the details from your mom."

"Goody. I want you to be there," Kelly said.

Jan gave her an extra squeeze and turned to Avery, who was twelve. "What are you up to, Avery?"

"Dad built me a balance beam so I can practice in the garage."

"Wow." Jan looked anxiously at Paula, who smiled and nodded.

"It's not regulation or anything," Avery said, "and it's only a foot off the floor, but the width and length are right."

"I hope you have plenty of mats down on that cement floor," Jan said.

"We do," Paula assured her. "Come on, girls. We'd better find seats. It looks like the program is about to start."

Sarah had prepared a themed devotional for the occasion, and soon after two o'clock, Elaine called for attention. The room had filled, and a few stragglers were still entering. The women who had been chattering in small groups hastily found seats.

"Ladies, thank you all so much for coming out today," Elaine said. "It's wonderful to see so many mothers and daughters here together for our tea. We have a special treat for you. Sarah Ryder is our speaker, and she will come now with a few words before we enjoy the refreshments."

Jan stayed in the kitchen with Kit so they would be ready when the moment came to take the steeped tea out to the serving area, but she could hear every word. Sarah seemed poised and well prepared, even though she had had a difficult week and was worried about her husband and the outcome of the vandalism of the church and theft of the historic letter.

Sarah took her text from Ruth 3:1, where Naomi said to Ruth, "My daughter, shall I not seek rest for thee, that it may be well with thee?" She brought to mind what a blessing mothers are, and the many ways in which they seek to ensure their children's well-being. Jan found herself tearing up as she recalled some of the sacrifices her own mom had made for her.

When the devotional ended, Jan and Kit carried out pots of steaming tea. Elaine joined them behind the table. Jan was fully occupied for a while, pouring several types of tea, while Kit handled other beverages and Elaine kept refills of dessert trays and teapots coming from the kitchen.

"I see your grandfather's medal is back in the case."

Jan looked up to see Pearl gazing at Kit pointedly.

"Oh yes. I saw that too," Kit said as she poured lemonade for Marcella.

Pearl's brow knitted. "Do you know anything about it?"

"Who, me? I was asking Jan and Elaine about it before you came."

Pearl began to smile. "Well, I guess it doesn't matter, so long as it's back. Your grandpa will be glad when I tell him."

Annie Richardson was next in line, with her two girls, Dori and Ella. "Everything looks beautiful, Jan," Annie said. "The girls especially love the favors."

"And the cupcakes for my birthday party were yummy," Ella added.

"Aw, thank you, sweetie," Jan said. "I'm so glad you and your friends enjoyed them."

After the refreshments, Elaine went around collecting the used disposable dishes. She wasn't being very efficient about it, Jan thought. She ought to just put a trash bag out there. Jan shook her head and went on helping Kit clear the china. Sarah volunteered to wash up the teacups and pots. In the fellowship room, Bristol led a few games and gave prizes to the mother-daughter teams that won. The women lingered to talk. When the tea was over, several women stayed to help with the cleanup. To Jan's surprise, they were done before five o'clock.

"Oh, look," Leanne Ryder called from the far end of the fellowship hall. "Mom, the medal is back in the display case."

Sarah nodded and smiled.

"I didn't know it was missing," said Rue Maxwell.

Jan looked at Elaine across the kitchen, and Elaine winked at her. Jan edged up beside her.

"Do you know something?"

Elaine's eyes widened. "Well, I know I've been collecting fingerprints all afternoon." She took Jan to a corner, glanced over her shoulder, and opened the top of a white garbage bag. Inside were several plastic cups and plates and a few plastic spoons with initials printed on them in black permanent marker.

"I couldn't be obvious about it, so every time I saw someone with an empty cup or plate, I'd offer to take it from them. I'd get a couple things and come back here and put the initials on them, then go get a few more."

"Oh, you sneak," Jan said. "I love it. Maybe someday we'll learn how to test DNA."

"I WAS TALKING to Maureen Oakley this afternoon," Elaine said to Jan as they drove home.

"I saw her, but I didn't get a chance to talk to her." Jan drove into the driveway and hit the button on the garage door opener. "How's she doing?"

"Fine. I was tempted to ask her about the gun application, but after what happened with Pearl and the Great Bible Quiz Medal Fiasco, I decided I'd better not mention it to her."

"Oh, you were a little *gun* shy, huh?"

Elaine winced. Jan's puns were often funny, but sometimes they were almost too appropriate. "Yeah."

Jan drove in and turned off the engine. "I think you're right. If you ask anyone about it, you should go straight to Alan."

"What if he doesn't want to talk to me about it?"

Jan looked over at her. "I think that's obvious. You let it go."

Elaine nodded slowly. "Maybe I should just forget it."

"But you can't."

"Right. I keep thinking about it."

Jan opened her car door, so Elaine did too. They had a lot of things in the backseat and trunk—dishes, leftovers, and teapots among them. Also in the trunk were the precious fingerprint kit and Elaine's bag of evidence.

"I can't wait to get to work on this project," Jan said as she picked up the kit.

"Me neither. And I'm glad we gave away goodie bags at the end, so we don't have as much to put away," Elaine said, stacking four plastic containers to carry in.

"Yeah, we had way too much food left. I sent Paula home with a lot of stuff." Jan took a box of teapots out and balanced the kit on top of it carefully while she shut the trunk.

When Rose and Archie had left for the day, Jan asked Elaine, "Do you want to eat supper?"

"I am so not hungry," Elaine said.

"Still thinking about Alan?"

"You know me too well."

Jan leaned on the counter. "We could box up some treats and go over there."

Elaine thought about it. Part of her wanted to jump at the offer, but another part wanted to stay as far away from Alan as possible. She had upset enough people in Lancaster already.

"How about if we see them tomorrow? I know you're itching to check all those fingerprints we brought home."

Jan grinned. "Now you're talking."

She set up the equipment on the long dining room table, and Elaine hefted the bag of trash next to it. They both worked at lifting the best prints off each item. It was slow work, but at the end of an hour, they had almost forty samples, each card marked with the owner's name.

"Now comes the fun part," Jan said. "We compare all these to the prints from the medal and the door of the trophy case."

Elaine frowned. "We're only going to eliminate women though. If a man did this, we won't know it."

"True," Jan said, "and most of the suspects for taking the letter are men. Pastor, Alan, Chris and Nick, Felix Prior…But I don't think the same person took both the letter and the medal. The medal came back just a few days after disappearing. The letter didn't."

"Okay," Elaine said. "I'm willing. And I guess if we don't get any matches, we can start asking the men at church to let us fingerprint them. Dan didn't think that was worthwhile, but it might be."

Jan nodded firmly. "It might be the only way to solve this thing." She took out the marked cards with the prints from

Will's medal and the door. She gave Elaine the one from the medal. "Just go through them systematically, and yell if you find a match."

They worked in silence for several minutes, until Jan said, "Well, guess what? My prints are on the door. Rats! I don't remember touching it before I put the powder on it. But the good news is, I also got a match for one other person. That leaves me two unknowns."

"Who's your match?" Elaine asked. "Because I've got one from the medal. If they're the same as yours, maybe we have a culprit." She turned around the card in her hand.

Jan smiled. "I think we have our medal thief. Shall we pay her a visit?"

# CHAPTER NINETEEN

R ussell Edmonds opened the door of his house and gazed at the cousins through his glasses with a bemused look. "Hello, ladies. May I help you?"

"Is Kit home?" Elaine asked.

"She's tucking Marcella in, but I'll tell her you're here. Won't you come in?"

"I'm sorry we called so late," Elaine said as they followed him into the comfortable living room.

"You're not late. It's only eight o'clock. Take a seat." Russell disappeared down a hallway.

Elaine looked around, taking in the green plush sofa and armchairs, a rocking chair, several full bookcases, and a watercolor of Chickadee Lake over the brick fireplace. Jan sat down on the couch, and Elaine took a seat in one of the armchairs. A moment later, Kit came in. She was wearing jeans and a plaid blouse, and she looked tired.

"Hello there. I think I know what you're here for."

"Will's medal?" Jan asked.

Kit let out a big sigh. "You got me. I hoped I could get Grandpa's medal back in the case without anyone knowing. The original plan was for no one to even realize it was missing, but that went out the window when you noticed."

"Pastor Mike noticed," Jan said, "but yeah, I was there."

"So you did take it," Elaine said.

"Yeah." Kit looked very unhappy at the admission. "I don't know how you knew, but you're right."

"Pearl didn't seem to be aware of it when I mentioned it to her at the tearoom," Elaine said.

"She wasn't," Kit said glumly, "and I didn't want her to be."

"I'm sorry I messed up your plans," Elaine said. She looked over at Jan.

Jan shrugged. "What's going on, Kit?"

"Do you remember that my dad flew up here last weekend?" Kit asked.

"Sure," Jan said. Billy had come to church with Kit and his parents, Will and Pearl Trexler, last Sunday. He was a couple of years younger than Jan and Elaine, and worked as a commercial pilot out of Newark, Jew Jersey. "We spoke to him."

"Well, Dad and I are planning something for Grandpa and Grandma."

"What kind of something?" Elaine asked.

"Their fifty-fifth wedding anniversary is coming up. Dad and I wanted to surprise them with a party. Dad's putting together a 'This Is Your Life' slide presentation, and he had me get the medal for him so he could photograph it. I guess

Pastor saw that it was missing before I could get it back in the display."

Jan nodded. "It wouldn't have mattered, but we were concerned at first that whoever took the General Knox letter took your grandfather's medal too."

"I didn't think of that." Kit brushed back a strand of her hair.

Elaine smiled regretfully. "I'm sorry I blabbed to Pearl about it though. I had no idea what you were up to."

"It will be all right," Kit said. "She did get upset yesterday. I told her it wasn't stolen and begged her not to say anything to Grandpa about it, but then she told me she already had, and they had gone over and talked to you about it together."

"Yeah. I'm sorry," Elaine said.

"Well, they're definitely suspicious, but it wasn't your fault." Kit laughed. "So you can quit apologizing, okay? I should have told Pastor Mike I was taking it. But I do appreciate your being so concerned about it in the first place."

"I hope your party isn't spoiled," Jan said.

"It would take more than this to spoil it. I'm sorry if it caused you trouble with my grandparents."

Elaine touched her hand. "You had every right to do this. In fact, I think it's a wonderful idea. It just never occurred to me that someone had a legitimate reason to take the medal, unless it was Will."

Jan nodded. "Unfortunately the same can't be said about the famous letter."

"No," Kit said. "Whoever took that had other motives. I hope they find out who took it soon."

JAN FELT A bit sluggish on Sunday morning. Since the tearoom would be closed all day, she decided to forgo her usual early rising and allow herself an extra hour of sleep. When she took her Bible out to the screened porch overlooking the lake, it was nearly seven o'clock, and Earl Grey was meowing on the back steps.

"You're hungry, poor thing. Wait just a minute, and I'll get you some breakfast." Jan laid down her Bible and went for the cat food. She filled Earl's dish and set it down on the deck a few steps below the porch. "There you go."

"Good morning," Elaine called from above her.

"Well, hi." Jan straightened and climbed the steps.

"Have you eaten?" Elaine asked.

"No, I was a lazybones this morning. Just got up."

"What would you like? I'll put the kettle on."

A few minutes later, they sipped tea and nibbled their breakfast together on the porch. Jan read the passage she had earmarked for her daily devotions, while Elaine looked over the day's Sunday school lesson. When she put her lesson book down, she sighed.

"I shouldn't leave it until Sunday morning. Most people are more organized." She lifted her teacup and took a swallow.

"I don't think it's a matter of organization," Jan said. "I'm sure a lot of people don't read it at all."

"Well, I like to be able to join in the discussion."

Jan finished the scrambled egg on her plate and took the last bite of her cinnamon toast. When she had chewed it, she said, "Have your little gray cells done any more work on the Knox letter mystery?"

A smile flitted across Elaine's lips. "If they're working, they're not showing much of a result. I was thinking just now about something totally unrelated."

"Like what?" Jan asked.

"Friday night."

"That was fun."

"Yeah," Elaine said.

"That T-shirt is pretty large," Jan said. "Do you care if I give it to Brian?"

"Go right ahead. But did you notice Greg Payson was in the Grill during part of the game?"

"I saw him. Didn't think anything of it. Why?" Jan looked out through the screen as a herring gull swooped past and landed on the marina dock.

"He was with another young man, a kid about his age."

"Okay," Jan said. "I didn't take much notice. They were eating something, I think."

"Yes, and the other guy gave Greg some money right before he left. I didn't see how much, but it looked like quite a bit. At first I thought he was giving Greg money for his part of the check. But then, on his way out, he stopped at the cash register and paid."

"That's interesting," Jan said.

"And Greg didn't pay when he left, so I'm guessing the other guy paid the tab for both of them."

Jan inhaled deeply. "I can think of at least half a dozen explanations."

"Yeah, I'll bet you can. But you agree that it's weird? I mean, shouldn't Greg have given his friend money to pay for his share, not the other way around?"

"Maybe. Let me think on it for a while." Jan looked at her watch. "Come on, we'd better get dressed if we're going to Sunday school."

Dan Benson attended church that morning, and between Sunday school and the worship service, Jan saw him heading for the fellowship hall.

"Do you want to get a cup of tea?" she asked Elaine.

"No, thanks, I'm good."

Jan went downstairs and scanned the large room. Dan was just pouring cream into his foam coffee cup. She walked to the table and chose a tea bag and a cup.

"Hello, Dan." She started filling her cup with hot water from a carafe.

"Hi. How are you doing, Jan?"

"Fine. I wondered if you had any new information about the vandalism here or the stolen letter."

"Not much," Dan said with a grimace.

"I think Pastor Mike said you tried for fingerprints?" Jan asked.

"Yeah, but it looked as though the letter's frame had been wiped. The case itself had just about everyone in the church's prints on it."

"So it's okay to hit it with the glass cleaner next time we clean?"

"I don't see why not." Dan stepped away from the refreshment table, and Jan followed him so they wouldn't be in the way of others getting their coffee.

"Do you think whoever broke in here had a key?" she asked.

"Maybe. Or maybe the door was already unlocked. Or it could be it was picked." Dan raised his cup to his lips.

"Were there marks that made you think the lock was picked?" Jan knew people who picked locks sometimes left behind telltale scratches near the keyhole, especially if they weren't experts at the task.

He swallowed. "Not really. There were a couple of tiny scratches, but I couldn't be sure. They might have been made by someone fumbling with their key. Let's call it inconclusive. But an awful lot of people come in and out of here during the week. The pastor made me a list of people he knew had been in, but there are times when the door is just left open—like when the Murphy boys were cleaning up the yard."

Jan thought about that. "What about that Felix Prior guy?"

"I talked to the Athertons. He'd checked out of his cottage and left Lancaster almost a week before the vandalism occurred." Dan took a sip of his coffee.

"Yeah, but what if he came back?" Jan asked.

"That seems unlikely. I mean, he lived clear down in a suburb of Boston. Why go home and come all the way back here a week later?"

Jan swirled her tea bag around in her cup. "How do you know he went home?"

Dan chuckled. "Seriously?"

"Well, yeah. I was. Serious, I mean."

Jan could have sworn Dan started to roll his eyeballs, but maybe he was just looking heavenward for guidance.

"Okay," she said. "I was just curious. Since you don't seem to have many other suspects."

"I wouldn't say that." Dan frowned. "Look, I shouldn't really discuss this with you."

"Sure," Jan said. "Sorry. I'll see you later." Disappointed, she took another gulp of tea and dropped her cup in the trash can. She looked around and wondered if she could get away with collecting men's cups the way Elaine had women's at the tea, but decided not. The worship service would start in a few minutes.

She went up to the auditorium, but she couldn't forget about the conversation. After lunch, while Elaine settled down with a mystery novel in their upstairs living room, Jan took her laptop to her favorite armchair. How many colleges could there be in the Boston area? she wondered. Sarah had said Mr. Prior worked at one. Maybe she could track him down through his employer. A quick search told her there were way too many— thirty or forty that she would have to check out if she started from that angle. She decided to begin with a search for anyone named Felix Prior in Massachusetts.

She turned up six, though she thought two might be duplicates, and another who spelled it "Pryor." She eliminated one who lived in western Massachusetts—too far out for a commute to the metropolitan area. Of course, a lot of computer types worked at home these days, and even some college professors taught their classes online. But Macy had thrown a possible residence in Boxborough out there, and Dan had said a Boston suburb, so Jan concentrated on that town.

She was left with two identities that she thought were feasible for the man who had stayed at Green Glade Cottages. Time to look for them on social media. Within half an hour, she was fairly certain the two Felixes she'd zeroed in on were father and son. She toggled between their Facebook pages. The older one looked to be in his seventies. The younger one looked closer to her age. His hair was showing a little gray at the temples, and his face bore fine lines. He wasn't overly handsome, but not bad looking. His brown eyes were a bit nondescript—forgettable, if Sarah's account could be trusted, and Jan thought it could.

A little more browsing took her to a photo of the two men together. "Happy birthday, Dad," read the caption. So she was right, the two Felixes belonged together.

She scrolled to the top of the younger Prior's home page, got up, and carried her laptop over to where Elaine was sprawled on the sofa.

"Excuse me a minute. Can you look at this?"

Elaine looked up, then put her bookmark in the novel and sat up straight. "Sure. What have you got?"

"Is this the guy who visited church a couple of weeks ago? The one who wore the Tommy Hilfiger shirt?"

Elaine took the laptop and peered at the photo at the top of the screen. "That's him, all right."

"Felix Prior," Jan said.

"How did you find him?"

She shrugged. "It's kind of an unusual name, and Macy told us where he lived."

"Good work," Elaine said, "but how does this help?"

"I thought maybe we could find out if he was down in Massachusetts when the church was broken into. If so, we could rule him out as the vandal."

"True. But he was interested in the letter, and we don't know when it was stolen."

Jan sat down on the sofa. "I know. But I'm thinking, one thing at a time."

Elaine nodded. "If you can find out anything, I guess it's better than nothing. Were you able to find out where he works?"

"Not yet, but that's a good thought. If he worked the Friday before the church was broken into, it would be pretty hard, but not impossible, for him to come back here in time to do that." Another thought occurred to Jan. "I think I'll see if he'll let me be his friend online."

"You're kidding!" Elaine pulled back and stared at her. "We know nothing about him."

"Actually, I know quite a bit, since I've been cyber-snooping on him and his father. If I send him a message and say I belong to the church in Lancaster, where he visited two weeks ago, who knows what will happen?"

Elaine was silent for several seconds. "Don't you think that could be dangerous? What if he's the vandal?"

"He's hundreds of miles away," Jan said.

"You think."

Jan huffed out a deep breath. "Well, it's no more danger- ous than some of the stunts you've pulled."

"Like what?"

"Like sneaking downstairs when there was a burglar in the house."

Elaine held up both hands. "Okay, okay. But let's think this through before you do anything."

Both sat in silence, mulling over the situation.

"I know," Elaine said. "What if we ask Pastor Mike to friend this guy? He could tell him he was sorry he didn't get to meet him personally when he was at the church. I'll bet Mr. Prior would answer and tell him anything he wanted to know."

Jan thought it over. "Okay, that idea has merit. What would you say to me calling Pastor Mike and putting it to him?"

"Sure. And if he's agreeable, he can approach it as he sees best." Elaine picked up her paperback book. "Now, if you'll excuse me, the detective is about to confront the main suspect."

"Okay. Oh, by the way, Dan told me this morning that he didn't get any prints off the letter's frame. He thinks it was wiped."

"Too bad," Elaine said. She sat up suddenly. "Jan! I meant to give Dan that pocketknife again today, but I forgot! Am I a dope or what?"

"Where is it?"

"In my room."

Jan cocked her head to one side. "We could check it for prints, now that we have the powder."

"You mean there's some left after all we did yesterday?"

"Yup."

Elaine sighed and set her book aside. "I guess I can't say no."

# CHAPTER TWENTY

O kay, so we've got two distinct prints," Elaine said a short time later.

"Yeah, and from their position, I think the owner is right-handed," Jan said.

Elaine frowned at her. "Do we have any left-handed suspects we can rule out?"

"Not that I know of." Jan stood and put the card with the pocketknife prints in the box with the others they had collected. "Unless we get some more comparison prints or we find something else to lift prints off, we're out of luck."

"Do you feel like visiting the Oakleys now?" Elaine asked, watching her closely. If Jan minded, she would just forget about it.

But Jan seemed energized by the suggestion. "Come on."

They went down to the kitchen and packed a couple of take-out boxes with cookies from the freezer. Jan looked at the thermometer on the splashboard near the sink. "It's cooled off—only forty-five degrees outside now. We'll want coats."

They gathered their things and got into Elaine's car. At the Oakley house, Alan opened the door. He wore a gray cardigan sweater over a dark button-down shirt, and his white hair was neatly combed over his balding top, as usual.

"Hello, ladies. Maureen's in the kitchen. I'll get her."

Before Elaine could say anything, he had ambled off toward the back of the house, leaving the door open. She and Jan stepped inside and shut the door. Elaine walked over to the Chippendale sideboard in the entry hall.

"I've always loved this. And the mahogany mirror." She smiled at herself in the beveled glass, but she still felt nervous.

"What if Alan doesn't come back?" Jan whispered.

Elaine had wondered the same thing. "I don't know. After what happened with Pearl, I don't want to bring up the subject to Maureen without him there."

At that moment Maureen entered, walking with her usual slight limp.

"Hi! What brings you out?"

"We brought you some leftovers from the tea." Jan held out the cookie boxes.

"Oh, that was thoughtful of you," Maureen said. She peered through the cellophane on the top one's lid. "Those look delicious."

"We had so much left," Elaine said. "We froze everything last night, but they thaw quickly."

"Come on in." Maureen led them into the living room.

To Elaine's relief, Alan hovered in the kitchen doorway, obviously curious.

"Honey, why don't you bring your coffee in here?" Maureen invited. "The girls brought cookies."

"Oh, are we interrupting your meal?" Elaine asked.

"No, we just finished, and I didn't fix any dessert for tonight, so this is perfect. Would you like some coffee? Oh, silly, I'll bet you'd like tea. It won't take but a minute."

"If you and Alan are both having coffee, I'll have some," Elaine said.

"Half a cup," Jan said.

Maureen went to help Alan, and Elaine heard one of the dogs yip in the kitchen.

"Why don't you put them in the backyard?" Maureen suggested. Elaine was glad because, while Dot and Dash were beautiful, they were not very calm dogs, especially Dash, the German short-haired pointer. She would just as soon drink her coffee without him and Dot, the Brittany spaniel, sniffing about in the living room.

A few minutes later, Maureen and Alan returned with extra mugs of coffee and distributed them. Alan set a small tray with a sugar bowl, pitcher of cream, and a couple of spoons on the steamer trunk that served as their coffee table.

"I thought the tea went very well yesterday." Maureen sat down in an armchair and opened one of the cookie boxes.

"So did I," Elaine said, sitting back on the comfortable striped couch. "Sarah's talk was so heartfelt. Just what I needed."

Alan took two cookies and settled into his easy chair, seeming content to let the women talk.

"Wasn't your daughter here from out of state this week?" Maureen asked. "I thought she might come to the tea."

"Yeah, she was," Elaine said. "She had to go back though. She flew out Friday morning."

Maureen nodded. "Well, it was good to see your mom."

"Thank you." Elaine glanced at Alan, wondering how to bring up the gun shop.

"Did you know that Sasha competes in biathlon?" Jan asked, smiling at the Oakleys. She apparently saw the mention of Sasha's visit as the perfect opening.

"No," Maureen replied. "What's that?"

"It's skiing and shooting," Jan explained.

"Oh, they have it in the Olympics."

"Yes." Jan turned and wiggled her eyebrows at Elaine.

Elaine nearly choked on her coffee. She lowered her cup and watched Alan as she said, "Can you believe it? Sasha actually had me at a shooting range on Wednesday. We went to that one in Augusta."

"*You* were shooting?" Maureen asked.

"I sure was. It was sort of fun," Elaine said. "Of course, we wore ear protectors and everything."

"Is that the same place where you bought your new pistol?" Maureen swiveled to meet Alan's gaze.

Elaine held her breath. Maureen had asked her question for her.

"Eames's?" Alan asked.

Elaine nodded. "Have you ever used their shooting range?"

"Yeah, just the other day, as a matter of fact, before I settled on the pistol I wanted to buy. I used to keep a handgun, but I sold it when we started having the grandkids around a lot. But now..."

"There've been a lot of burglaries lately," Maureen said.

Alan nodded. "Several ice-fishing huts were burgled last winter, and they had some robberies in Augusta. I figured it was time to get another gun."

"You two even had a break-in last summer, didn't you?" Maureen asked.

"Well, yes," Elaine said. "It was shortly after we moved in. But that man was looking for a particular item he thought was in our house, not just out to steal valuables."

"Still a burglary," Alan said with a note of stubbornness.

"And now there's all that business over at the church." Maureen shuddered. "It's got me a little jumpy. Do they still think the Murphy boys were involved?"

Elaine said quickly, "From what I can tell, Chris and Nick just happened to be over there in the front yard a short time before we discovered the mess inside."

"We think it was someone from outside the church family," Jan added.

"*Hmm.* We were away Saturday," Maureen said. "We went to the museum in Searsport. But I heard about the break-in after we got home."

"Whoever did it, we'll feel safer with a gun in the house," Alan said. He took a bite of a cookie. "Just for protection."

Elaine nodded.

"So how *are* your grandchildren?" Jan asked, flicking Elaine a glance.

Elaine agreed with what her cousin seemed to be thinking— time to change the subject.

"Oh, they're good." Maureen smiled, happy to talk about the kids. "We're going to take them to Strawbery Banke next month."

"I've never been there, but I'd love to see it," Elaine said. The restored village in New Hampshire had become a regional attraction. "I hear the educational programs there are wonderful."

"Oh, they are," Jan said. She was opening her purse. "I have a picture of my daughter Amy's twins. They're just adorable." She passed it to Maureen, who exclaimed over Max and Riley's adorable photo.

Elaine felt much better after hearing Alan discuss his gun purchase openly and calmly. He and Maureen had been out of town Saturday too. That wasn't scientific proof that he was innocent, but it seemed unlikely that he was involved in the theft or vandalism.

She relaxed to enjoy her coffee and a nice chat with friends—one that had nothing to do with the theft of the General Henry Knox letter.

ELAINE RECONCILED HER financial records for the tearoom on Monday morning and then stopped by the kitchen, where Jan was helping Rose prepare customers' trays.

"I thought I'd run over to the town office and register my car, if you don't need me. It expires at the end of this month."

Jan looked her way. "No, go ahead. I have a little finger-printing job to do once I get a minute free."

"Oh?" Elaine asked.

"Tell you later," Jan said.

Rose smiled at Elaine. "Go do your car registration. We're fine."

"Did you talk to Pastor Mike about Mr. Prior?" Elaine was still concerned that Jan would put herself at risk if she got sloppy in her eagerness to solve the mystery.

"Not yet," Jan said. "Maybe later, when I'm not busy."

"Okay. Just be careful." Elaine went out to the garage, got into her car, and backed out on to the street.

"I should have just walked over there," she told herself in the mirror. But she was out now, and the front of her red Malibu had reached the edge of Main Street. It would be as much trouble to turn around and drive back into the garage as to take the car, so she pulled out and drove the short distance.

Several other cars were already parked in front of the town hall. Maybe Monday morning wasn't the best time to do business here, Elaine reflected. But she wasn't in a big hurry, so she took her insurance card and registration from the glove compartment, got out, and went toward the front entrance. Bristol Payson was coming out. Elaine started to give a cheerful greeting, but it died on her lips. Bristol's face was red and puffy, and tears streamed down her cheeks.

"Bristol, are you all right?" Elaine asked.

"Y-yes. I just came over to talk to Mark. Excuse me." Bristol all but ran past Elaine, down the steps to her car.

Elaine turned and looked after her, an uneasiness settling in her chest. Her friend was obviously disturbed. She watched as Bristol pulled out of the parking lot and on to the street. She seemed to be driving with care, and it was only a short distance to the Bookworm, if that was where she was headed. Elaine turned and went inside.

Mark was hunched over his desk to one side, seemingly immersed in paperwork. The town manager, Linda Somes, stood behind the counter. She was just finishing with another customer, and Elaine stepped up. Linda quickly helped her complete her registration. When Elaine turned toward the door, Mark looked up.

"Hi, Mark."

He gave her a sober nod and went back to his work without speaking. Elaine decided this was not the time to ask questions.

She drove back to the tearoom praying silently for the couple. As she passed the Bookworm, she saw Bristol's car in the parking lot. Bristol hadn't gone inside the store. She sat in the driver's seat, resting her head on her hands on the steering wheel.

Elaine couldn't help it. She turned in and parked beside Bristol. When she opened her friend's passenger door, Bristol turned her head and looked at her.

"Honey, are you okay?" Elaine asked softly.

Bristol sniffed. Her lovely face was ravaged by her recent weeping.

"If you want me to go away, say the word," Elaine said. "I'm worried about you though."

Bristol let out a long, shaky sigh. "I got a disturbing call this morning, and I went to tell Mark. It's Greg."

Elaine caught her breath. "I'm sorry. Is he all right?"

Bristol groped on the console for a tissue. "So far as we know. It has to do with his schooling."

"Oh. I'm sorry. I hope everything works out."

Elaine started to turn away, but Bristol held out a hand. "It's all right. I trust you, Elaine. I just don't know what we're going to do." Her tears gushed freely and splashed on the front of her ivory gauze top. She grabbed a tissue and held it to her nose.

"Is there anything I can do?"

"Maybe tell me if I'm overreacting or not?"

"Sure." Elaine took that as an invitation, and she slid into the passenger seat and closed the door. "If you want to talk, I'm here. If you don't, that's okay."

"Mark was just—oh, I don't know. He went into the 'It's my kid' thing and the 'It's costing me umpteen thousand dollars to educate him' part. Not to mention the 'How could he do something so stupid?' part."

Elaine remembered Mark's shell-shocked expression. She reached over and squeezed her arm gently. "Kids can do that to you."

"Yeah." Bristol wiped her face.

"And how are *you* doing?" Elaine asked.

"I don't know. None of it makes sense to me." Bristol cleared her throat. "The college phoned this morning. It was about Greg's bill. We pay on a twelve-month schedule. This last school year is all paid for, thanks to my income from the store and Greg's scholarships and Pell grants, but we'd started making payments toward next fall. It's easier for us that way."

"Sure," Elaine said, remembering the lean years when Jared and Sasha were in college.

Bristol sniffed. "Well, the bursar's office called me, and they said Greg had given up his scholarships for next year, and they wanted to know if we wanted them to return the payment we'd made this month."

"He turned down his scholarships? But why?"

"I don't know," Bristol said. "He went out this morning and I couldn't ask him. He was going job hunting. He took Mark's car. I tried to call him on his cell, but it went right to voice mail." She ran a hand over her disheveled hair. "His grades last semester were okay. Not as good as last year, but...I just don't understand it. This has got to be a mistake."

"Maybe he has his phone turned off while he talks to people about jobs," Elaine suggested.

"He needs his own car but he can't afford it yet." Bristol dabbed at her eyes with another tissue. "He hopes to get a summer job that will pay him enough so he can buy a used car by the time school starts again."

"What did Mark say?"

"He's going to call the school. He said it might just be a mistake. Maybe somebody put an error into the system without realizing it."

"Sure," Elaine said. "That could happen."

Bristol drew in a deep breath. "He said he'll call me when he knows something." She looked toward the store. "I'd better get inside. Katelyn is probably wondering what's taking me so long." She reached over and squeezed Elaine's hand. "Thank you."

"I didn't do anything."

"You were there."

Elaine smiled. "If you need anything, let me know. I hope this turns out okay."

"Thanks. And you can share this with Jan if you'd like. I'm sure she'd want to know what's going on." They both got out, and Elaine went to her Malibu. Bristol went into the bookshop, and Elaine drove over to the tearoom and into the garage.

Jan wasn't in the kitchen, but Rose told her to look down back. From the back porch door, Elaine could see her sitting on the lower deck with her plate and glass on the wrought iron table. Elaine made a sandwich and walked down the wooden steps. Over sandwiches and iced tea, Elaine told Jan about her encounter with Bristol.

Jan shook her head. "I hope that boy hasn't lost his scholarship because of somebody's goof."

"I know," Elaine said. "Mark and Bristol work so hard to keep him in school."

"I thought he was looking for a summer job to help out."

"Yes, and he told me he had some leads—a callback, even—but apparently nothing's gelled yet. Bristol and Mark were both upset, I could tell. Let's keep them in prayer." Elaine took another bite of her turkey and lettuce sandwich.

"I have a small bit of what I hope is good news," Jan said.

Elaine arched her eyebrows as she chewed.

"I located Felix Prior."

Elaine swallowed. "Literally?"

"Yeah. I found out the college he works at and everything. He's legit. He lectures on history."

Elaine nodded, picturing him in her mind. "He looks like one. And he wasn't up here when the vandals broke into the church?"

"Nope. He was at a symposium on Boston in the Revolutionary War that weekend."

"Wow. Wait a minute." She narrowed her gaze at Jan. "How do you know that?"

"I called him."

"What?" Elaine's squawk sounded like a something an irate herring gull would make. "I thought you were going to let Pastor Mike contact him."

"Relax. It's fine. So, anyway, as I was saying, he was at this symposium on the weekend in question."

"Sounds like fun."

"You would say that. I think it sounds boring." Jan grinned. "I wish you'd talked to him. He was really interesting, in an intelligentsia sort of way. And he's writing a book about Henry Knox."

"A book about the general?" That startled Elaine. "Is that why he came up here?"

"No, he was really on vacation, but he did go over to Thomaston while he was here and toured the Knox house. He was quite enthusiastic about it."

"I should get over there someday," Elaine said. "Have you ever seen it?"

"Yeah, Peter and I took the kids once, years ago. It's not the real house, you know."

Elaine frowned. "What do you mean?"

"The real Knox house—Montpelier—was torn down in 1871 to make way for the railroad. The one that's there now is a reconstruction."

Elaine stared at her. "Are you sure?"

"Uh-huh. Mr. Prior even mentioned it when I talked to him."

"Wow." Elaine studied her closely. "So you just cold-called him?"

"Yup. I found him listed on the Internet in Boston University's history department. They had a phone number for the department office. I worked up my gumption for a while first, but when I made up my mind and did it, they put me right through to him."

"You're turning into quite an investigator, Jan."

Her cousin smiled. "Thank you. Coming from you, that's a great compliment. Anyway, Mr. Prior and I are now friends, and he was shocked to learn that the letter had been stolen. Oh, by the way—he's certain the one Sarah showed him was the real deal, so I guess that narrows down the time of the theft. It wasn't stolen months ago."

"Right. It has to have been taken between the Sunday when Felix Prior visited and the Tuesday when you and Priscilla spotted the fake."

"Nine days."

Elaine nodded, looking out over the lake. "Either the vandal took it, or somebody else went into the church and stole it."

"Did I tell you that Dan Benson said it's possible the lock was picked?"

"No." Elaine swiveled her head to meet Jan's gaze.

"Yeah, when I was talking to him Sunday."

"So it could have happened any time—well, any night, at least—during those nine days."

"Yeah." Jan picked up her dishes. "Dessert?"

"No, thanks," Elaine said, thoughts of all they had learned recently tumbling through her mind. "It's really hard to resist, but living in a tearoom can be hazardous to the waistline."

Jan chuckled and patted her stomach. "I've noticed that too."

They both went back to work, Jan in the kitchen and Elaine in her office. Elaine's thoughts kept straying to Bristol. She tried to concentrate on other things, but she couldn't shake it off. Finally she went to the kitchen.

"Are you busy now?" she asked Jan. "I thought we might stroll over to the Bookworm and see how Bristol's doing."

"Good idea. She's probably got some new puzzle magazines in too. That will be my excuse for tagging along."

They checked in with Archie and let him know where they'd be, then walked over to Bristol's shop. Several people were browsing, and Katelyn waited on them, but Bristol sat behind the counter on a stool, apparently idle for the moment.

"Hi!" She stood to greet them. "I should be making out an order, but instead I'm sitting here wishing Greg would call."

"Did Mark find out anything from the college?" Elaine asked.

"Unfortunately, yes. The academic office said Greg also canceled his class registration for fall."

"No," Jan said.

Bristol nodded, her face grim. "He's got some explaining to do, I'll tell you."

"I'm sorry," Elaine said. "Can you think of any reason he might decide not to go back to school?"

"I've been trying to come up with something that makes sense, and I can't."

Elaine patted her hand. "Let us know if we can help."

"Just pray," Bristol said. "Right now, I admit, I'm furious. How could he do something like this and not tell us?"

"Is there any chance of reinstating him once you and Mark have a chance to talk things through with him?" Elaine asked.

"I don't know. I just wish he'd call home. Whatever he's up to, we need to know. Even if he wants to quit school, he needs to tell us."

"Sure," Elaine said. "It wouldn't be the end of the world if he wanted some time off."

One of Bristol's customers headed for the counter with a couple of books in her hand.

"Excuse me," Bristol said.

"We'll see you later," Jan said.

They went out and walked home.

"You forgot your magazine," Elaine said.

"I'll go over tomorrow when she's had some time to process everything."

Elaine nodded, but she couldn't shake her concern for the Paysons. Although the sun glittered on the placid lake and the flowers in their yard were outdoing themselves with bright blooms, the heavy feeling of sadness hung over her.

ELAINE STAYED IN her office most of the afternoon. The tearoom wasn't too busy, and she was able to work on planning for an upcoming bridal tea and their Fourth of July specials. When she was ready for a break, she took a roll of quarters and one of pennies out to the cash register to see if the change needed restocking.

The pennies in the drawer were low, so she cracked the roll and poured the coins into the compartment. In one of the little spaces to the right, a few miscellaneous items had collected: paper clips, a foreign coin, a rubber band, and the poker chip she had picked up off the floor the previous week.

She took it out, holding it carefully by the edge. She closed the drawer and carried it out to the kitchen, holding it by its edges.

"Jan, do you think it's worth dusting this poker chip?"

"Maybe." Jan said. "Although...we know none of us dropped it, so it had to be a customer. We don't have any customers' fingerprints to compare with."

"We don't have Nick and Chris's prints," Elaine said. "I should have bought something other than frozen lemonade the other day, and we could have gotten Chris's prints after he checked me out."

"I think I can get them to give them to me voluntarily," Jan said. "Same with Pastor Mike. I'm not so sure about Alan, but he said he wasn't around during the vandalism. And we can't get Felix Prior's, but I'm pretty sure he's alibied out."

"Okay, that will be a good project for this evening," Elaine said. "I don't want to get into it with the tearoom open. They might need me out front at a moment's notice."

Jan nodded, her gaze fixed on something farther away than the kitchen walls. "If you want to lift prints from the chip after closing, I'll go around to the Murphys' and the parsonage and see how many fingerprints I can cajole from people."

"Deal," Elaine said.

Their evening was spent on the project. Jan came home with Chris, Nick, and Des's fingerprints, and Elaine was surprised to learn that Jo knew about it. Pastor Mike and Asher had also given their inky prints on two of Jan's cards. All they had to do was compare them to the prints from the pocketknife and the ones Elaine had taken off the poker chip.

Jan made a face and looked at Elaine.

"So much for that exercise. Nobody matches."

"But we didn't expect them to," Elaine reminded her. "We didn't *want* them to."

"True. But I really had hopes for that pocketknife. I just wish that one time we could catch the criminal this way."

"We got Kit for taking the medal."

"Not the same," Jan said, smiling.

# CHAPTER TWENTY-ONE

J an was baking muffins early the next morning when the phone rang in the kitchen. She wiped her hands on a dish towel and answered it.

"Hi, Jan. It's Kate Pierce. I just got a heads-up from the senior citizens' group in Waterville. They're bringing a busload of members to Lancaster later this morning. They wanted to make sure the diner was up to handling forty for lunch. I told them the ice cream stand's not open yet, but I'd alert you and the Pine Tree Grill."

"Wow, thanks," Jan said. "Isn't it early in the season for that?"

"That's their point," Kate replied. "They want to be able to poke around the gift shops and antique stores before the summer crowds move in."

"Sounds like I'd better whip up an extra batch of the cookie of the day. Thanks, Kate."

She was cracking eggs a few minutes later when Elaine breezed into the kitchen.

"Busload alert," Jan said. "The Waterville senior citizens are having an outing today, and they picked our quaint little town."

"I thought I heard the phone earlier," Elaine said. "What do I need to do?"

"Just hang around in case Rose and Archie need help serving. Rose should be here any minute. She was going to make cream puffs for me this morning."

Elaine walked to the back door and peered out through the screened porch. "I think I see her boat coming down the lake. I'll make some extra napkin wraps and check the sugars."

Rose came in a few minutes later, windblown from her short cruise from her father's dock, and went right to work. Jan decided to make extra scones as well as the six dozen pistachio-raisin cookies and four dozen peanut butter shortbread she had run through the oven that morning.

By the time Archie arrived, every surface in the kitchen was covered with cooling racks. Elaine was carrying containers of muffins into the dining room just to give them more space on the counters.

"Did I miss something?" Archie asked. "Queen coming to tea with her entourage?"

"No, a bus full of seniors," Rose replied, not looking up from the miniature cream puffs she was filling.

"Shall I fix some flower vases for the tables?"

"Wonderful idea," Elaine said. "Jan, do you think we have enough flowers?"

Jan looked up from her work. "The lilac out back is coming into bloom, and with the tulips, narcissus, and hyacinths, there should be enough. Oh, and you might find a few wildflowers down near the deck."

Without another word, Archie put on an apron, took kitchen shears from a drawer, and lifted a basket down from on top of the refrigerator. He went out the back door humming.

"What were you working on last night?" Elaine asked Jan.

"When?"

"I saw you working on your computer, after we were done with the fingerprint project, and you were concentrating as if it was very important."

"Oh," Jan said with a chuckle. "I thought maybe I could find out something about that poker chip, since we weren't able to match the fingerprints to anyone we've printed so far. Turns out it's about as generic as you can get. Manufactured by a big game company, and you can buy them in just about any department store or toy store."

"Not all your investigations can yield high results," Elaine said.

"That's true. It probably fell out of someone's pocket when they were pulling out some change."

"I think our work last night was worthwhile, even if we didn't match any prints to the knife or chip," Elaine said. "Well, except Rose's on the chip, but we knew that would be there."

"The chip is probably incidental," Jan replied, "but we've shown that the prints on that knife don't belong to Pastor Mike or any of the Murphy men. That's important."

She smiled, remembering how Des had encouraged his boys to take part in the process and then practically begged Jan to take his prints too. She figured he was showing the boys it wasn't anything to be leery of, and also that he wanted to be in on solving the case that had caused his family grief. Jo had declined to take part, but that was all right. Jan was sure she had nothing to do with any of it.

Twenty minutes later, when Jan peeked into the west parlor, Archie was setting small vases with two or three stalks of blooms in each on the tables.

"Lovely," Jan told him and went back to the kitchen.

After Rose flipped over the Open sign at ten o'clock, she reported to Jan, "The community center bus is parking down at Murphy's."

"Terrific," Jan said. "I think we're ready."

Elaine had laid out containers of several special tea blends she had developed, and she started filling tea balls with some of the most popular ones on the menu. She looked up at Rose. "They'll probably start their shopping at A Little Something and Sylvia's Closet and work their way up here. Now, Rose, these folks will want everything nostalgic, so use the oldest teapots and cups first."

"Got it," Rose said with a wink. "The older the customer, the older the dishes."

Jan mostly stayed out in the kitchen, loading trays for the servers, but when it got busy, even she ventured into the parlors to do whatever was needed. She manned the checkout in the entrance hall during the biggest rush, while Elaine helped ferry teapots and pastries to the customers.

She was headed back to the kitchen about eleven o'clock when the front door opened and four women entered together. Not part of the seniors group, Jan thought, although one of the quartet was probably in her sixties. She stepped forward to greet them.

"Good morning. Table for four?"

"Yes," said a tall, brown-haired woman about Jan's age. She looked very stylish in her ivory sweater set and green linen pants, with a jade necklace at her throat, but her face was open and friendly.

"Are you in Lancaster for the day?" Jan asked.

"We're on our way to see the summer exhibit at the Colby College Museum of Art," said the youngest of the four. She appeared to be about thirty, and her long blonde hair was caught back in a ponytail. "We're from Marble Cove."

"Well, we're glad you stopped in," Jan said. Usually people from Central Maine went to the coast for their day trips, not the other way around. "Let me just take a peek—we have a lot of folks in this morning, and we want you to be comfortable." She stepped to the west parlor doorway. She could only see one free table in Rose's station. The rest were crowded with older people, who seemed to be thoroughly enjoying themselves, but Rose had her hands full. She walked across to the east parlor door. Archie had a bit more free space, and Jan could see two or three tables that would do.

"This way," she said, smiling at the newcomers. "I'll turn you over to Archie, our British server."

As the women followed her into the parlor, Archie looked up and caught Jan's eye. He came toward them looking entirely English and capable, which he was—and which was why Jan and Elaine had hired him.

"Good morning, ladies," he said with a little bow. "Would you like to sit near the window?"

"Thank you. It's lovely," said the older woman.

As Jan headed back out to the checkout, she heard them ask Archie about his background and his accent. Another cluster of seniors was coming through the door, and Jan hurried to greet them.

"What an adorable house," one of the women exclaimed. "How long has this tearoom been here?"

"About a year," Jan said. "Welcome. Table for three?"

She led them into the east parlor and designated a table near the decorative fireplace screen. As they passed the party Archie was waiting on, one of the women was saying, "Our friend Margaret here is an artist, and she owns a gallery in Marble Cove."

Jan made a mental note to tell Elaine. She would certainly want to meet the artist and chat with the other visitors for a minute. That reminded her of the painting Elaine had recently purchased. It was still wrapped and sitting upstairs in the sewing room. They really ought to get that hung.

As her customers sat down, she handed them menus. "Archie will be right with you. I hope you enjoy your tea."

ELAINE WAS THRILLED by the business they were getting, but she hoped the usual noontime lull didn't pass them by. They all needed a chance to catch their breath and sit down for a lunch break, even if it was short. She was helping Archie by cleaning off the tables in his station as quickly as parties vacated them.

She had thought Jan was overdoing it a little with her extra baking that morning, but her cousin was right. These day-trippers were hungry! She assumed some were planning on a full lunch at the diner or the Grill, but you couldn't tell that by the amount of pastries they put away in the tearoom. Several people asked for plates of goodies, and some ordered takeaway boxes as well.

Not only that, but she had met an accomplished artist and a published mystery author this morning. She had Diane Spencer's business card and a brochure for Margaret Hoskins's Shearwater Gallery in her apron pocket, and she intended to look up both on the Internet tonight. Maybe she and Jan could take a drive to Marble Cove later in the summer and return the women's visit.

She ran into Jan once in the kitchen. Elaine was carrying a tray of dirty dishes, and Jan was heading out bearing one with two plates of pastries and a steaming teapot. Both pulled up short in the doorway, and Elaine stepped aside.

"After you."

"Thanks," Jan said and walked through the swinging door, holding it open for Elaine.

As Elaine set down the tray of dirty dishes, she noticed a can of wood stain on the counter. What on earth was Jan doing with that?

No time to think about it. She loaded the dirty dishes, took the tray, and headed back to Archie's parlor. Jan was now at the checkout, cashing up a party, and another couple stood in line, waiting to pay.

None of Archie's tables had emptied in the last few minutes. The people cashing out must have been seated in Rose's station, Elaine presumed. She started to turn away and see if

Rose needed a hand, when movement outside the side window caught her eye.

They hadn't used the tables on the side porch much this spring. They'd been popular last summer, but that was mostly after the temperatures warmed. But someone was sitting at one of them today—a man with his back to her. She wondered if anyone had been out to serve him.

Archie came her way, and she jerked her head, signaling him to come to her.

"There's a man outside. Has anyone asked if he wants to order?"

"Oh." Archie peered toward the side windows. "I didn't see him."

"I'll go," Elaine said. "You're busy enough in here." She went out to the entrance hall and grabbed a menu from the rack by the checkout. Jan was making change for the couple, and another woman had joined the line.

"I'll be on the porch," Elaine whispered to Jan. She bustled out the door and around to the side porch. About the same time she recognized the customer was Greg Payson, she realized he was talking on his cell phone.

"No, don't do that," he said sharply. His free hand rested on a manila envelope on the table.

Since he was on his phone, Elaine greeted him with a wave and set the menu on the table. She smiled and mimed that she'll be back to take his order in a bit. She assumed he must have come back home last night, and she hoped Greg, Bristol, and Mark had had a productive conversation.

Greg nodded to her and she began to walk away. "No, don't go there," Greg said into the phone. "Come to the tearoom next door. Yeah. I'm waiting there now, on the side porch. Right." As he closed the connection, he glanced at her and sat up straighter. "Sorry, Mrs. Cook."

Elaine turned on her heel and headed back to the table. "Hi, Greg. No problem. Can I get you something?"

"Uh...no, thanks."

"Are you sure? It's kind of chilly out here. How about a cup of coffee?"

"Well..."

"On the house," she said. Apparently he had asked a friend to meet him here, but he hadn't said so. Given what she learned from Bristol yesterday, she knew money was tight, which was probably why he wasn't ordering anything. She planned to text Bristol and ask how her chat with Greg had gone last night.

"Sure," Greg said, avoiding her direct gaze. "Thanks." He looked so young in his Bowdoin T-shirt and jean jacket.

Elaine walked inside and went into her office to text Bristol. Then she went into the kitchen and placed a small pitcher of real cream, a spoon, a napkin, and a pressed glass sugar bowl with an assortment of sugar and sweeteners on a tray. She put one of Jan's pistachio-raisin cookies on a saucer and added it to the tray. A mug of fresh Colombian coffee came last. Jan came in from the hall.

"Hey! What's up with the can of stain?" Elaine asked.

Jan took a white disc from her pocket. "Remember this?"

"The poker chip?" Elaine asked.

"Yeah. The fingerprints on it are Greg's. I matched them to the ones on the can of stain he used when he fixed the steps."

Elaine stared at her for a moment. "He's on the porch. Should I ask him about it?"

"If you want." Jan slipped the chip into the pocket of Elaine's apron.

Elaine went out the back door and around to the side porch. Greg was sitting where she had left him, looking toward Main Street.

She spoke before she quite reached the table, so she wouldn't startle him.

"Here we go. Nice and hot. Is someone joining you?"

"Uh, well, yeah. That's okay, isn't it?"

"Sure," Elaine said with a smile. "It happens a lot. I'll try to keep an eye out so that if your friend wants to order anything, one of us will be here."

"Okay." He looked doubtful, and Elaine got the impression he would rather that she didn't take notice of his friend. She reached in her pocket and drew out the white poker chip. "Greg, is this yours? We found it on the floor in the tearoom the day you fixed the steps."

Greg's eyes widened. "Yeah. I didn't realize I'd lost it until later, and I didn't know where."

"I'd forgotten you sat there when you had your snack, and I hadn't made the connection," Elaine said.

"It's mine. Thanks." He took it from her. "It's my lucky chip. It's like a keepsake."

"From a poker game?"

"Yeah, at the dorm. But please don't tell my folks. I don't want them to freak. They're already a little bit upset with me, and they're not big fans of gambling."

Elaine eyed him keenly. Something was definitely up with Greg.

"I'll check on you in a little bit and see if you need anything." She walked around to the front door and went inside. She slowed her steps as she walked through the entrance hall. The poker chip, she thought. What was he into? She paused by the checkout, thinking.

Two women came out of Rose's parlor, chatting together.

"Ready to check out?" Elaine asked with an automatic smile.

"Yes, thank you."

Elaine went through the motions, but her thoughts were elsewhere. When the women left, she walked across the hall and paused at the doorway to the east parlor. She ducked a little for a better look out the window across the room from her. Someone else was out there with Greg.

# CHAPTER TWENTY-TWO

J an was brewing a pot of chai tea for one of Rose's customers when Elaine walked swiftly through the kitchen toward the back door. The sweet, spicy smell hung in the air.

"Hey," Jan said.

"Sorry, gotta run," Elaine replied. "A friend just joined Greg out there."

"What kind of friend?"

It must have been the sharp tone in her voice that stopped Elaine.

"I don't know. He asked some guy to meet him here." She recalled his instructions on the phone: *"Don't go there. Come to the tearoom next door."* "And he didn't want Bristol to know."

"I don't like the sound of that," Jan said.

Elaine stared at her for a moment. "Maybe we should call Bristol and tell her that Greg's here."

"Want me to tell her?" Jan walked over to the back door. Out on the water below, a cabin cruiser was headed in toward their dock, or more likely the marina.

"Yes, I guess so," Elaine said. "She'd want to know, don't you think?"

"I do." Jan watched her go out and around to the side porch. Before she shut the back door, she confirmed for her own satisfaction that the boat she'd spotted was Jack Weston's. She hoped he would dock at the tearoom's pier, but he veered toward the marina instead, slowing to keep his boat's wake at a minimum. Jan closed the door and stepped toward the phone just as Archie dashed in.

"Quick, quick! Marcella just spilled her hot chocolate all over the table."

"Oh, here!" Jan tossed him a dish towel. Archie ran out, and she grabbed the roll of paper towels from its holder under the upper cabinet and followed him.

As she had suspected, six-year-old Marcella was crying quietly, her face bright red. She tried to hide it in her mother's sleeve.

"Hey," Kit was saying, "it's going to be okay."

"That's right," Archie said, patting the worst of the puddle on the table with his towel. "And as soon as we get this mopped up, I'm going to fetch you a new cup. Now, look, there's a clean table over there." He nodded toward the corner near the teapot display. "Why don't you and your mum go sit over there, and we'll bring it to you right away."

Marcella gulped and let Kit lead her to the other table.

"Oh, thanks," Archie said, taking the roll of paper towels from Jan. "I can get this. Would you mind fixing a fresh cuppa for her though?" While he spoke, he bent and retrieved a peppermint stick off the floor—Marcella's usual stirring stick in her cocoa.

"Sure." Jan took the candy in a soiled napkin and hurried back to the kitchen. There was just too much going on today.

ELAINE ROUNDED THE corner. The man sitting across from him was much older than Greg. He wore a tweed sports jacket with patches at the elbows and jeans—extra large, if Elaine was any judge. Definitely not the young fellow she'd seen him with at the Pine Tree Grill on Friday evening. One hand rested possessively on a sheet of paper on the table between them, and the two appeared to be deep in conversation but kept their voices low.

She pasted on a smile as she approached the table. She hadn't thought to bring a menu or a sales pad.

"Hello," she said. "Welcome to Tea for Two. May I get you something? Tea? Coffee, perhaps?" She stood at the side of the table, between them.

Greg was looking a little out of sorts. In fact, if she knew him better, she would ask if he felt ill. Again she wondered why he had chosen the tearoom as a meeting place. He didn't have his own car. Did he want a place that was close to home, so he could get there on foot or by bicycle, but not so close that his parents would see whom he met?

The older man held her gaze for a moment. His craggy chin was dark with stubble, and his deep brown eyes seemed to bore into her.

"Coffee. Black coffee."

"Coming right up." It sounded inane, and her smile was about to crack the skin on her cheeks. Her gaze swept downward, to the paper the man shielded with his hand.

The top of it was covered, but the bits she could see around his wrist looked like old paper, not the crisp white they used today, and smaller than a sheet of copy paper—perhaps only half as large. The words on it were handwritten in wispy script, and the ink had faded to a brownish hue.

She turned away, for some reason toward the front of the house, not the back, though it was farther to the kitchen by that route. She just wasn't thinking—but she wasn't about to turn around and walk back past them to the door of the screened porch.

When she got to the front porch, she did a quick scan of their small parking area. Five cars sat there, and a couple more were parked at the edge of the street. She didn't recognize most of them—just Kit's car and Archie's. Rose had brought her dad's boat this morning, and Elaine and Jan's cars were hiding in the garage. The tearoom was packed with customers, but a lot of them arrived via the senior citizen center's bus.

Her gaze swept the opposite side of the street, what she could see of it—Gift Me, the library, a house, Murphy's store. The memory of Greg pumping gas came to her suddenly, filling the tank on Bristol's car. And then he'd come over to Diane's shop and picked the lock on the front door for her. They'd praised him at the time.

But that was before Dan Benson said someone might have picked the lock on the church door.

Elaine pulled in a shaky breath and went in the front door of the tearoom. Archie was headed into the east parlor with a fresh tray, and Rose was disappearing into the kitchen.

"Archie."

"Yes, Elaine?"

She walked over to him, and they both stopped in the middle of the entrance hall.

"Could you please serve black coffee to the man on the porch right away—the one sitting at the table with Greg Payson?"

"Certainly."

"Top off Greg's coffee too, and maybe take them a few cookies. I don't want them to rush off while I call the police."

Archie's eyes flared, but he quickly resumed his neutral expression.

"Very good."

Elaine hurried across the hall and into her office. She closed the door so that there would be no chance of customers overhearing her and dialed 911.

"What is your emergency?" a female voice asked.

"This is Elaine Cook at the Tea for Two tearoom in Lancaster, and..." She mentally scolded herself for wasting time. They could tell where the caller was now, since she had dialed 911 on a landline. "I think there's a criminal transaction taking place on our side porch."

"You think there are criminals at your place of business?" the woman asked.

"Yes. If you could put me through to Trooper Dan Benson, he lives near here, and I think this has to do with a case he's investigating."

"One moment. Please stay on the line."

Elaine could think of a thousand reasons why Dan wouldn't answer his phone right away. He could be in court in another town today, or he could be on his day off, or lending his services at a car accident on the interstate highway or—

*Stop it,* she told herself. Instead of coming up with more scenarios, she sent up a silent prayer. *Lord, please let Dan—or somebody—get here fast.*

"Elaine?"

"Dan!" She was so relieved, her breath whooshed out of her. "Greg Payson's here at the tearoom, and he had another man meet him here, and something's not right. Dan, I think they have General Knox's letter. I saw an old, handwritten document. I don't know what's going on, but..."

"I'll be right there. Don't do anything to alarm them."

The line went dead, and Elaine hung up. Her hands shook as she opened the office door. She stepped around the corner into the kitchen. Archie was just lifting a tray with a mug, a coffee pot, and a plate of cookies on it. Jan stood at the sink, her hands in soapy water, staring at him.

"Let me take that out, Archie." Elaine whisked the tray from his hands.

"But you said..."

"Dan Benson is on the way," she told him. "Make sure when he comes that he goes right to the side porch, where Greg and that other guy are sitting."

"All...all right," Archie said.

Elaine went out the back door before anyone could say more.

JAN OPENED HER mouth to say something, but Elaine was already shutting the porch door. She took her hands from her dishwater and wiped them on a terry towel.

"If something's going on, we can't let her go out there alone."

Archie hesitated. He didn't often appear helpless, but today was an exception. "If we all descend on them, we'll scare them away. I suppose I could go out and wipe down another table, just to lend my presence."

Jan clenched her teeth together. She didn't know why Elaine had called the police, but it had something to do with Greg and that man he was drinking coffee with.

"Dan Benson could be twenty minutes getting here," she said.

"Oh, I don't think..." Archie frowned. "Well, yes, if he was at home or on the other end of town."

Jan dashed out on to the screened porch, and Archie followed her. Why couldn't Jack have docked here? His cabin cruiser was still tied to the marina dock. She could hustle across the shore in less than two minutes.

"Here." She whipped off her apron and stuffed it into Archie's hands. "Jack Weston's at the marina. He'll know what to do." Jan opened the back door and ran down the steps to the deck below.

# CHAPTER TWENTY-THREE

H ere we go," Elaine said brightly, setting the mug in front of the stranger. He'd been studying the paper intently, but he lowered it as she approached, laying it down face-up. She could see part of the signature clearly. Definitely a letter, but in her quick glance she couldn't tell if it was signed by Knox or not.

She poured out the coffee for the customer, pleased that her hands were steady. She got a better glimpse of the paper as the man edged it slightly away from the coffee mug.

"Greg, can I heat yours up?"

"Sure," Greg said, not looking at her.

Elaine poured, and Greg mumbled, "Thanks."

She set the plate of cookies on the table between them. "Anything else I can get you gentlemen?" She smiled at both the men, who were studiously avoiding eye contact.

"No, that's all," the big man said.

"Okay, great." Still Elaine hesitated. The paper was close to him, mostly hidden under his tweed sleeve now. "Is that an old document?" she asked. "I took a workshop once on reading antique handwriting. Isn't it odd? Sometimes it's almost indecipherable."

The stranger looked up at her blankly. He moved his hand so that it covered more of the paper.

"And nowadays, they're not even teaching kids cursive in school. How will anyone be able to read those old documents twenty years from now?" Elaine knew she was blathering on when she shouldn't. In fact, she knew with certainty that she ought not to have mentioned the letter.

"Well, if you need anything else, we're close by." She turned toward the front end of the porch, reasoning that she would be between them and their exit. She could watch out the front windows so that if they left, she could tell Dan when he arrived which way the stranger went, and possibly what his car looked like.

Behind her, Greg said, "What...?"

The older man interrupted him. "Just a minute, ma'am."

Elaine turned around, balancing the tray with the coffee-pot, and her smile froze on her lips. Greg was staring open-mouthed at his companion, who was leveling a gun at her—a modern semiautomatic pistol, much like the one her husband had carried during his military service. Her throat went dry, and when she spoke, her voice quivered.

"I don't understand."

"I think you do." The man stood, keeping his gun trained on her. "I think you understand perfectly, and I don't want you making any calls. You come over here please, where I can keep an eye on you. We'll be done in a minute, and we'll be out of your hair."

Elaine didn't move.

He moved the gun slightly. "Now."

She swallowed with effort. "Greg, this is a mistake."

"Shut up," the man said. "Get over here."

Elaine's legs didn't want to move. It was as though her pant legs were full of lead. She had read somewhere that pioneer women sewed rows of lead shot into the hems of their skirts as they crossed the prairie, to keep them from flying up in the wind. She almost laughed at the random thought. Here she was, leaden-legged, wanting to conceal not her petticoats and pantalets, but her fear and helplessness. She managed to take a couple of steps toward them.

Greg still sat at the table. His terrified gaze whipped from her to his companion. "Charlie, you can't…"

"Zip it, kid." The big man reached inside his jacket and rummaged for a moment, keeping the gun trained on Elaine. He produced an envelope and tossed it on the table. "There's your money. Put the letter back in the envelope you brought it in."

Elaine listened hard. Shouldn't she be hearing a siren by now? Or was Dan approaching in silence, so as not to tip off his quarry? Movement at one of the parlor windows caught her attention. Rose was peering out at them, her face pale and her cell phone at her ear. Two other people crowded next to her, looking out.

*No*, Elaine wanted to yell. *Get away from the windows. Get back, all of you!* If only the stranger with the gun wouldn't look their way.

"Elaine? Everything okay?" Elaine and the gunman shifted their gazes toward the back of the porch, and Greg swiveled in his chair. Jack Weston stood, solid and charming, just outside the door to the screened porch. Unfortunately, the gunman's body had blocked the view of his weapon until he turned toward Jack, and it was too late for Jack to pull his gun.

Jack didn't twitch a hair.

"What's going on here?"

"Stay back." The big man took a step toward Elaine and grasped her arm, still pointing the pistol at her. He pulled her closer, against his side, and she felt the barrel poking her ribs.

"What are you? A rent-a-cop?"

"No, sir," Jack said. "I'm a game warden."

"Ah." The man looked Jack up and down, his upper lip curling in disdain. "I'm doing business with this guy, and we just want to end the transaction and leave."

Jack looked at Elaine. "What does Elaine have to do with this?"

"Nothing. Not yet, anyhow. I'd like to keep it that way."

Jack sighed. "See, you've already involved her. Now, whatever you came here for might be all right—I don't know. But holding a gun on someone, that's different. Put the gun down, and we'll talk."

"I don't think so."

Jack glanced at Greg, who was still seated, but turned toward him now, away from Elaine and the big man, closer to Jack than they were.

"Greg, what's this all about?" Jack asked. He sounded so calm, Elaine wondered if his heart was beating seventy beats a minute, or if it was galloping at twice that, like hers was. He looked so handsome and capable. His uniform didn't show one wrinkle. Did he have to iron those summer shirts, or did they come out of the dryer looking like that?

Elaine realized she was losing touch with reality. It was so much nicer to think about Jack's life as a bachelor than the lethal weapon sticking into her side or the fingers of the gunman's left hand, digging into her upper arm through the thin cotton layer of her blouse.

Greg was still fumbling with the envelope and the letter. "I…uh…"

"You know this guy?" Jack asked.

"Well, he…uh…not really, but…"

"Stow it," the gunman snarled. "Now you, Smokey Bear, just take your gun out nice and easy and lay it on the table there beside you."

Jack hesitated. He was standing beside an empty table that had two white chairs pulled up to it.

The big man poked the muzzle of his pistol harder into Elaine's side. "What, you think I don't mean it? Put the gun on the table."

Jack's gaze shifted, and he seemed to reach a decision. "Sure. I'll put my gun on the table, and you can walk away. Nobody gets hurt."

"Now you're talking," the man said, so close to Elaine's ear his breath fanned her cheek. He smelled like Colombian coffee. Had anyone ever picked a suspect from a lineup based on his breath? She almost laughed, but she knew she would never forget this man's face, so his coffee breath wouldn't be a requirement when the time came to give her statement.

She saw Jack as if from a vast distance, slowing reaching with fingers extended to release the safety catch on his holster and pull out the gun, fingers on the butt. He laid it gently on the little table and then moved his outspread hand away from it.

"Okay," he said. "You can go now."

"Step away from the table," the big man said.

Jack took a step sideways, toward the railing.

"Give me the letter, kid," the gunman said.

"Greg, don't do it." Elaine tried to keep her voice calm. She was surprised she could speak at all.

He paused and threw her a panicky look. Greg was more afraid than either she or Jack was, Elaine realized. He was afraid this man would kill her, and he would be responsible.

"You don't have to do it," Elaine said.

"Shut up." The man poked her ribs with the gun. "Kid, you give that to me and then get outta here."

"Wh-where to?" Greg asked.

"Don't go, Greg," Elaine said. "You stay right here."

Greg swallowed hard. He had at last got the paper into the envelope—without damaging it, Elaine hoped. He pushed his chair back.

"I can't face my folks. I'm sorry." He looked pleadingly at Elaine, as though begging her to understand.

"They will forgive you," Elaine said.

"She's right," Jack said. "Just stay where you are, Greg. We'll figure this out. Don't run now, or it will be a whole lot worse."

"I...I can't." Greg shut his eyes for an instant, and when he opened them again, Elaine saw the glimmer of tears on his lashes.

"Nobody's been hurt, Greg," she said softly. "If you run now, it will shape your life forever."

"Look, I've had enough out of you." The gunman shoved her toward the porch railing and reached toward Greg. "Give it to me now."

Greg seemed unable to move.

"It's okay, Greg," Jack said, behind him. "Give him the envelope. Let him have it. Just stay here. Don't run away."

At that moment, footsteps sounded behind Elaine on the board floor. Bristol charged on to the porch and strode over to stand in front of her and the gunman.

"What do you think you're doing?" Her voice came out louder and higher than her normal pitch as she glared at the stranger.

"Mom!" Greg started to rise.

Elaine opened her mouth to speak, but Bristol was quicker. She drew back her hand and slapped the gunman across the face.

"Hey! Lady!"

Elaine jumped forward, pushing Bristol with her, toward the windows and away from the man.

Jack saw his opportunity. When Elaine whirled around, she saw him spring forward with his own pistol aimed directly at the gunman's chest.

"Drop it. Now."

Elaine realized the man had fumbled with his own gun in the chaotic moment of Bristol's fury. He was caught off guard, with it pointing down toward the floorboards.

"Police," came Dan Benson's deep, authoritative voice from the front end of the porch. "Do what he says. Put the gun down."

The big man drew in a breath, hesitated just an instant, his stare glued on Jack, and then he bent his knees and carefully laid his weapon on the floor.

"Hands up," Dan said. "Shoulder high."

The gunman obeyed. Dan walked over and kicked the pistol gently toward Jack, who picked it up.

"Turn around and put your hands on the railing," Dan told the prisoner. "You're under arrest. You have the right to remain silent."

He went on with the recitation while Greg, his face drained of color, plunked down into his chair.

"Gregory Thomas!" Bristol sprang toward her son, not yet emptied of anger and fear.

Jack held out a hand to stop her.

"He's okay, Bristol. Just let us handle this."

"I'm sorry, Mom," Greg cried, his tears spilling over and running unheeded down his face.

Bristol shrank back against Elaine, and Elaine put her arms around her.

"It's going to be all right." She patted Bristol's shoulder and sent up a silent prayer of thanks.

In less time than she would have thought possible, Dan had handcuffed the man and headed out toward his patrol vehicle, which he had parked at the curb. As they went down the steps, Elaine heard Dan talking into his shoulder mic, asking for backup and help transporting two suspects.

Jack holstered his pistol and put a hand on Greg's shoulder. "Greg, do you have any weapons on you?"

"What? No. Well, a jackknife." Greg turned his head and stared at Jack, his lips trembling.

"Okay, stand up slowly and empty your pockets. Put everything on the table."

Greg shoved the chair back and stood. He fished out his wallet, pocketknife, and a few coins and set them on top of the manila envelope.

"Good," Jack said. "Now, what's in the envelope?"

Greg's eyes darted about, as if he still wished he could run away. His mother glared at him, and he pulled in a deep breath.

"It's the old letter from the church. The one the general wrote."

"Okay," Jack said, as if that was perfectly normal. "I want you to put your hands on the railing over here, nice and easy. I'm going to pat you down. It's what we call standard operating procedure."

As he finished frisking Greg, Dan returned. "Good going, Jack. You got handcuffs?"

"Yeah." Jack unsnapped the case on his belt and took them out. "What did you do with the other guy?"

"He's secure in the vehicle. I've got another trooper on the way to transport him. Did you Mirandize him?"

"No. Why don't you go ahead?" Jack gave Dan his handcuffs, which Dan exchanged for a bag. "Okay, if you'll put everything off that table in here. And unload the pistol and bag it too, would you?"

"Sure." Jack picked up the prisoner's gun, unloaded it, and dropped it, the clip, and the cartridge from the chamber into the sack. Then he gathered the envelopes and Greg's wallet and other things off the table. He came over to stand by Elaine and Bristol. "Are you ladies all right?"

Elaine nodded.

Tears coursed down Bristol's cheeks. "Where will you take him?" she choked out.

"Probably the county jail, in Augusta."

"Will we be able to see him tonight?"

"I don't know. I'm guessing not, but Greg can call you after he's booked."

Over his shoulder, Dan said, "We'll try to get him a bail hearing tomorrow, Bristol. I'll try to call you or Mark later."

"Th-thank you," Bristol said.

Dan turned Greg around. "You got anything you want to say to your mother?" he said a bit harshly, in Elaine's opinion, but maybe that was what Greg needed right now.

Greg's face contorted, his tears still flowing. "I'm sorry, Mom. Really. Tell Dad—tell him I'm sorry."

"But why?" Bristol raised her hands and then let them fall. "You stole the letter?"

"I needed money." Greg's head sank and he looked down at the floor. "I owe a lot of money. I didn't mess up the church though. I swear. I went in Friday night after I got home, and it wasn't like that. Everything was fine."

*He picked the lock,* Elaine thought, remembering the ease with which he had opened Diane's door. *He must be the person Dr. McInnis saw in the church parking lot the night before we discovered the vandalism.*

"Get the best lawyer you can," Dan said more gently to Bristol. "Maybe Bob Claybrook?"

Bristol nodded, and Elaine squeezed her shoulders.

Dan led Greg away. "Come on. Time to take your lumps, Greg."

"Here, sit down, Bristol." Jack pulled over one of the white chairs.

Bristol sank into it, and her sobs wrenched out of her.

A moment later, Jan, Rose, and Archie rushed out on to the porch, followed by what seemed like the entire town, but Elaine realized it was probably the dozen or two customers who had been in the tearoom when the drama began.

"Bristol, dear!" Jan knelt beside her chair, and Bristol fell into her arms, sobbing uncontrollably.

# CHAPTER TWENTY-FOUR

A re you okay?" Rose hurried to Elaine's side, her face pale and her blue eyes troubled. "He was holding a gun on you."

"I'll be fine," Elaine said, giving her a quick hug.

"Are you sure?" Rose looked past her. "And what about poor Bristol?"

"She's a little shaken," Elaine said.

Jan rubbed Bristol's shoulders. "Sweetie, I'm sorry. I was going to call you, but things got intense really fast."

"I was going to call too, and tell you Greg was here," Elaine said. "Then that other man showed up, and I thought it was more important to keep an eye on things. How did you know to come over?"

"Elsa told me," Bristol said, looking off toward the lake.

"Elsa Leon?" Elaine looked inquiringly at Jan.

Bristol nodded with a sniff. Archie stepped forward and gave her a neatly pressed and folded white handkerchief.

"Elsa was in the tearoom when this started," Rose said. "I was getting her and her friend some tea, and I saw out the window—well, I saw the guy pull out a gun. I should have kept quiet and just called the cops, but I'm afraid I said something. Elsa looked out and saw Greg. She said, 'Oh no! What's Greg up to? Bristol's got to get over here and talk to him.' And she ran out the door." Rose had tears in her eyes. "I'm sorry, Mrs. Payson. Everyone started crowding the windows to see after that. Archie and I tried to get them to stay back, but..." She turned helplessly to Elaine. "I'm sorry."

Elaine patted her shoulder. "It's all right, Rose. I could have handled things out here better too."

"We all could have acted more wisely," Jan said. "Bristol, let me drive you over to the town office. You'll want to talk to Mark."

Bristol clapped a hand to her mouth. "Mark. Oh no." She struggled to stand.

"Why don't I call the office and ask Mark to come here?" Elaine asked. "The two of you can have some privacy upstairs in our living room."

"Sounds like a good idea," Jan said.

"No. He took the day off and is running some errands in town," Bristol said, her eyes stricken. "He and Greg had a long talk last night, not all of it cordial. Mark woke up with a splitting headache, and I suggested he just take the day off."

Elaine put her arm around Bristol. "Come on. We'll call him and see if he's up to discussing it with you."

She guided Bristol inside and up the stairs, while Archie and Rose attempted to calm the guests and steer them back to their tables inside. As soon as she had Bristol settled in a comfortable recliner, Elaine went to her room and dialed Greg's cell phone number.

"Mark, this is Elaine. I have some news," she said when Mark came on the line. "Bristol is here at my house. It concerns Greg. Would you be able to stop by?"

"Is Greg okay?" Mark asked. "What happened?"

"He's not hurt," Elaine said quickly. "I think it's best if we explain in person."

"Okay," Mark said uncertainly. "I'll be right there."

When she got back to the living room, Jan was placing a mug of coffee and a plate of cookies and scones on the coffee table where Bristol could reach it.

"Mark's on his way," Elaine said.

Jan nodded. "Archie will watch for him and bring him up. And I've got a fresh pot brewing." She smiled mournfully at Bristol.

"Thanks," Bristol said. She wiped her eyes with Archie's handkerchief. "Greg said he owed someone money. To that awful man, I suppose."

"I'm not sure he's the one," Elaine said. "It seemed to me that Greg was selling the Knox letter to him. The man gave him some money in an envelope. Jack took it off the table for evidence, along with the Knox letter. I think Greg was going to use that money to pay off his debt. And I saw another guy—a young man—give him some money Friday night at the Pine Tree Grill."

"He went out with one of his friends Friday night," Bristol said. "His roommate from last year. We know the kid. He seems decent."

"Maybe he was repaying a loan or something," Jan suggested.

"How could he owe so much money?" Bristol wailed. "He's not into drugs. He can't be. I'd have noticed something funny, and his grades would have suffered."

"I'm sure you'll have some answers soon," Jan said gently.

"But he wouldn't tell us why he left school. He just said he wanted to try something different. He never said anything about being in debt."

"I have an idea what the money was for," Elaine said.

"What?" Bristol demanded.

Elaine almost didn't want to voice the thought, but it might ease Bristol's mind if she had a credible alternative to drug dealing for consideration.

"I think it could possibly be a gambling debt."

"Gambling." Bristol sat still, her eyes focused on something far away. "He likes games. Plays cards with his friends, I think. And he mentioned once that he and a couple of buddies went to Foxwoods one weekend. Mark chewed him out for it and asked how much he lost. Greg just said, 'Not much,' and we never heard any more about it."

"We found a poker chip on the floor in the tearoom," Elaine said. "At the time, we didn't put it together, but that was the day Greg was here to fix our back stairs to the deck. Today he told me it was his lucky chip. I'm guessing he got in over his head, Bristol. I think he was terrified that you and Mark would find out. I'm afraid it's a large debt, but I don't know how much."

At a quiet knock on the doorjamb, they all turned toward the entrance. Archie stood in the doorway.

"Mr. Payson is here."

"Thank you, Archie," Elaine said.

Archie stepped aside, and Mark strode into the room. "Bristol! What's going on?"

Bristol jumped up from her chair. "Mark, Greg stole the general's letter from the church."

"What?" Mark's eyebrows shot up and he pulled Bristol into his arms. "Why?"

"He was here, trying to sell it to some thug. He told me he owes a lot of money. Elaine thinks he's been gambling."

"Slow down, slow down." Mark pulled her over to the sofa and sat down next to her. "Now, start at the beginning."

"I didn't see the beginning," Bristol confessed. "Elsa Leon ran into the store and said Greg was at the tearoom and some man with a gun was out on the porch with him and Elaine."

Jan walked over and placed a hand on Mark's shoulder. "I'm going downstairs to see if Rose and Archie need help, but I think Elaine can fill you in on most of it."

She left the room, and Elaine walked over to the chair where Bristol had sat earlier. She looked at the couple. How much heartache was she about to inflict on these friends? But she knew Mark needed as much information as possible before he talked to the police or Greg or a lawyer. She pulled in a deep breath.

"It started when I saw Greg sitting at one of the porch tables, talking on his phone."

JAN AND ELAINE arrived at the Paysons' house early in the afternoon a couple of weeks later. The one-story brick house looked warm in the rays of the setting sun.

"Bristol's flower beds are going to look fantastic in about a week," Jan said as they walked slowly to the front entrance.

"If it doesn't get too cold again," Elaine said. She paused to look closely at the plants sprouting from the dark earth. "Her phlox is coming right along. Is that foxglove?"

"Looks like it." Jan rang the bell, and Bristol opened the door, smiling.

"Hi. Thanks for coming over."

She took them into the living room, where Mark rose from the sofa. Across from him, Greg got up from his chair.

"Greg!" Jan was delighted to see the young man. "This must mean your hearing went well."

"Yes, thanks." Greg clasped the hand she held out and turned to greet Elaine.

"It's wonderful to see you at home again," Elaine said.

"It's great to *be* home." Greg started to reach for her hand but pulled back. "Can I hug you?"

Elaine grinned. "You sure can."

Greg gave her a clumsy bear hug. "I can't thank you enough for helping me that day."

"It was nothing," Elaine said.

They all sat down, and Bristol fixed Elaine with a sober gaze. "It most certainly was not *nothing*. If you hadn't intervened..."

Greg nodded. "At the time, I was furious that you'd seen me, and you kept hovering around. I was really scared. But when you told me not to run, and..." He looked sheepishly at his father, and his face flushed. "When you said my folks would forgive me, I wanted to believe you so bad. But I wasn't sure."

"We may have been angry," Mark said, "but we still love you, and we always will."

"Of course we forgive you." Bristol swiped at a tear with the back of her hand. "I only wish you'd told us earlier, before you got in so deep."

Mark cleared his throat. "Elaine, Jan, we figure the two of you may have saved Greg's life. You certainly helped steer him away from a life of crime and despair. Elaine, you called the police, and you put your life on the line when you went out there to wait on Greg and that gangster. And Jan, you ran over to the marina and got Jack Weston. Between the two of you—well, and Jack and Dan Benson—we figure we owe a lot of thanks."

Elaine's lips quirked. "Thank you, but don't forget Bristol's part. If she hadn't shocked that man when she slapped him, he might not have given up his gun."

Mark shook his head and slid closer to Bristol. "She could have been shot. Or you could have."

"Yes," Elaine said more soberly. "I'm so thankful it turned out the way it did."

Bristol sighed. "I can see now that I was reckless, but I was so mad. I wasn't going to let him do anything to my son. Or to you, Elaine."

"So, anyway," Mark said, "I think she's learned a lesson from that. And the judge released Greg in our custody."

"That's wonderful," Jan said.

Greg nodded, looking down at his size 12 sneakers. "I'll be doing restitution for the church this summer."

"Two hundred hours," Mark said. "Cleaning, painting, whatever the trustees can find for him to do."

Bristol nodded. "We didn't want him to take away Chris and Nick's yard work, but Des and Jo said they need them quite a bit in the store in summer. They said it's okay if Greg does the mowing and trimming. He'll be tending the flower beds too."

"What about the Knox letter?" Jan asked.

"The church will get it back after Charles Masden's trial," Mark said. "And with all the publicity surrounding the case, a lot of interest has been generated in it."

"What do you mean?" Elaine asked.

"Several historical societies and antique dealers have contacted the pastor and the board about possibly buying or borrowing the letter for display."

Jan stared at Mark. "You mean they're going to sell it after all?"

"They're thinking about it, yes," Mark said. "The loan comes due in about three weeks. The bank agreed to waive any penalties if we have a signed offer that will cover the balance."

"How much is it?" Elaine asked. "And how much would the letter bring?"

"Well, the state museum has offered five thousand dollars."

"That's a lot," Jan said.

"But still." Elaine frowned and eyed Mark carefully. "I think Pastor Mike said we still needed about ten thousand beyond what the church has to pay it off."

He nodded, his lips pressed in a thin line.

"There could be a higher offer," Bristol said. "We hope, after all this, that people will donate more."

"I'll get my checkbook," Jan said.

Mark smiled. "We're having a special business meeting after church on Sunday. Be prepared."

"I will," Jan promised.

"Me too," Elaine said.

"The worst thing is, it wouldn't have paid the twelve thousand dollars I owed," Greg added glumly. "I never should have touched that letter."

"So..." Jan looked hesitantly from Greg to his parents. "What's going to happen with that?"

"We're going to pay it off slowly," Mark said, "and Greg is going to pay us back. Shane Atherton came over yesterday and offered Greg a job for the rest of the summer at Green Glade Cottages if he was released, so he'll start work tomorrow."

"Wow." Elaine looked Greg up and down. "That *and* your restitution work. That's a big obligation."

"If he's busy, he'll stay out of trouble," Bristol said.

Mark's lips twitched. "Well, that may be the worst thing, son, but I think the best thing is that you're going back to school in the fall."

"Really?" Elaine cried.

"Hooray!" Jan said.

"Yeah, I…" Greg shrugged. "I had figured there was no way Mom and Dad could keep paying for my schooling with the debt I had, and even if I got away with not telling them, every cent I earned would have to go toward the debt, so I wouldn't be able to pay anything toward tuition. It seemed like it would be better to quit school and get a full-time job to pay it off if the people I owed would let me do that."

"Is that apt to get nasty?" Jan asked.

"The police provided a liaison with the casino," Mark said. "We think we can work things out."

"I'm going to repay you," Greg said. "Even if it takes me ten years, I'll pay you back, Dad. And no more gambling. Ever."

Bristol smiled. "Music to my ears."

"You'll pay me for the lawyer's fees too," Mark said.

"Right." Greg was very subdued.

Jan decided to plunge in and ask one of the questions that had niggled at her for weeks. "How did all of this start anyway, Greg?"

He huffed out a deep breath. "Some of the guys in the dorm got up a poker game one Saturday night. It seemed like innocent fun, and I won. Only a hundred bucks or so, but it felt great. I kept playing with them every week, then twice a week. I won often enough that I thought I was pretty good. When one of the guys suggested we go to a casino, it sounded exciting. Maybe I could win big time."

"Did you?" Jan asked.

Greg shook his head. "No, I lost a little. Forty bucks. It wasn't that much, but I was determined to go again and do better. I really thought I could. But that time I lost eight hundred dollars."

Bristol winced. "Why did you keep going back?"

"I couldn't stand that I'd lost that much. I was sure I could win back at least part of it. But my debt kept getting bigger and bigger. I started making more bets in the dorm to get enough cash to go to the casino again." Greg's face flushed a dull red. "Pretty soon I was betting on anything—ball games, academic competitions, even on what day it would snow. And if there was a card game on campus, I was in it."

"When did you study?" Jan asked.

"My grades dipped a little," he admitted, "but for the spring semester I made sure my load wasn't too heavy. I only had one class I had to write a paper for, and I made sure I got that done on time. I knew Mom would disown me if I blew it off."

"You've got that right," Bristol said.

"But I'm done," Greg said firmly. "No more cards, no more betting."

"It might not be that easy," Mark told him.

"I know. But the system we talked about..." Greg looked his father in the eye. "I *will* call you when I'm tempted, Dad. I promise."

Mark nodded. "And we'll pray about it and find something else to distract you if we have to. I'll even pick you up from the school and bring you home for a few days if you need to get away. You're going to beat this."

"I think now that I can."

Jan smiled. "We'll be praying for you too, Greg."

"That's right," Elaine said. "And you can come have a cup of coffee on us anytime, if you promise never to bring any thugs to our place again."

Greg held up both hands in surrender. "I won't. I only picked the tearoom because Charlie was going to come to our house. I knew Dad had had that day off, and I was afraid he'd be home. I didn't want Charlie anywhere near there, but I hadn't asked to use Mom's car that day, so I needed someplace in the open, but a place we could talk that was within walking distance. I'm sorry, Mrs. Cook, Mrs. Blake. That was a really bad idea."

"Or a really good one," Bristol said. "If you'd gone somewhere farther away, where nobody knew you, we might not be having this conversation now, and I shudder to think what that would mean down the road."

Greg drew in a deep breath. "You could be right, Mom. Maybe that's why I thought of the tearoom, I don't know. But I'm really sorry I put you in danger, Mrs. Cook."

Jan had never seen Greg look so humble, except for the moment when Dan Benson led him off the porch in handcuffs.

"If there's anything I can do to help you ladies, let me know," Greg added. "I feel like I owe you one."

"You don't owe us anything, Greg." A glimmer shone in Elaine's eye. "Although there is one small thing you could do for me."

"You name it."

Elaine smiled. "I have a painting over at the house. I bought it several weeks ago, and I never got around to having it hung."

Jan had a brief oh-no moment, realizing that she had completely forgotten to call Brian and have him come hang Elaine's new painting. Maybe that was for the best.

"I'll come over tomorrow morning and do that for you," Greg said quickly.

Jan winked at Elaine. "Come before you go to Green Glade," she said.

"Shane told me to be there by nine."

"Great. We'll see you at eight thirty."

Bristol leaned forward on the sofa. "That's perfect. I'll bring him along with me when I go to the store, and he can walk over to Green Glade from there."

Greg swallowed hard and nodded. "I'll be there."

On their way home, Jan looked over at Elaine, who was driving.

"I was thinking."

Elaine grinned. "You're always thinking."

"Well, yes, aren't we all? But this is about Pastor Mike and Sarah."

"Oh?"

Jan nodded soberly. "I do want to give toward the church mortgage, but if I can, I'd also like to give something toward the Ryders' medical bills."

"I was thinking the same thing," Elaine said. "Maybe together we could pay their next installment. Once we get past the church mortgage, maybe we could do something bigger."

"Yeah." Jan slid her fingers up and down her seat belt, thinking about that. "The mortgage is more urgent. But maybe in July or August we could host an event to benefit them."

Elaine shook her head. "They'd hate that. They're so self-effacing. You heard them. They haven't told anyone about their debt."

"Well, maybe we could just hold a special event—like the Teas around the World, something along those lines—and give the proceeds to them."

"Anonymously?" Elaine asked, putting on her turn signal for their driveway. "Cash in an envelope?"

"Sure, if you like," Jan said, "but they would know it was from us."

"I suppose they would, if no one else knows about Sarah's medical bills. But we don't know where they make the payments, so we can't just go pay it off."

"Maybe what you suggested is best. We could give the envelope to someone else to deliver. The treasurer, maybe. Even if the Ryders knew it was from us, they couldn't make a big fuss, or then everyone would know about their medical bills."

"Sneaky, but I like it."

As they passed Murphy's General Store, Elaine noticed a group of boys huddled near the air hose with their bicycles. She quickly pulled into the store's parking lot, in a spot that left a couple of cars between her and the boys. She switched off the engine.

"What are we doing?" Jan asked.

Elaine peered past her, toward the air pumping station. "See those boys?"

"Yeah."

"On the day Sasha and I went to the shooting range, we were coming home, and those boys came tearing out of the

Penzance boat landing without even looking for traffic. I nearly hit the redheaded boy."

"Okay," Jan said.

"It was a school day," Elaine said. "I don't know. It just made me think of the boys Caleb Ryder said he saw talking to Nick and Chris. Kids on bikes. And the fact that we still don't know who vandalized the church."

# CHAPTER TWENTY-FIVE

J an eyed the group of boys soberly. "Hold on."

She got out of the car before Elaine could ask questions and walked over near the group of boys. Elaine rolled down her window.

"Hello, boys," Jan said.

One of the kids, the blond boy, muttered something. His friends snickered.

"Have a great day," Jan said. She came back to the car and opened the door. "The carrottop kid who's putting air in his tires—when he knelt down, I saw his shoe treads."

"Are they similar to the ones in the pictures you took at the church?"

"I think it's worth investigating. How about if I run home and get the fingerprinting kit?"

"Go," Elaine said.

Jan headed across the street. Elaine got out of the car and went into the store. Des was cleaning the glass doors on the refrigerator case.

"Des, those boys out front," Elaine began.

"What boys?"

"Boys on bicycles. They're using the air hose, and I've seen them before, running loose during school hours like this."

Des tossed his cleaning rag into a bucket and walked with her to the exit door. He opened it and looked out. Elaine peeked beneath his arm. The boys were headed for the street, leaving the air hose dragging in the dirt.

"Hey!" Des yelled.

They stopped and looked back at him.

"Put the hose away, Tim!"

"You know them?" Elaine asked softly.

The redhead rode his bike back and hopped off to coil the hose.

"Yeah. They go to school with my boys. You're right. They should be in the classroom."

Jan hurried across the street a moment later carrying their kit. The boys were disappearing toward the ice cream stand.

"Mind if we do a little investigating?" Elaine asked.

"Go ahead." Des followed her out and watched with interest.

Jan pulled up short beside the air hose. "Hi, Des."

While Jan explained what she was doing, Elaine searched the ground to the side, where the parking lot pavement ended. Bike tracks ran through the dirt toward the street, and where the red-haired boy had stopped and turned back, she found what she wanted. She took out her cell phone and clicked several photos.

She walked over to Jan. "Take a look at these. Do you think they match your pictures?"

Jan looked and then brought out her own phone and pulled up the best footprint photo. She scrutinized both and handed the phones to Des.

"What do you think?"

Des looked at them and whistled softly. "I'd call that a match."

"We should measure the new ones to make sure," Elaine said.

"I'll get a tape measure." Des headed inside.

Meanwhile, Jan dusted away with her powder at the air hose handle and the metal box with the control switches. "Tape please."

Elaine handed it over.

"There we go."

Elaine had a new card ready for her. Then she held it beside the card with the fingerprints from the pocketknife. She and Jan looked at each other and smiled.

"Time to call Trooper Benson," Elaine said.

GREG ARRIVED AT the same time Rose did the next morning. Elaine was out on the porch with a wet cloth in her hand when they climbed the front steps. A chipmunk had scampered up to the railing and sat scolding her for invading his territory. She shook out her cloth over the railing when she saw the young people arrive and walked out to meet them by the front door.

"Hi, Greg. Thanks for coming. Morning, Rose."

Rose grinned. "Good morning."

"You drove today?" Elaine asked.

"Yeah, it looked as though it might rain later," Rose said. "I hate being out on the lake in rainstorms."

"Good choice," Greg told her. "I heard on the radio that we're in for some thunder and lightning around noon."

"*Hmm.* That could mean nobody comes to the tearoom, or it could mean a dozen people take shelter here at the first sprinkle." Elaine shrugged. "You never know."

Rose opened the front door, and they all went in. Elaine turned to Greg. "The painting I mentioned is up in our sewing room. Why don't you come up with me and carry it down, if you don't mind?"

"No problem," Greg said. He nodded at Rose.

"See you later." She headed for the kitchen, as she usually did in the morning.

Greg followed Elaine up the staircase to the second floor, where she turned right in the hallway. The sewing room and her bedroom and bath were on this end, at the back of the house.

"Ever been up here?" she asked.

"No. In fact, I had never been in here at all until that day I worked on the steps a few weeks ago."

"Well, here's our sewing room. Most of this is Jan's craft stuff, but that"—she pointed to a large, rectangular package on the worktable—"is my painting. It's got bubble wrap around it under the sheet." She whisked off the old twin sheet she had folded around it to keep the dust off.

Greg hefted it cautiously and smiled. "Oh, this is no sweat."

She laughed. "Glad you think so."

"Where do you want it?"

"In the west parlor downstairs. Oh, by the way, Greg, I have some good news."

"What's that?" he asked.

"Yesterday, Jan and I found out who vandalized the church. You don't have to worry about that anymore. We know it wasn't you."

Greg paused, resting the edge of the frame on the table. "Who was it?"

"Some boys from Penzance. They biked over here that Saturday morning and saw the Murphy twins working on the church lawn. They said they needed to use the bathroom, and Nick told them the church was unlocked."

"So the Murphy kids let them in and then lied about it."

Elaine frowned. That was the most painful part of the story. "They didn't realize what the kids had done. Apparently Nick and Chris never went in. After the bike boys had been inside fifteen minutes or so—longer than seemed reasonable—Nick was going to go check on them. He said that just as he got to the door, they came out, so he figured everything was okay."

Greg shook his head. "From what I heard, that was a lot of damage for fifteen minutes."

"Yes. There were three of them though." Elaine sighed. "When the twins heard later about the vandalism, they were afraid to tell anyone about the other boys. They told Trooper Benson that they were afraid they would be suspected, so they just kept quiet."

"I'll bet Des loved that."

Elaine nodded. "He's not happy, and the twins are being punished. Grounded for three months is what he told me. But Dan said they won't be charged with anything."

"I'm glad, for their sake, but I hope they've learned a lesson."

"There's no doubt about that. They were very contrite, and I think their guilty knowledge had been eating away at them. The Penzance boys confessed when Dan confronted them with the evidence in front of their parents, and they said the twins didn't go inside, so Dan thinks it's true."

"What kind of evidence was it?" Greg asked.

"Fingerprints, footprints, and a pocketknife one of them dropped in the church." Elaine smiled.

"Did they think it was funny, making a mess like that?" Greg asked.

"I guess so. And Dan is trying to link them to another break-in in Penzance. Apparently they'd been cutting school and getting into mischief." She turned toward the door. "Come on. Let's get this picture hung."

She led him down and showed him the spot on the wall where she thought it would look best. "Why don't you go ahead and get the bubble wrap off. I'll get my toolbox from the office."

She had bought some hanging brackets when she and Jan were decorating the previous year. She brought the leftover ones, as well as a hammer, a level, and a handy gadget called a stud finder.

"Do you know how to use this?" she asked Greg, holding it up.

"Yeah. That's great that you've got one. I was just thinking I should have brought my dad's."

"Wouldn't want you hanging it on plaster with nothing behind it," Elaine said. "Although there's a lot of wood in these walls. We saw some when the remodelers worked on the kitchen last year. I think all of these walls are that old lath and plaster."

"Cool. So about here, if there's something solid behind it?"

After some discussion, Elaine went to the kitchen to enlist Jan and Rose's help in making sure they hung the painting straight.

Greg held the frame against the wall, and the three women stood back a dozen feet to consider exactly how high it should hang.

"I don't know," Rose said. "Maybe you should put it out in the entrance hall."

Greg groaned, which Elaine took to be a protest.

Jan came to her rescue. "I like it there, but it's a little high. Remember most of our customers' eye level is at least six inches lower than yours, Greg."

He slid the frame downward about three inches as the front door opened. Elaine looked over her shoulder to see Archie coming in.

"Rose, can you take this?" Greg asked. "I want to mark the spot."

"Sure." Rose stepped forward as Archie came to the doorway.

"Hello, folks. What's the attraction?"

"Oh, we're trying to hang this painting that I bought at the flea market," Elaine said. "Come see what you think."

Archie stepped into the parlor doorway smiling. As usual, he was impeccably dressed and cheerful. Rose had set the painting on a nearby table, and he walked over to look at it.

"Isn't that nice? Why..." His expression froze, and he leaned forward, his gaze glued to the painting. "Oh, I say!"

"What is it?" Elaine looked from him to the framed scene and back.

"It's just—that mark over the fireplace." Archie stared a moment longer then turned to face her and Jan. His face had paled. "Where did you say you got it?"

"What is it, Archie?" Jan asked. "Is something wrong?"

"No, I don't think so, but..." He turned his gaze back toward the painting. "That's my father's mark."

Jan and Elaine looked at Archie in astonishment. "What? How? How do you know?"

Archie's face looked as confused as theirs. "That thing over the mantel in the scene, the thing that looks like a small abstract painting—that's my father's special mark. It's formed from his initials, and he used to put it at the end of notes and letters to me."

"Do you think he painted this?" Elaine asked.

"I guess I don't know. But I can't think of any other explanation." Archie's face was glazed with confusion.

"So," Greg said uncertainly, looking at Elaine, "do you want me to put up the hanger or not?"

Elaine looked back at Archie and down at the painting. "I don't know. Let's sit down and talk about this before we decide."

She loved the painting she had bought. But was it leading into another mystery?

# ABOUT THE AUTHOR

Susan Page Davis is the author of more than sixty novels and novellas in the historical romance, mystery, and suspense genres. She is the mother of six and grandmother of ten. A Maine native, she now lives in western Kentucky with her husband, Jim. Visit her Web site at susanpagedavis.com.

*From the Tea for Two Kitchen*

# JAN'S COCONUT-OATMEAL COOKIES

1¼ cups butter, softened

½ cup sugar

¾ cup packed brown sugar

1 egg

1 teaspoon vanilla extract

1½ cups all-purpose flour

1 teaspoon baking soda

2½ cups rolled oats

¾ cup flaked coconut

1 cup white chocolate chips

Preheat oven to 350 degrees.

In a medium bowl, cream together butter and sugars. Mix in the egg and vanilla.

In a separate bowl, whisk together flour and baking soda and then blend into creamed mixture. Stir in the oats, coconut, and white chocolate chips.

Drop dough by rounded tablespoons on to ungreased cookie sheets. Bake for ten to twelve minutes or until lightly browned. Cool on wire racks.

READ ON FOR AN EXCITING SNEAK PEEK
INTO THE NEXT VOLUME OF TEAROOM MYSTERIES!

## Mystery and Macarons

Jan Blake looked around the east parlor. Nearly every table was full. Guests were laughing, chatting, and drinking tea from delicate china teacups. Soft classical music played in the background. Bright summer sunlight streamed in through the open window, and a light breeze fluttered the curtain gently. Archie Bentham, one of the tearoom's two employees, came through the door from the kitchen, balancing on one arm a giant silver tray stacked with bone china teapots and an array of finger sandwiches.

Jan sighed happily. It was the second summer season running Tea for Two, and so far, it was going along perfectly. The tearoom had been busy every day since Memorial Day, and Jan truly loved keeping the kitchen stocked with pastries and interacting with the regulars and visitors alike. Running this tearoom with Elaine was a dream come true.

Jan looked around once more and saw that everything was in order, so she crossed the hallway and poked her head into the west parlor. Elaine was chatting with a pair of elderly sisters as she cleared their table. The other tables of guests all seemed to be doing well. Maureen Oakley was sitting with her daughter Shannon by the door to the dining room. Jan waved, and Maureen waved back. Jan spotted another table of regulars over by the window, and she made her way to where Rue Maxwell and Macy Atherton were seated.

"Hello, hello," Jan said, smiling as she approached the table. Both Rue and Macy looked up.

"Hi, Jan." Rue set down her Royal Albert Old Country Roses teacup and a tiny splash of Irish breakfast tea spilled out onto her saucer. Rue had perfectly styled hair and was dressed in a tailored jacket and skirt, even on this midsummer day. "It's a beautiful day, isn't it?"

Jan had to smile. Rue was bubbly and outgoing, and it was always a pleasure to see her here.

"Hello," Macy said, a hint of a smile spreading across her face. She was crumbling a blueberry scone with her fingers.

"How is everything today?" Jan asked. Rue and Macy were two of their most loyal customers, though Macy most often found something to complain about.

"The scones are a bit dry," Macy said. "But the tea is good."

"I could get you some extra jam or clotted cream," Jan volunteered. She'd made those scones this morning, with just picked blueberries, and she knew they were fresh, moist, and soft.

Macy shook her head. "Too many calories."

Jan pasted a smile on her face. She knew to expect this sort of thing from Macy, and it honestly didn't bother her, because she had come to enjoy Macy's company. Jan turned to Rue.

"How are those sandwiches? I got the watercress at the farmers' market on Saturday. I love shopping there at this time of year. There is so much beautiful produce in season."

"I love it too." Rue nodded. "And the sandwiches are wonderful. Is that dill mixed in with the cream cheese?"

"It is." Jan nodded. "So how are things going for you both?"

"Oh, well, you know. We were just talking about the thief that's been terrorizing the town," Macy said, giving Jan a significant look.

It took Jan a moment to process what she'd just said. "Thief?"

Macy nodded. "It was all over the paper this morning. Didn't you see it?"

Jan had read the *Penzance Courier* this morning, but hadn't seen anything about a thief terrorizing the town.

"It was a small piece in the local section," Rue clarified, giving Jan a smile. "Both Macy and I have guests who've been robbed."

"Robbed?" Jan felt her eyes widen. "What do you mean?"

"Someone came into one of my cabins and robbed one of my guests. Just took her wallet right out of her purse." Macy was shaking her head. Her scone was crumbling into smaller and smaller pieces.

"When was this?" Jan asked. How had she not heard about this?

"Saturday," Macy said. "She was at the pool with her kids, and when she came back, the door of her cabin was open and her wallet was gone. Can you imagine?"

Jan couldn't imagine. What a terrible thing to happen to a guest. That poor woman must be so upset, and scared, and—

"Just think of the bad reviews I'm going to get now." Macy sighed. "Who wants to stay at a place that's unsafe? It will probably take months to recover."

Jan wasn't quite sure how to respond to that. "And after all that trouble last year too," Jan finally said. A few months back, one of Macy's cabins had been accidentally set on fire.

"Yes, it does seem like someone has it out for me." She picked up a piece of her scone and popped in it her mouth. "At least Rue's guest wasn't robbed at her inn," she said after she'd swallowed her bite.

"You had a guest robbed too?" Jan asked. Rue and her husband, Ned, ran Northwoods Bed-and-Breakfast, an old, rambling farmhouse that they'd converted into a charming, cozy inn.

Rue took a sip of her tea and set the cup down gently. "It's so terrible. It was a lovely couple who had just checked in Friday evening. I feel so bad for them."

Sometimes Jan had trouble understanding Rue and Macy's friendship. Aside from the fact that they both ran places to stay in Lancaster, she couldn't see what they had in common. Rue was so sweet and bubbly and always thinking of others, and Macy...well, Macy was an integral part of the Lancaster community, Jan reminded herself.

She turned to Rue. "Where were they robbed?"

"They went out to eat at the Pine Tree Grill," Rue said. "And while they were out on the deck watching the sun set, someone took her wallet right out of her purse."

"Oh my goodness. That's terrible." Jan felt awful. What a thing to happen on the first night of your vacation. "Does Dan Benson have any clues as to who is behind all this?"

Trooper Dan Benson was an officer of the Maine State Police who lived in Lancaster, and he dealt with most of the petty crime that happened around these parts.

"He's been out to see my cabin that was robbed, and Rue was just saying he's been talking to her guest as well, but so far there doesn't seem to be much headway." Macy picked up a finger sandwich and examined it from every angle.

"I certainly hope they find this person soon." Jan hated to think there was someone out there on the lookout for wallets to steal.

"I just hope it doesn't get out beyond the local papers. It would be a shame if tourists stopped coming to town."

Once again, Jan didn't know how to respond, so she turned toward a noise at the far end of the room. She realized it was a woman's voice breaking through the quiet din of the busy tearoom.

"It was just here," she was saying, digging into her purse. Jan didn't recognize the woman. She looked to be in her late thirties or early forties, and she had a long mane of red-dish-blonde hair and freckles. She wore the sleeveless shirt and capri pants combination that signaled that she was on vacation. She had a large leather bucket purse and was pawing through it, pulling out one item after another, obviously looking for something.

"You had it when we came in," the woman who sat across from her said. She had the same hair and freckled skin, and

Jan was certain they were sisters. "I saw you tuck the business card into it. Did it fall out?"

A few of their other guests had turned and were now watching them.

Jan saw that Elaine had already appeared from the other room and was on her way over to the women, a calm smile on her face, but Jan excused herself and headed toward them as well.

"Is everything all right?" Elaine was asking as Jan approached. "Did you enjoy the lemon verbena?"

The woman didn't seem to hear her. She pulled a pair of sunglasses and a folding map of Maine out of her purse and peered into the bottom of her bag. "I can't find my wallet," she said. "I know it was here when I came in."

"It *was* here," her sister added.

"But it's not here now," the woman continued, looking up at Jan. Jan didn't want to believe it. She would have given just about anything to be able to rewind this scene a few minutes so that it never happened. But a sinking feeling was already spreading throughout her body.

"Somehow, in the time I've been sitting here, my wallet has disappeared."

# FROM THE
# GUIDEPOSTS ARCHIVES

This story by Jeffrey Minick of Waynesville, North Carolina,
originally appeared in *Guideposts*.

During the longest summer of my life—the summer of
1992—there was a painting of my house hanging in the
gallery across Main Street from our bookshop. Friends kept
stopping by, asking, "Have you seen the painting? It's beautiful."

My wife, Kris, returned from the gallery impressed. "I wish
your mom could see it," she said. "You know how she loves
the house."

Mom, sadly, was too ill to leave her home, and I was busy
helping take care of her. But one afternoon in early August
I went to the gallery to take a look. The walls were drenched
with color, filled with beautiful depictions of our town—Main
Street, walkways, gardens, older homes.

Then I saw the painting. Though many people had photographed, sketched or painted our turn-of-the-century house,
no one had captured its whimsical character the way that artist, Ann Vasilik, had. She had shown it from what might be

considered its ugly side, where the stack pipes and rambling renovations were visible. But in Ann's soft, warm colors, our house looked just as I fancied it—a dowager in genteel poverty, her fortunes down but her pride undiminished.

As I studied the picture, I felt for the first time in weeks an interest in something other than my own troubles. But one glance at the price told me the painting was beyond the means of a small-town bookseller.

The summer had begun on a high note. I had finally decided to make a major commitment to my faith and join the Catholic church. Just a week later, however, I got some terrible news: My mother was dying of cancer. Ever since, I had lived in a haze, as if the world's sights and sounds came to me through gauze.

I left the art gallery without giving the painting further thought. In the midst of making Mom's last days comfortable, I didn't even notice when the exhibit closed.

After Mom's death in early September, I settled into a routine that helped me get through each day. Prayer brought me some comfort, but my grief went deeper than I imagined possible. Without Mom—the soul, the center of our family—I felt overwhelmed by the dark forces that accompany grief…loneliness, emptiness, despair and isolation.

In November our good friends Henry and Julie Nathan asked us to supper at their house. Kris and I were surprised at the large buffet spread out in the dining room. Julie explained that she had invited a few other friends to join us. We chatted in the living room, greeting others as they entered.

As more and more guests arrived, anxiety gripped me. This wasn't a small party. The room was filling with people. Although they were all friends of ours, I couldn't make the connection between some of them and the Nathans. Why were they there?

Never before had I felt such an extraordinary tension in the air, a sense of an impending event. Finally, Julie came into the room with a large object wrapped in a blanket. "Attention, everyone!" she called. Then she turned to Kris and me: "We all chipped in to get it for you."

Julie whisked away the cloth. There was a watercolor, like a bright jewel, all sunlight and shimmering warmth. I was so overwhelmed it took me several seconds to realize it was the painting of our house.

The rest of that evening remains vague in my memory. Our friends applauded. I got to my feet and stammered a few remarks of gratitude. My wife cried. I scarcely remember eating supper or visiting afterward.

What I vividly recall, however, was an amazing sense of blessing, of knowing God's grace was at work. For weeks I had thought I was alone, cut off from others, yet here was proof of the love and friendship that filled my life.

Today the watercolor hangs above the mantel in our living room. Guests often ask about it, and then I gladly tell them how it came to me. I never tire of the story. Because each time I tell it, I look at the painting and see not simply a picture of my house. I see instead the faces of my friends.

# A NOTE FROM THE EDITORS

We hope you enjoyed Tearoom Mysteries, published by the Books and Inspirational Media Division of Guideposts, a nonprofit organization that touches millions of lives every day through products and services that inspire, encourage, help you grow in your faith, and celebrate God's love.

Thank you for making a difference with your purchase of this book, which helps fund our many outreach programs to military personnel, prisons, hospitals, nursing homes, and educational institutions.

We also create many useful and uplifting online resources. Visit Guideposts.org to read true stories of hope and inspiration, access OurPrayer network, sign up for free newsletters, download free e-books, join our Facebook community, and follow our stimulating blogs.

To learn about other Guideposts publications, including the best-selling devotional *Daily Guideposts*, go to Guideposts.org/Shop, call (800) 932-2145, or write to Guideposts, PO Box 5815, Harlan, Iowa 51593.

# Sign up for the
# Guideposts Fiction Newsletter

## *and stay up-to-date on the fiction you love!*

You'll get sneak peeks of new releases, recommendations from other Guideposts readers, and special offers just for you . . .

### *And it's FREE!*

**Just go to Guideposts.org/Newsletters today to sign up.**

**Guideposts**  Visit Guideposts.org/Shop
or call (800) 932-2145

# Find more inspiring fiction in these best-loved Guideposts series!

## Sugarcreek Amish Mysteries
Be intrigued by the suspense and joyful "aha" moments in these delightful stories. Each book in the series brings together two women of vastly different backgrounds and traditions, who realize there's much more to the "simple life" than meets the eye.

## Miracles of Marble Cove
Follow four women who are drawn together to face life's challenges, support one another in faith, and experience God's amazing grace as they encounter mysterious events in the small town of Marble Cove.

## Secrets of Mary's Bookshop
Delve into a cozy mystery where Mary, the owner of Mary's Mystery Bookshop, finds herself using sleuthing skills that she didn't realize she had. There are quirky characters and lots of unexpected twists and turns.

## Patchwork Mysteries
Discover that life's little mysteries often have a common thread in a series where every novel contains an intriguing mystery centered around a quilt located in a beautiful New England town.

## Mysteries of Silver Peak
Escape to the historic mining town of Silver Peak, Colorado, and discover how one woman's love of antiques helps her solve mysteries buried deep in the town's checkered past.

**To learn more about these books, visit Guideposts.org/Shop**